Bound Through Time
~Present~

By Twyla Turner

D1113379

To,
all the women who were told they are too dark, too tall, too
something…
You are perfectly made.

Table of Contents

Prologue

1051 A.D, Iceland

A cold chill ran down Jerrik's (YEH-rik) spine, and it had nothing to do with the frigid air that surrounded him and his men. It was a feeling of foreboding.

His clan was crouched and ready to raid clan Bjorn to exert dominance over them. The word had spread to Jerrik, that Bjorn wanted to overthrow him and steal the lands he occupied. Jerrik's land was the richest in Iceland. The soil was black and deep and produced the most food compared to other lands on the island made of volcanic rock. Their inlet also brought in the most trade. His father and his father before him had practically discovered the island and built it with their bare hands. Jerrik would die before he let anyone take what was rightfully his.

He had his clan and his family to worry about. Two of which were next to him. His baby brother Thorin and his bastard half-brother Dag, who was born only a few months after Jerrik. They were raised close and Jerrik loved them and his mother more than anything. Once clan Bjorn was put in their place and he married his betrothed, Sassa, he hoped he could relax a little.

Jerrik and his brothers were a formidable trio. All tall, broad shouldered, and blond-haired. Dag was the fiercest of the three. He was their greatest warrior and best trainer with a long scar down his face to match. Thorin was free-spirited, chasing lasses and glory in battle. Jerrik was just as fearsome, at six-feet-six with corded muscles honed to bring destruction like Hel the Goddess of Death. But often his quiet side yearned for peace.

As chieftain he was tired of defending his lands. He wanted to farm them. To fish. He wanted to travel, building relationships in the farthest reaches of the world to trade with. If he strayed too far now, he'd come back and have no home. Jerrik hoped that once he married Sassa and united with clan Magnus, he'd be able to rest. Magnus, Sassa's father, was the second wealthiest chieftain in Iceland. With the two clans forming into one, others would be less likely to try to usurp them and Jerrik would have more freedom to just be.

At least he hoped.

Thorin looked over at him. Jerrik could barely make out his brother's dark blond hair hanging loose around his shoulders. Jerrik nodded. He was ready. He watched Thorin look over at Dag. Jerrik couldn't see his middle brother's scarred face in the darkness of the new moon. All he caught was the glint in his silver eyes. Jerrik knew Dag was ready. He could feel the bloodlust radiating off of him. It was the same before every battle.

Jerrik rose up, and began to run quietly. His ax clutched tightly in his hand. His broadsword, passed down from their father, ready at his hip. His men followed just as silently behind him. As they approached the sleeping village, Jerrik let out a soul-stealing roar before they ripped their enemy from their sleep.

A man ran out of his home with sword drawn. Jerrik toyed with him for a while, letting the smaller man believe he had a chance. Finally, Jerrik caught the man's sword with his ax. He brought his ax down and flipped it back up again. The sword ripped from the other man's hands and flew up into the air. Jerrik caught it on its descent and spun around with the sword extended. The blade sliced perfectly through the man's neck. A look of shock was frozen on his face as his head rolled back and fell to the ground.

Jerrik didn't have time to celebrate his small victory. Men ran at him from every direction. He fought off several men at a time. His brothers and his other men stepped in to help when they could.

The target would always be him. He was chieftain. He was the one wanted dead.

Jerrik cut down one man and spun on his heels slashing through another. The blood of his enemies ran down his face and dripped from his blond beard. He made a gruesome sight. Enough to give even the most seasoned warrior nightmares.

Then a smile broke across his face as he overheard Dag and Thorin bicker. The white of his teeth stood out against the red blood that looked inky black in the darkness. The happy expression should've broken the sinister look of him. It only made him look more deadly and insane.

His brothers were at it again, and he couldn't help but laugh.

"How many is that for you, brother?" Dag shouted over the sound of steel and screams.

"Five!" Thorin shouted.

"Ha! I am at seven. Better hurry or ye'll never catch up!" Dag tossed back.

Thorin chuckled under his breath as he sliced his enemy down the middle of his chest, and he collapsed in agony. Thorin plunged his sword into the man's heart to swiftly end his misery. It was his and Dag's ritual to count the lives they took to see who the better warrior was. Dag usually bested him.

"Only seven! By now, you'd have ten or more. Must be getting slow in your advanced years, old man," Thorin shot back.

"Oh, ho!!! We shall see, young brother." Dag announced as his ax swung and decapitated his challenger.

"Oh, would you two stop carrying on like a pair of old wedded people." Jerrik scolded them.

They knew he wasn't serious. He loved playing mediator and big brother to them, and they knew it.

The sounds of clashing steel and screams had dissipated to a few last skirmishes in the village. Jerrik turned to make sure there was no one left to put up a fight. Most of those who fought for clan Bjorn were either dead or wounded. Then the sound of steel whistling through the air reached their ears, but Jerrik and his brothers were too slow to react. Jerrik's eyes widened in shock as a battle ax sailed through the air and headed straight for his heart. Jerrik tried to pivot out of the way, but the ax still sliced his chest before implanting itself in the ground.

Jerrik breathed a sigh of relief and looked down at his chest.

"Are you alright brother?" Dag asked as Jerrik touched the bleeding flesh wound on his chest.

"Aye…" Jerrik said.

Suddenly his legs felt numb and his mind fuzzy. He swayed and then collapsed on the ground.

"NOOOOO!" Thorin bellowed as his eldest brother and chieftain dropped to his knees.

A look of shock crossed over Jerrik's face before he fell back to the cold, hard earth. Thorin was there to catch him. Dag ran over to them to look over his brother.

"I…I can't feel my legs or arms," Jerrik whispered. Terror ran through his blood, and he was sure colored his voice.

Dag reached for the ax that had seemed to only nick Jerrik. He sniffed the blade. His eyes rose to Thorin's. Jerrik wasn't sure, but it looked like fear that crossed his half-brother's face in the faint firelight that broke the darkness. Jerrik had never seen fear in Dag's eyes. He didn't think it was possible.

"Poison," Dag whispered.

Dag slowly rose from the ground before turning and charging over to the man who had dealt their brother a fatal blow. He went berserk, killing the man swiftly. Brutally. Dag's anguished cries intermingled with the death gurgle of the dying man. Once the man dropped to the ground dead, Dag raced back to Jerrik's other side. Both Thorin and Dag each held onto his hands. Jerrik squeezed his youngest brother's hand slightly, and Thorin looked down into his eyes.

"Thorin…" he whispered.

"Aye, brother," Thorin answered gruffly.

"T-Take c-care of the village in m-my stead," Jerrik said haltingly. "I know you do not believe it, but father was proud of you. He was only hard on you because he knew you had potential to be great."

He then sluggishly turned his head to his other brother. It was becoming increasingly hard to move or keep his eyes open. "Dag."

"Aye, my jarl," Dag responded respectfully.

"W-Watch after our l-little brother. He'll need your help."

"I will."

Dag may have been the bastard son of their father, birthed by Rolf's mistress only months after Jerrik was born. But their father made sure he raised them to be close. They were not only brothers. They were best friends.

Unable to keep his eyes open any longer from the weight of his lids, Jerrik's eyes closed and his hands went slack. Thorin and Dag both squeezed his lifeless hands tighter, not wanting to let go.

Jerrik could feel nothing, but he heard everything.

"You four." He heard Thorin say. "Tie up the survivors before we sack their village. The rest of you prepare one of the smaller ships for Jerrik. He shall have a funeral fit for a king."

But I'm not dead. Jerrik tried to speak, but the words only ran through his mind. Silence came from his lips. *I'M NOT DEAD!*

He sensed the weightlessness of being lifted and being set down again. He could hear his people talking solemnly. The sound of the shieldmaidens around him. Jerrik sensed the rhythmic rock of a boat. He knew what was to come next.

I'm not dead! Odin, help me to move so they know that I still live!

After a few moments, the distinct whistle of an arrow reached his ears. The sound of its sharp head piercing the wood of the boat somewhere above his head made Jerrik flinch internally. The soft crackle and pop of a fire spreading, soon surrounded him. The acrid smell of it filled his nostrils.

Jerrik was helpless. He could not speak. He could not open his eyes. He could not move. All he could do was hear and smell the flames drawing nearer. He prayed to Odin that the blaze of his Norse funeral did not consume him.

To scream in his head as he slowly burned alive…

A worse death Jerrik could not think of.

But if Valhalla awaited him, he'd surely go.

****

Present Day, Harlem

Jett stood in the doorway of her bedroom stock still. Her eyes were wide and her mouth popped open on a silent gasp. Her heart roared in her ears and she felt her blood rush to her face, heating it. Her keys slipped from her fingers and hit the hardwood floor.

The sound startled her unsuspecting husband and her twin sister who was in the middle of riding his mediocre dick.

Nicolette gasped. She quickly scrambled for the sheets to cover herself as she simultaneously rolled off Shawn's husky body. Nic rolled too fast and too far. A yelp expelled from her mouth. Her body hit the hardwood with a thud, in a tangle of caramel limbs and white sheets. Jett thought it would all be pretty comical if it weren't happening to her.

"Jett! I…I…I'm so sorry!" Nic said as she stood. "W-We couldn't help ourselves."

Jett looked from her sister to her husband. He'd arrogantly put his hands behind his head lounging. As if he was waiting for the show. The catfight.

"Baby, you had to have known I had a little crush on your sister all these years. It was only a matter of time. Hell, you should join us." Shawn said casually as if he were discussing dinner. "You're already sisters, it would be easy to be sister-wives."

Jett supposed that it was her own fault. She'd always deferred to him. Never wanted to rock the boat. She'd felt as if she was lucky he'd wanted to marry her at all. That was all before.

"Get out," she said softly. Calmly. Too calmly.

"Now, bab-"

"Don't call me baby. Now. Get. The fuck. OUT!" Jett enunciated each word, ending on a scream.

"Bitch, this is my house too." Shawn grumbled as he rolled out of bed. "As if you didn't know I wanted your sister from the start. I only dated your black ass to get close to her."

"You're literally only a shade lighter than me, asshole. And you don't own shit. My dad bought me this house. Now, get your shit and my trifling ass sister and get the fuck out! She can have your baby dick."

"Baby dick!" He bristled and stormed towards her.

"Do it," Jett lifted her chin and stared him directly in the eye. It wasn't hard since he was a few inches shorter than her. "Give me a reason to beat your ass in front of my sister."

Jett may have battled with low self-esteem because her looks had made her a target her whole life. But because of that she'd fought women and men tougher than her husband. She'd tried to make herself smaller, meeker, all to make him feel more like a man. That obligation died the moment she walked into their bedroom and saw him fucking her sister.

Shawn backed down like she knew he would. Nic swiftly pulled on her skintight dress and thigh-high boots while he gathered up a few of his belongings. Jett watched the scene with a raised brow and stoic face.

To look at her, they'd never know that she was reliving moments from her childhood that would later define her. Her twin sister was literally the exact opposite of Jett in every way. Short, slender, with their father's hazel eyes, sandy-colored hair, and light skin. Everyone around them never let Jett forget it either…

"You're twins?!?!" One of their classmates exclaimed.
"No way!" The others surrounding them shouted in unison.
"We're fraternal twins," Jett shot back.
"What's that?"
"It means we're not identical. Duh."

"No shit!" The main little boy who started the whole scene on their elementary school playground said. "You got hit with the ugly stick and your sister didn't."

"Shut up!" Jett barked.

"You're so black that if you closed your eyes and mouth at night, no one would see you." The boy joked.

Everyone in the circle of hecklers laughed. Jett's eyes scanned the crowd. None of their laughter mattered as much as one person's. Jett's eyes landed on Nic. Her twin sister. Her eyes danced with delight as she laughed with them. The ultimate betrayal.

If there was anyone who would have her back, it should've been her twin sister. The pain was intense, but Jett knew she couldn't attack her sister. Nicolette was her mother's favorite. If she came home with even a scratch, Jeanette would get her butt beat.

Jett turned to the main bully and charged him instead. She was a whole head taller than him, so it wasn't hard to overpower him quickly. She used her weight to hold him down and pummel his face.

Unfortunately, her looks and the rumors about her ability to fight would place a target on her back that she'd never get rid of until she went to college.

"I like this dress," Jett said as she searched for her size on the rack of prom dresses. "But...there's none in my size."

"Jett, I told you, you should've been dieting way *before now." Her mother, Gloria, scolded her. "You knew it would be impossible to find your size. Let alone finding the right color to suit your skin tone."*

"How about this one?" Nic chose that moment to walk out of the dressing room in yet another prom dress that looked like it was tailored for her.

So far Jett had only found one dress in her size and it looked like a shimmery potato sack. As Nic twirled around in her 9ᵗʰ dress, Jett held back her tears.

She seriously considered staying home and watching 'Carrie' instead. It wasn't like her prom was going to be the traditional prom where she went with her boyfriend and lost her virginity. No, she had to ask a friend to go to prom with her. He didn't have a date yet, and neither did she. Jett figured they could just go together instead of alone or not at all. She wasn't the slightest bit attracted to him. He was scrawny and only reached her chin. But she was willing to give it a shot.

She searched through all the beautiful dresses until she found a shapeless, floral print dress. On the plus side, it hid her plump body. But according to her mother, 'did nothing for her skin tone, except make her look even darker.' Dejected, she stood next to her mom and sister as they chattered happily about the gorgeous dress Nic had found. She looked like a princess in it.

Jett blinked back tears as she came back to the present. They weren't tears for her failed marriage. They were tears from feeling inadequate in comparison to her sister once again. She fought to build her self-esteem every day in a world that continually told her she wasn't good enough. And this setback was a devastating blow to her fragilely built confidence.

Jett stepped to the side to let Shawn and Nic pass as they hurried from her bedroom. She turned and watched them stumble down the stairs and out of her Harlem brownstone.

After they'd gone, Jett pulled out her cell and sent a text to her best friend, Desiree.

Jett:
911! Found Shawn cheating with Nic.

It took under a minute for her to respond.

Dez:
The fuck?!? On my way!

Desiree made it to her place in record time. She burst through the door like a cop doing a drug bust.

Jett's best friend was stunning. Honey skin. A fashionable, natural tapered cut with dyed blonde curls that hung to her forehead. A thick, hourglass figure to die for. And a tomboyish style with the right girlie accessories to make her ensembles the envy of everyone she passed.

"I knew that lowdown, worthless motherfucker was no good! Where is he, so I can cut off his limp dick?!" She growled as she slammed the door.

Jett couldn't help smiling at her friend, even as her life was falling into a million little pieces. Dez always had that effect on her.

"Are you okay?" Dez asked a little gentler as she wrapped Jett in a warm hug.

"Surprisingly…yes." Jett pulled back to look her friend in the eye. "I haven't even really cried yet. I mean, I got a little upset feeling inadequate next to my sister once again. But as far as Shawn goes. I feel kinda hollow. Or relieved even."

Jett walked into her kitchen, opened the refrigerator, and grabbed a bottle of white wine. She poured herself and Dez a glass. Dez took her glass and looked at Jett candidly.

"First of all, that's because you never loved his basic ass. He's not that attractive, he's a short shit, he puts you down, he hops from job to job expecting you to hold it down in between, and he's a terrible lay. You just settled for him because you thought that's all you could get or deserved."

"All true."

"Which brings me to my second point. How many times and for how many years do I have to tell you that you're drop dead gorgeous? More gorgeous than your sister. On the outside *and* inside. Just because society and our own damn community has fucked up views of dark skin doesn't mean that it actually makes you unattractive. Your sister wishes she was as beautiful as you are. Which is why she's always doing and saying things to put you down. She doesn't want you to realize your worth or your power. And neither does your trifling husband."

Dez had always been her biggest fan. Ever since they met in grade school. She'd jump gladly into a fight to defend her friend. She was just as light-skinned as Nic, but she never once made Jett feel inferior to her. Most times, she sighed with envy at Jett's smooth, even-toned ebony skin.

"Oh no!" Jett let her head drop into her hands.

"What?"

"My mother." Jett rubbed her hands over her face wearily. "I wonder how she's gonna spin this to make it my fault because Saint Nic can do no wrong?"

Dez rolled her eyes so hard, Jett wasn't sure they'd come back down. Jett often had to hold her friend back from strangling her mother. It wasn't an easy feat since Jett wanted her to do it as well.

"That woman. She is the poster child for self-hatred. She acts like you didn't get your gorgeous ebony skin from her." Dez reached across the countertop and grabbed Jett's hand. "You do realize it's not about you, right? It's always been her fighting her demons about hating her own dark skin."

"I know." Jett hunched her shoulders. "But it's still hard when your own mother can't stand the sight of you."

"I know, sweetie." Dez sighed. "Well, at least your dad has your back. You being daddy's girl and all."

Jett smiled thinking of her dad. While her mother doted on Nic, her father, Morris, adored his 'little chocolate drop.' Well, she hadn't been 'little' for some time now. By high school she was the same height as her father. Six feet even. One more thing to add to her torture growing up...

Jett slammed the front door closed and ran up to her room. She slammed the door to her bedroom and collapsed on her bed before the waterworks burst in a torrential downpour.

She heard a knock on the door over her sobs.

"Jett, what's wrong? Why are you slamming doors like you pay the bills?" Her mother asked through the door.

"Leave me alone!" The words burst through her lips before she could stop them.

"Look here…"

"Gloria, I got this," her dad said on the other side of the door.

"That girl has a lot of nerve."

"Sweetie, she's obviously upset. Let me handle this."

"Fine."

A few moments passed. Jett assumed her dad was waiting for her mother to go back downstairs.

A soft knock came from the other side before he spoke.

"Jeanette, can we talk?"

Jett sat up and walked to the door. She unlocked it before going back to lie on her bed. She felt the bed dip as her father sat next to her hip. He rubbed her back soothingly, which made the tears start fresh.

"What's the matter, Nette?" His voice was filled with sympathy.

Her father never called her Jett. It was a nickname that had stuck when she was a baby. Everyone in the family thought it was a cute way to shorten her name. But her father had his own nickname for her. And she loved it. It was their thing.

It took Jett a few minutes to calm down. She was finally able to speak around her hiccups.

"On the bus home, the boys were talking about a list of girls and whether we were…good enough to hook up with."

It was actually called a 'Fuckable List.' But Jett couldn't very well say that to her dad.

"Go on," he encouraged.

"Well, Nic was on the top of the list, of course. But when they got to me…" Jett sighed before continuing over the lump in her throat that made a reappearance. "They said I was the most unhookupable. They said I'm too tall, too fat, too dark, and too ugly. Then they started calling me Dark and Ugly instead of Lovely like the beauty product.

~ 12 ~

Morris's jaw muscle ticked rhythmically. Jett knew he was mad, but he couldn't do anything about it. It was her battle.

"Let me tell you something, sweetie. You're absolutely gorgeous. You always have been. Sometimes even in our own community, the self-hatred and desire to align themselves with lighter or white is their problem. Only small-minded men will be unable to see your height, your size, and your color are just as beautiful as any other woman. You make them feel inferior. But one day, you will meet a man who finds every inch of you perfect. Just like your dear old dad. You're perfect just the way you are, baby girl."

"You have to say that because you're my dad." Jett rolled her eyes.

"I don't have to do anything other than work, pay the bills, and feed you."

"True. But how am I going to find anyone when Nic is the one who gets all the guys' attention?"

"First of all, you're both only 16. Please wait a few years before you go looking for 'the one.' Give your dad a few more years of peace."

"Tell that to Nic."

"As far as your sister goes, I worry about her all the time. I don't have to worry about you like I do her."

"What do you mean?"

"You're smart and observant. You can spot a bullshitter from a mile away. You're gonna go to college, get a great job, and even if a man doesn't come along, you'll be able to take care of yourself." He blew out a harsh breath before continuing. "But your sister, bless her heart, isn't as bright as you. Or she is but refuses to apply herself, because she thinks she has her looks to fall back on. As they say, 'beauty fades.' You can only get by so long on charming people with looks. I fear she might have to live off me and your mom or some lowlife man for most of her life. I'll be performing surgeries long after I should've been retired, just to support her. While you'll be free. I know it's hard for you to see it right now at 16, but you've been blessed, Nette."

Jett came back to the present.

"My dad might have my back, but he still lets Nic get away with murder. He never wants to rock the boat and piss my mom off." Jett frowned.

"So, what are you gonna do," Dez asked.

"Start over. It's the only thing I can do." Jett sighed.

"Maybe now you can find a man actually worthy of you."

Jett shook her head vigorously. "Nope. It's gonna be a long while before I get back out there. If ever. I see what you go through dating in these online streets. I can't."

"Take all the time you need. But Jett, please *overstand* something. You really are gorgeous. Like model-gorgeous. Sky-high cheekbones. Big Bambi eyes. Full, lush lips. Smooth, flawless ebony skin. And legs that go on forever and ever. And to top it off, you have a heart of gold. Every year, your students adore you because you care. Any man worth a damn will see all that."

Dez reached over and hugged Jett tightly.

"Thanks, Dez." Jett blew out a harsh breath. "But first things first. I gotta get rid of the last man, and I use the term 'man' very lightly. And the Lord only knows what drama Nic and my mom are gonna throw at me."

Chapter 1

"No...you...DIDN'T!!! Dez screeched.

Her best friend turned her from side to side in Jett's doorway.

Jett had taken the plunge, went to a barbershop, and had all of her natural hair buzzed off into what she liked to call a Black girl pixie. She'd started to grow out her natural hair shortly after getting married. It was five years of baggage she had cut from her head and life.

"Why am I picturing you standing in front of the mirror and taking the clippers to your head like *Nappily Ever After* or *G.I. Jane*?"

"Almost. But I wanted to get lined up in the back, so I went to the barbershop."

"You look stunning. Like a model."

Jett gave her friend the side eye.

"Girl, don't cut your eyes at me! I'm telling you, 'you look like a model.' So, you look like a model. I said what I said." Dez scolded.

"Alright. Alright." Jett held up her hands in surrender. "Come in. We can chat in the kitchen."

Jett led Dez into the house and Dez stopped and looked around. There were different sized boxes everywhere.

"Um...did I miss something?"

"My hair isn't the only change I've made." Jett smiled nervously as she went back to packing up her kitchen.

"So...you're moving in with me, right?"

"Uh...no."

"Next to me?"

"Nope."

"Jersey?"

"No…I'm moving to Maine."

"MAINE!" Dez shouted.

Dez watched her with wide eyes as she placed newspaper wrapped flatware into a box marked 'Kitchen.'

"Did you really say Maine?"

"I did." Jett continued packing to avoid eye contact.

She'd put in her resignation at the elementary school she taught at, shortly after getting hired at a school in a suburb just outside of Portland, Maine.

"But…but…"

"But what?"

"But…*why*? What's in Maine? Other than a *lot* of white people."

"Actually, and surprisingly, the principal who interviewed me was a sweet older Black lady. Plus, they have a great program up there. They're looking for teachers, among several other fields like nursing, and if you come to work there, they'll pay off your student loans. It's a no-brainer. Hint…hint."

Desiree was a nurse and Jett would love nothing more than for her friend to come live near her.

"Hint not taken." Dez shook her head before continuing. "So then, riddle me this, Batman. Why do they even need a program like that?"

Jett shrugged, feigning ignorance.

"Don't play dumb. You know why. Because there's no one there! They're desperate for people to come there because their population is declining because young people are leaving because there's shit to do there!"

"That's a lot of becauses."

"Because it's true!"

"Well, I can't stay here. And quite frankly, I want to get as far away from Shawn, my sister, and my mother as I can. I need a fresh start. And what better place to do it than where they're offering to pay off the rest of my loans?"

"Was it really that bad?" Dez asked, referring to Jett meeting with her family.

"You can't even imagine."

"Can you really blame Shawn though. Men have always fallen at your sister's feet. And after you cut off all of your hair it's no wonder. You know men like long hair." Her mother, Gloria said with a look of disdain.

"Mom, I cut my hair after I found them having sex in my bed! My hair has nothing to do with it," Jett said.

"Well, you can't blame your sister for falling in love with Shawn. He's a good man." Gloria said.

"Ma, are you kidding me? She's my sister! Sisters don't sleep with their sister's husband. And he's quite obviously not a good man if he cheated on his wife. Make it make sense." Jett looked over to her father. "Dad?"

Per usual, although she might be her father's favorite, he almost always deferred to her alpha female of a mother, when making decisions about anything.

"I'm not happy with Shawn. But you know how your sister can be."

"Yeah, an attention whore. Not to mention a real whore."

"Fuck you, Jett!"

Jett took a step towards her sister. Their father immediately jumped in front of her.

"Don't protect her," Jett growled.

"You both need to watch your mouths," Gloria warned. "Jett, you need to swallow your pride and give them your blessing. If only just to keep the peace in the family."

"When will Nic ever be held accountable? When will she have to apologize? When will you stop giving her the world? When will you say no? You literally raised her to believe that everything was hers. Even what was mine. I had to share to keep the peace, instead of you telling her no and teaching her how to cope with disappointment. Now look where we're at!" Jett raised her arms and let them fall heavily. "You let her get away with everything for

so long, she felt it was okay to steal my husband. And once again, you don't have a damn thing to say about it, other than, 'Protect poor helpless Nic.'"

"I didn't have to steal anyone. He came willingly."

"Because you don't know how to cover your ass. Always hanging around him like a bitch in heat."

"That is enough!*" Gloria lifted her chin defiantly.*

"Yeah, it is. I've had enough of this family."

"Nette," Morris stepped towards her.

"No, Dad. I'm done." Jett looked at Nic. "You can have him. But I'm assuming just like all the toys you stole from me, the moment he's all yours the appeal will wear off. Because what's the excitement of the toy when Jett doesn't want it anymore?"

"I want to be selfish in this moment and tell you to stay. But yeah, you need to get the fuck away from them. That's some toxic shit right there," Dez said.

"The only reason my dad gets a pass is because he's helping me pay for my new place in Maine. At least until the brownstone here gets sorted out in the divorce. I can give my dad the money when it sells."

"Alright, I guess Dr. Johnson gets a pass this time. But throwing money at everything won't fix the problem. So, I'mma really need him to stand up for you in the future."

"Well, I'll always have you to stand up for me. You'll come visit me, right?" Jett blinked back tears thinking about being so far away from her best friend.

"Abso-fucking-lutely! I gotta make sure the *Village of the Damned* doesn't snatch you up." Dez joked but was dead serious.

"You ain't right for that." Jett laughed.

"But…uh…what are you gonna do about dick?" Desiree tried to ask nonchalantly. "You know all the dudes up there are either gonna be old, married or country bumpkins."

"The last thing I'm thinking about right now is dick. Dick is what got me into the mess I'm in now."

"Yeah, but it was little dick. So, it doesn't count. And I highly doubt you're gonna find some of that Mandingo dick up there. What do we even know about New England dick?" Dez scrunched up her face.

"I hate you. You know that, right?" Jett said as she squeezed her lips and tried not to laugh.

"Which is why you're gonna miss me," Dez grinned.

"I really am." Jett choked back tears as she blinked rapidly.

She hugged her best friend, and then they continued the job of packing her life into various sized cardboard boxes.

Chapter 2

Nicolette turned her head this way and that. She pulled back her sandy brown-colored, curly afro as she looked at herself in the mirror.

Jett had transitioned from her straight relaxed hair to natural, five years ago. Her black, coily curls had grown in so beautifully. Nic had immediately ran to the Ghanaian lady around the corner to get her hair braided in a protective style to grow out her own natural curls. Once they grew out and Nic went fully natural, her curls were never quite like Jett's. No matter how many ways she tried to get her curls to pop. Twist outs. Roller sets. Bantu Knots. Flat twists. Nothing. Nothing gave her the luster and curl pattern Jett had.

Nic kept her hair natural though. If Jett's hair was natural, so would hers. Even if she hid it under protective styles sometimes out of frustration.

She looked now. She felt her scalp. Checked for lumps or misshapen spots. She wanted to know if she too could pull off the buzzed Black pixie look, like her 2-minutes older twin sister.

Nic sighed in frustration at her reflection. She followed whatever her sister did but buzzing off all her hair was too far outside of her comfort zone.

So many people within the Black community subconsciously favored Nic over Jett. Especially the men. They told Nic she was beautiful all the time. In school, they always said how much prettier she was than her darker sister. Even their mother favored her. But it didn't feel that way to Nic. She only saw that her father favored Jett and that Jett had their beloved mother's dark skin.

My skin is never smooth enough. Nic looked at her acne prone skin, even at thirty, partially hidden under makeup. Jett had her last blemish at nineteen, and had smooth ebony skin ever since.

My nose is too masculine and my lips are too thin. Nic flared her nostrils and pouted her lips. Jett's lips were insanely plump and her nose perfect and feminine.

She has the career and the man. Jett had excelled in school. Nic just liked to socialize there. They'd both gotten into college. Well, Jett had gotten into NYU and Nic had gotten into community college. Jett had told her it was nothing to be ashamed of. But, once again, Nic had felt unable to compare. And Jett had gone on to graduate with a degree in Education. While, Nic had dropped out of school after the first semester.

Nic hopped from job to job. She couldn't find what she wanted to do with her life. She couldn't even pretend to like teaching in order to follow her sister like usual. She'd hoped that Shawn would be able to take care of her. It'd never crossed her mind that Jett had been taking care of him the whole time.

"Nicky," her father called out.

Nic opened the door to her parent's powder room and walked into the kitchen where Morris was waiting for her.

"Come sit." He pointed to one of the stools at the kitchen island.

Her father crossed his arms and leaned his hip against the counter. Nic expelled a breath. Whatever was to come, it wasn't good.

"Your mother and I have been providing for you your whole life. When you didn't finish college, instead of making you fend for yourself, we got you your own apartment. You didn't have to pay rent or utilities as you galivanted all across this city. You hopped from job to job, never keeping anything for longer than two months when things got too hard. You've been chasing fun and your sister for too long. So, it's time for some tough love." Morris shifted hips.

"Daddy, a friend is gonna get me a job at one of the New York fashion houses." Nic blurted out desperately.

"Good. I hope you take this one seriously then. Because you have three months. Three." He held up three fingers. "That's enough time for you to save up several paychecks. After those three months are up, you're cut off. No more help from us. You're thirty. It's long past time for you to take care of yourself. If you're grown enough to take your sister's husband, you're grown enough to take care of yourself."

"You're punishing me for sleeping with Shawn?" Nic whined.

"You bet your ass I am." He leveled her with a disappointed look. "You had no right to do what you did. I know you look up to your sister, but this isn't the way to follow in her footsteps. You find your own life. Your own man. You don't take hers."

"You always take her side!" Nic shouted.

"I don't take her side. I take the side of what's right. If you get on the side of right for once, I'll be on it," Morris said.

"Does mom know about this?"

"She does. She's not happy about it. But since I'm the main one paying your bills, she doesn't have much say."

"You paid for Jett's brownstone and now her new house in Maine."

"Yeah, but she pays the bills. And I'll get the money back for the brownstone when it sells. Be glad you don't have a mortgage or rent to pay. All I'm telling you to do is pay your utilities and other bills. But if you keep testing me, I'll sell your apartment, and you'll have to find someplace else to live and will most certainly have to pay rent," Morris said.

Nic scowled as her mind whirled with ways to get out of her predicament.

"Do we have a deal?" Morris asked.

"Do I have a choice?" Nic asked petulantly.

"Actually, no."

Nic huffed as she got up from the stool. She grabbed her designer purse and stormed towards the front door.

"You can always find a sugar daddy, but your real daddy is done paying for you." Morris shouted at her retreating back.

Nic ripped the door open and slammed it closed behind her.

Chapter 3

Jett collapsed on her couch and Dez sprawled across the loveseat. Both limp and exhausted.

"This really is a cute townhouse in an adorable town. It's like right out of a postcard." Dez said after catching her breath.

They'd been unloading Jett's moving truck, and hadn't stopped until it was completely empty and her new home was filled with furniture and boxes strewn everywhere.

Jett cracked open her eyes to look over at her best friend. "It is, isn't it? I think I might actually love it here. Well, that is if the people are cool."

She'd moved to Cape Elizabeth. A quaint town outside of Portland, Maine. The outside of the townhouse looked like a large, two-story single-family home but divided into three parts, in the classic Cape Cod style. Gray shaker shingles with white trim. Jett's side had two bedrooms, one and a half baths, and a medium-sized but modern kitchen with an open concept that led into the living room. It was the perfect size for just her. And maybe a guest if Dez wanted to come to visit.

She couldn't even wrap her head around family coming to visit. She wasn't ready to see them.

"Hopefully, they will be." Dez paused. "Do you hear that though?"

"What?" Jett said as she listened closely. "I don't hear anything."

"Exactly! It's quiet as shit out here. Too quiet. No chattering. No shouting. No cars or honking horns. No sirens. Nothing. All this quiet is so...*loud*." Dez finished.

"I think it'll be nice to have some peace and quiet. I *crave* some quiet for a while. My life has been so loud. Or more like the people in it have been," Jett said.

Dez gave her a look.

"Not *you*!" Jett grinned. "I mean, yeah, you're loud. But you're always so positive and the best hype person a friend could have. But the negativity that everyone else has been radiating my whole life is so loud that I can't hear myself think even when they're not around. It's a struggle to uplift yourself when you have naysayers screaming 'you're not good enough.' I need some separation."

"Well…while you have some separation and much needed YOU time, I have a gift for you," Dez said.

She hopped up, grabbed her overnight bag, and dug through it. A sly smile spread across her face when she found it. Jett's best friend pulled out a wrapped medium-sized box. Dez's hand extended out to her and Jett took the gift hesitantly.

"What is it?" Jett asked dubiously.

Dez was known for buying her friends over-the-top stuff.

"Just open it." Dez waved away her skepticism.

Jett ripped the sparkly rose gold paper. Her mouth fell open and she gave Dez a scathing look.

"What?!?" Dez gave an innocent shrug. "Your piece of shit ex-"

"He's not my ex yet." Jett cut her off. "He still hasn't signed the papers."

"As far as I'm concerned, he became your ex the moment he stuck his dick in your sister. So, as I was saying, your piece of shit *ex-husband* wasn't taking care of business, and God only knows how long before you find a man up here in Mayberry. So, I figured you needed something to get you through the rough nights. Besides, every lady needs a good toy. You're thirty. You should've *been* had a vibrator. If it were up to me, all girls would get vibrators on their 18th birthdays. No one should be walking around not knowing how to pleasure themselves." Dez finally finished her speech.

"I guess I should be glad I didn't have to go in the store to buy it myself. I'd die."

"How a freak like me and a prude like you ever lasted as friends this long is beyond me." Dez smiled warmly at her.

"We balance each other. I keep you out of trouble…sometimes. And you get me in it." Jett looked down at the clitoral sucking toy and sighed. "I guess I should say thank you."

"If you don't now, I assure you, you will later." Dez winked.

Jett rolled her eyes at her oversexed friend. She let out a deep exhalation and looked around at all she had left to do. *This is the physical representation of what my life looks like. A mess.*

She smiled to herself anyway. *But now I have the time and the peace and quiet to rebuild the life I've always wanted.*

~~~

Jett laid in bed wide awake that night. The quiet was deafening. She heard nothing but crickets, the occasional owl, and a serial killer lurking outside.

"Shut up. Shut up. Shut up, brain! There isn't a serial killer outside my window. And damn you, Dez for putting that shit in my head!" Jett rolled over and punched her pillow.

Her bestie's speech about how quiet it was replayed itself in her head over and over again. She tossed and turned for another hour before Jett growled in frustration and reached for her phone. She pulled up her favorite music streaming app. She typed in "city sounds." Several options dropped down and she tapped "City Sounds for Sleeping."

The sounds of a city filled her room from the portable speaker on her dresser. They drowned out the quiet and unfamiliar sounds of nature outside her window. Cars, construction, honking, chatter, and footsteps quickly lulled Jett into a deep restful sleep.

Chapter 4

"So...you think you'll like it here?" Mrs. Pennyman asked from the doorway of Jett's new classroom.

Jett looked up from organizing the ten desks into a big circle in her new classroom. The principal of Lake Cove Elementary, Vivienne Pennyman, was a kind but firm older woman. She was average height with medium dark skin and an easy smile. She was dressed casually in jeans, t-shirt, and sneakers. Similar to Jett's denim capris, yellow tank, and white sneakers.

When they'd first met, Jett had been surprised that a Black principal was at the school in a small town in Maine. She'd told Jett that the Portland area was on a mission to bring diversity to their area. And schools were a great start.

"I think so. The people in town seem nice enough," Jett paused. "It's just so *quiet*."

Vivienne chuckled. "Yeah, it takes some getting used to. But you'll eventually acclimate. And the next thing you know, when you visit the city, it'll be *way* too loud and you'll be ready to run back to all this quiet."

"If you say so," Jett said skeptically.

Vivienne chuckled softly. "Alright, I'll leave you to it. Just know that my door is always open if you need someone to talk to. I've been here three years and have settled into the community. So, I should be able to help, if for nothing other than being a familiar face."

"Thank you, Mrs. Pennyman."

"Viv. Call me, Viv."

"Thanks, Viv."

Jett's new principal smiled before turning and walking down the hall. The squishy squeak of her all-white sneakers faded away on the linoleum floored hallway.

School was set to begin in a week. Jett had been working all morning to get the room ready for the first day of school. It was a small school and she'd only have ten 3rd graders.

A twinge of guilt at leaving behind her old school shot through her heart. The staff had been devastated by her resignation. They'd begged her to stay, knowing that inner city schools needed all the good teachers they could get. But for once in her life, Jett had decided to put herself first. So, while there was still guilt there, there was also a deep sense of rightness with her choice. Maybe she'd go back in the future, when her life and happiness were back on track. But for now, getting back to happy or technically finding happiness for the first time in her life was Jett's top priority. And as she looked around the classroom, her heart filled with hope and excitement. She felt happiness dancing along her peripheral.

~~~

"Good morning, ladies and gentlemen!" Jett said loudly over the cacophony as the students stampeded into the room.

There were only ten of them, which she was used to at least 30. Yet they still made just as much noise. She smiled as they hung up their bookbags on their designated hooks, in cubby holes with their names in it.

"Find the desk with your name on it. I set them up in a circle so you all can see each other. If you behave yourselves, we can keep them like this all year."

They all excitedly scrambled around the circle of desks to find their names. There were some squeals of delight when certain students found they sat next to each other. And a few grumbles when others found their neighbors weren't who they wanted.

Two kids in particular, a boy and a girl, appeared to be unhappy with the little boy seated between them. Their body language spoke volumes as they tried to lean as far away from him as their desks would allow. The boy had messy chestnut curls with big, sweet brown eyes that currently looked morose. He held his right arm close to his chest. It was skinnier than the other and his wrist and fingers were contorted limply. A brace leaned against his desk.

Jett had seen him limp slowly around the circle of desks as he used his brace to help him walk. His right leg bent awkwardly at the knee making it hard for him to walk normally.

And this must be Mason Mitchell, Jett thought to herself as she smiled at the boy.

She'd already been given information about the little boy. He had Moderate Cerebral Palsy. Classified as hemiparesis, where it affected the arm and leg on one side of his body. He was smart as a whip but spoke a little slower than the rest of the kids. Keeping up with the other kids physically was also difficult for him, but not impossible if given the chance.

Jett made a mental note to keep an eye on him. She didn't want to coddle him or give him more attention than the other kids. She didn't want him to feel babied. But she did want to make sure he wasn't bullied.

"Alright, everyone," Jett began and the class fell silent. "Now that you've all found your seats, I'm going to do roll call. I'm sure you all know each other. But you're all new to me. So, as I call each name, I want you to tell me something you did this summer that was fun, unique, or meaningful to you. Even if it's as simple as reading a good book. It'll help me remember your names and tells me a little about who you are as a person.

"I'll start. My name is Ms. Johnson. And this summer, for the first time in my life, I moved from Harlem, New York and came to this quaint little town in Maine. And now, I'm teaching all of you," she smiled as she finished.

Several hands shot up into the air.

"Is it scary in New York?"

"Are you married?"

"How tall are you?"

"You have no hair. Are you sick? My aunt is sick and she lost all her hair."

"Hold on. Hold on!" Jett gestured for them to settle down. "I'll tell you more about myself later. First, we have to finish roll."

She started calling off each name. There were lots of stories of pools, beaches, video games, and weeks at grandma's house.

"Mason Mitchell," Jett called out and smiled encouragingly at the differently-abled boy.

He raised his good arm.

"It's nice to meet you, Mason. What did you do this summer?" Jett asked gently.

"M-My mom told me if I finished all the *Harry Potter* books before summer was over, we could go to Disneyworld to visit the Wizar...Wizard...Wizarding...World of Harry Potter." He got out slowly. "After every book, I watched each movie."

"Oh wow! And did you finish them all? Did you go?" Jett asked.

Her encouraging voice made him finally look up. He smiled so brightly her heart melted. There were gaps between each tooth, all which looked way too big for his little face. But if he wasn't one of the cutest kids she'd ever seen, she didn't know who was.

"I did! We did! It was so fun!" He exclaimed.

"Yeah right," another boy, Caleb grumbled.

Jett had already figured out the hierarchy of the class. And it was obvious Caleb was the popular boy. Blond, blue-eyed and classically attractive for their age. The girls gave him googly eyes and the other boys looked at him like he was a celebrity and high-fived him often.

"What was that, Caleb?" Jett asked.

"Um...I said 'yeah right.'" Caleb lifted his chin defiantly.

Some kids laughed. Others nodded their head in agreement. Jett looked over at Mason and his head was down again.

"Mason, I bet it's something you'll remember for the rest of your life. And you don't need to prove to anyone that you were there. You know you were. Sometimes people get so jealous they can't help but say negative things to try to make you feel as small as they feel.

"I bet you got a magic wand," Jett winked at him.

Mason grinned and nodded hard.

"Well, when we eventually have Show and Tell, you'll have to bring it in to show us."

"I will."

Jett continued on with roll as Caleb crossed his arms over his chest, sunk down in his chair, and scowled at her.

She hoped that her set down of Caleb and defense of Mason was a warning to all the kids that Mason was to be left alone. But she knew that it could have also made him a target. She'd been bullied plenty in her life, so she knew the signs.

Sigh... I love 'em, but kids are a lot of work.

Chapter 5

"What are you gonna do to support us?" Nic asked Shawn.

"What about that job you told your dad about? The one your friend was getting you at that fashion house." Shawn threw back.

"I told you that my friend was *trying* to get me a job there. Not that she had." Nic rolled her eyes. "And what does that have to do with *you* getting a job. I'm not my sister. If you're gonna stay with me, you need to work."

"Well, I'm nobody's sugar daddy. If I have to work, so do you."

"We don't have time for this shit, Shawn! A month and a half have already passed. We've only got another month and a half to find something or we won't have any money to pay the bills."

"There aren't any good jobs out there. Call centers and shit like that is all that's available. I'm not trying to work for somebody else. You know I'm an entrepreneur."

"And what businesses have you tried to start?" Nic rolled her eyes.

"You know my ideas were stolen. I gotta start from scratch."

"Oh, you mean the food bike delivery service that never got off the ground because you were the only delivery guy and ate the customers' food because you were so hungry after biking to the restaurants to pick the food up? Are you talking about that business?" Nic said snidely.

"Fuck you, Nic!"

"Ugh! I can't believe Jett stayed with you so long. So, all that shit you talked about her and you paying all the bills were lies to get in my pants? The dates you took me on, those were on her dime, weren't they?"

"What if I told you I knew of a way to be set for a few years? At least until my next business venture gets off the ground." Shawn blurted out.

"And what way is that?"

"I took out an insurance policy on your sister. For 200 Gs." Shawn raised his brows.

"You mean…" Nic couldn't finish.

"Yeah, exactly."

"How?"

"I don't know. An armed break in. Car accident. Poison. There's all kinds of ways." Shawn shrugged.

"But it's my sister."

"Yeah, the sister you told me you hated over and over again."

"I mean, yeah. But that's taking it to a whole new level."

"Do you want the time to figure out what you wanna do with your life or not? Do you wanna try to start your own fashion line like you've mentioned? This could do it." Shawn coaxed as he sat next to Nic and held her hand reassuringly.

Nic sat in thought.

Money. My own fashion line. My parents being proud of me without my sister always upstaging me. Maybe it could work…

Chapter 6

Asphalt crunched underneath Jett's athletic sneakers as she took her daily walk. The crisp late-September air bit slightly at her face. Her nose a hint of red and runny. And brown eyes a smidge watery as she took in the bursts of color from the leaves on the trees. *I love fall.*

Walking was a part of her life in NYC. But in Cape Elizabeth, she drove everywhere. She knew that if she didn't get out and do at least some sort of exercise, she'd feared she'd gain even more weight. So, she'd taken up walking.

During the school week, she walked around her neighborhood in the evenings. On the weekends, she decided to walk further to see more of the town. Her favorite place to go was Portland Head Light lighthouse. It was a two-mile trek one way, which was why she chose the weekends to explore.

The old lighthouse was situated on a rocky seaside cliff. The roof of the museum and gift shop were a rust red color and the outer walls painted white. Construction was completed in 1791, yet the structure was in pristine condition and the lighthouse still functioned.

The first time Jett had found it, she'd smiled brightly. She couldn't imagine a more quaint, picturesque image if she tried. Each weekend, she took her walk at different times to see the lighthouse in all its various glory. The mornings were a sight to behold as the colorful dawn lit up the night sky and reflected on the endless sea. All which played as the backdrop for the pretty lighthouse. Afternoons the lighthouse itself was the star of the show, as it was bathed in the midday sunlight. And evenings, were lovely as well with dusk streaking through the sky from the western horizon.

Jett's favorite time was definitely morning. Everything was quiet. Few people were up at that time. The cool air felt good against her skin. And it felt like the lighthouse was hers as hues of purple, blue, pink, and orange painted the sky.

It was morning again, on the last Saturday in September, as she approached the lighthouse. A strange fog hung low around it. Jett frowned at the sight. She'd been there before during misty mornings. And while, the lighthouse looked like something out of a mystery or dramatic movie on those days, this was something different. The fog seemed to ripple and wave like it was alive. And it was so low that she could see over it, which seemed unnatural.

She approached the large rocks leading down to the water. The eerie mist began to recede, almost crawling over the rocks as it went back out to sea. As it cleared the giant boulders, Jett squinted and then her eyes widened in shock. On the rocks was a battered and broken boat. A longboat. As in Viking longboat, circa the 9th-11th centuries.

Jett wondered if someone had built it for a movie or something and it had gotten loose. Curiosity got the better of her and she walked forward. Gingerly, she climbed down the large rocks towards the capsized boat. The closer she got she could see that the boat was charred as if it had been burnt.

The bow of the ship that faced her had the head of a dragon on it. Jett came around to the side of the ship and gasped before stumbling a little.

"Oh my God!"

Lying in the middle of the boat was a man. Even lying down, she could tell he was massive. In height and width. She tried to get a good look at him to see if he was alive, but she couldn't be sure unless she got closer.

Jett placed her hands on the edge of the hull and awkwardly pulled herself over the side of the ship. Once she got her footing on the tilted ship, she leaned in a little closer to the man.

He had long, pale blond hair that must have been French braided back, because the braided tail lay next to his neck, wet and limp against the wood. A long blond beard added to his ruggedness. His face was smudged with ash, and his dark pink lips were cracked from exposure and possible dehydration. But even that couldn't detract from just how beautifully this man was created. Jett blinked in awe at the vision he made.

Her fingers trembled as she reached out to touch the man.

"What are you doing?" Jett asked herself as she balled her fist tightly right as she was about to touch him. "You have to see if he's alive, dummy!"

Jett loosened her fingers and reached the rest of the way to his neck. She placed two quivering fingers against the place where his pulse should be. The ash from the charred wood she'd touched smeared against his fair skin. Just as she felt his faint pulse, his eyelids shot open. With a yelp, she stumbled back. On shaky legs she stepped forward again. Deep set, arctic blue eyes looked back at her.

"Freya? Am I in Valhalla now?" His deep voice rasped in an accent that was both familiar yet different.

"What?" Jett asked.

His eyes fluttered closed and his head went limp.

"Oh no. Oh no. Don't die now!"

Jett pressed her fingers back to his neck and expelled a breath when she still felt his faint pulse. It was so weak she feared he wouldn't make it much longer. Fumbling for her phone in her yoga pants pocket, Jett pulled it out and swiped open her phone to call 911.

"Hello! My name is Jeanette Johnson. I'm at the Portland Head Light lighthouse. There's a capsized boat on the rocks and a man is in it." Jett rambled off quickly.

"Just keep calm, Jeanette." The female dispatcher said in a soothing voice. "Is he conscious?"

"No. He did open his eyes and spoke for a moment. But then he passed out again. I felt his pulse and it's there, but faint."

"What did he say?"

"Uh...he said, 'Freya? Am I in Valhalla?'"

"Huh. That's odd."

"You're telling me."

"Well, Jeanette, an ambulance and fire truck are on the way. It should be there in less than five minutes."

"Thank you so much!"

Jett hung up the phone and looked down at the man. She saw something silver peeking out from under the dais he was on. She bent down and slid out a broadsword.

"The hell?!?"

Her fingers wrapped around the hilt and she tried to lift it. Even using all her strength, she could barely get it a few inches off the floor of the ship. Jett gave up and instead reached for the man's hand. His palm was massive, the fingers thick and long. Her hands and long fingers had always felt so big, especially compared to Shawn's. This man's hand fairly dwarfed hers as she gripped it tightly.

Sirens reached her ears and she looked up to the rocks above. A few minutes later, firefighters and paramedics peered over the edge. Jett waved up to them.

A moment later, three fighters and two paramedics started to gingerly step down the rocks. They had one of those orange rescue stretchers to lay people on that looked like a long sled. And one held a hook with a wire tether attached and pulled it along behind him.

"Hello. Jeanette, right? You the one who called 911?" One said as the others climbed into the longboat.

"Yes, that's me."

"I'm Captain Stevens." He shook her hand. "Has he woken up again?"

"No, still the same."

The men started to work. It took four of them to lift the unconscious man onto the stretcher. He didn't really fit, so they strapped him in extra securely. When they were satisfied that he wouldn't fall out, they latched the hook to the metal bar of the stretcher above his head.

"Oh! Could someone get his sword?" Jett said. "I'm pretty sure it's his. But I can't lift it though."

One of the firefighters attempted to pick it up and dropped it. "Jesus!" he said.

"What?" what another looked at him.

"It weighs a ton."

"Lemme try." The other said.

He walked over to it and tried to pick it up. He got it up, but he struggled lifting the tip of the sword up. The other fireman who'd first attempted it, helped lift the tip and they laid the sword on top of the unconscious man's side.

"Wow! That was heavy as hell. But as big as this guy is, I bet he can lift it like it's a toothpick."

"Quit playing around you two. We've still gotta get him over the side of the boat," Captain Stevens said.

All five men used every ounce of strength they had to lift the stretcher over the hull of the ship and ease the big man down.

"Alright Dan, bring him up!" The captain called up to a fireman standing at the top of the rocks.

Four of the guys flanked either side the stretcher. Two on one side, two on the other as they held onto it and walked up the rocks. The other guided Jett back to the top.

Once at the top, Jett anxiously wrung her hands as they moved him onto a regular stretcher and loaded him into the ambulance. *Should I go home or should I go with him?*

"Do you have any idea who he is?" The one who had helped her up asked.

"Not a clue." Jett shook her head.

"Would you like to ride along to the hospital with him?" He shrugged. "You know…just to make sure he's okay?"

"Uh…yeah. If I don't, I doubt I'll be able to function until I know he's okay. Which I have no idea why. I've never seen him a day in my life," Jett frowned.

"Usually, people who help save others become invested. Human nature, I guess." He smiled at her.

The firefighter was a handsome man. Possibly in his late twenties. A few years younger than her thirty years. Under different circumstances, Jett could've seen herself try to flirt. 'Try' being the operative word.

The cute fireman helped her into the ambulance and they took off towards the hospital.

~~~

Jett sat in the waiting room as doctors and nurses worked on the man she'd found. When they'd arrived at the hospital, the staff had asked her several questions she couldn't answer. Who he was, what happened, if he had insurance, etc.? All she could say was that she'd found him and knew nothing else about him.

"Jeanette Johnson!" An Indian lady doctor shouted as she ran into the waiting room.

Startled, Jett looked up. "Yes, that's me."

"Come with me." The doctor waved to her urgently.

"What?" Jett asked as she got up. Her legs trembled.

"I'm Dr. Khatri. The man that you brought in had a relatively superficial wound to his chest. But the skin around it looked off. So, we did his bloodwork and it came back that he had tetrodotoxin in his system." Dr. Khatri explained as they walked.

"What is that?" Jett asked, not even attempting to say the word.

"Pufferfish." Dr. Khatri paused. "Which as I'm sure you know, is very toxic. We see this most of the time when someone ingests it while playing Russian Roulette with food. But I've never seen it come from a flesh wound.

"Anyway, it can cause temporary paralysis, lowered heartrate and breathing, and even death. Apparently, either not enough got into his bloodstream to cause death or his sheer size was enough to keep him alive. I'm beginning to believe the latter." Dr. Khatri said with a look on her face.

"So, if he's okay, why are we rushing back?" Jett asked.

"Well, he's awake." Dr. Khatri hesitated. "And he's, well…"

The doctor slowed down as they approached a room where shouts were spilling out into the hallway.

"Get away from me! What is this place?!? Where are my brothers?! Thorin! Dag!" A deep baritone voice colored with a thick Scandinavian accent bellowed from within the room.

The sounds of furniture and equipment smashing followed the shouts. Jett's eyes widened and she looked over at the doctor.

"Exactly. We were hoping that seeing you might help." Dr. Khatri informed her.

Jett shook her head vigorously. "He doesn't know me from Adam. What can I do other than catch a chair upside the head?"

"It's worth a shot."

"Yeah, a shot to my head!"

"Please! Orderlies and security are in there trying to subdue him, but if they can't, we'll have to call the police. We don't want it to escalate to that. Please?" She pleaded with Jett.

"Ugh! Okay," Jett grumbled.

She was surprised no one could hear her knees knocking together as she started forward.

"Start a new life they said. It'll be great they said. Now look at me." She whispered under her breath.

"What was that?" Dr. Khatri asked.

"Nothing," Jett mumbled.

She reached the room and peeked her head around the open doorway. The first sight that greeted her eyes was an impossibly tall, broad man standing with his back to her in a hospital gown. The gown gaped open in the back, giving anyone looking a feast for the eyes. And Jett feasted.

His back was wide and muscled with old, angry scars crisscrossing different parts. His thighs were thick tree trunks. Shapely, muscled calves flexed. And his wonderfully round, plump backside begged to be gripped during the throes of passion. Jett had to shake her head to rid herself of the visions that flashed in her mind unbidden.

This is neither the time nor place, pervert!

The men in the room who tried to calm him, looked over at Jett, which caused the man to turn his head to look back at her. He finally stopped mid-rage. He turned with a chair in his hands he'd been ready to throw. His eyes widened when he caught sight of her and he lowered the chair.

"You."

Chapter 7

Jerrik's eyes blinked rapidly as they opened. Harsh light nearly blinded him. He lifted his arm to cover his eyes as they adjusted. There was a prick of pain in his hand. He lifted it a few inches away from his face and looked up at it. He scrunched his eyebrows as he tried to understand the IV that was stuck in his hand and connected to the IV drip hanging behind him. He tugged and the tubing and tape holding it to his hand gave way. The needle slid from underneath his skin and he looked at it with a frown.

The other hand had a clamp on his pointer finger and he pulled that off too. The beeping noise that had filled the room and his head finally stopped.

His eyes searched the room. He laid in a bed and there was a chair near it. But they were unlike any bed or chair he'd ever seen before. Everything else in the room he couldn't recognize at all. The equipment. A flat black box bolted to the wall. Even the light overhead confounded him. Light from the sun, he understood. Light from fire, made sense to him. But the strange light glowing from the ceiling damn near frightened him. Jerrik hadn't been scared of much since he'd come of age.

A woman in strange blue clothing walked into the room.

"Uh oh. What did you do? Did you remove your IV and heart monitor?" she asked.

"Where am I? What is this place?"

"You're at Casco Bay Mercy Hospital."

Jerrik barely registered what the woman said. He was shocked by the language that tumbled effortlessly from his lips and that he understood every word she spoke.

What is happening to me? He thought to himself.

Jerrik quickly slid from the bed.

"Whoa! Whoa! Sir, you have to get back into bed." The woman said with wide fearful eyes.

Jerrik towered over her.

"Where are my brothers? Who are you?"

"I don't know your brothers. You came in with a woman. I'm your nurse."

"Find my brothers and find them NOW!"

The woman scurried from the room as fast as she could. A moment later two men in the same clothing as the nurse but in the color gray, ran into the room and grabbed either of Jerrik's arms. Jerrik emitted a loud bellow and threw the men against opposite walls. He picked up one of the machines and threw it against the wall. The men shook off the initial assault and charged at him again.

As Jerrik wrestled with the men, throwing them around like ragdolls, a woman with brown skin in green clothing came running into the room. Her eyes widened at the sight and she quickly left where she had come. Several minutes passed as Jerrik fought off anyone who came in to subdue him. He could go all day and he was just getting started.

"Get away from me! What is this place?!? Where are my brothers?! Thorin! Dag!" Jerrik shouted.

He lifted the chair and was ready to throw it at one of the men's head. Suddenly, they all looked at something behind him. Jerrik turned and saw the woman who he'd believed was a dream or Freya come to take him to Valhalla.

He lowered the chair and set it on the floor as he stared at her. "You."

She hesitantly stepped into full view of the doorway. She was lovely. Unlike any woman he'd laid eyes on before. She was tall and built thickly, like some of the shieldmaidens from his village. But her skin was dark and smooth. Her coloring reminded him of the wood of his ship or the fine furs he'd seen on his travels with his father.

Her eyes were large, a warm brown, and expressive. Her nose flared sweetly. And her lips were full and lush, more so than anyone he'd ever seen before. What little hair she had was black as night. The lack of hair framing her face made her feminine facial features stand out even more. Her high cheekbones, doe eyes, and plush mouth on display.

The clothing she wore left little to the imagination. Her pants were molded to her long legs. Their thickness welcoming. She wore strange shoes. And the shirt was loose but didn't hide the fullness of her heavy breasts.

She was more beautiful than any woman he'd had the pleasure of being in the company of. So, she had to be a goddess. Freya. The Goddess of Fate and Destiny. The goddess who represented beauty, love, and finery.

"Uh...*me*?" She asked.

"Who are-?"

Jerrik was cut short as he felt a sharp sting. One of the men had stabbed him in the thigh with a syringe. The 6'6", 290-pound Viking turned and grabbed the man by the neck and began to lift him. The other orderly quickly shot him with another dose of sedatives.

The world suddenly became fuzzy, and Jerrik went down like a lead balloon.

~~~

Jett had never seen anything like it. He keeled over like a felled tree. She literally felt the floor tremble when he landed.

That's gonna hurt when he wakes up again.

She'd thought that he was big when he was lying in the boat. But nothing had prepared her for him standing tall and proud. Most of the time, she felt enormous, dwarfing nearly everyone around her. She wasn't even close to him and she knew he had to be at least a whole half a foot taller than her. And his mass was insane.

She knew he had to weigh in the upper two-hundreds. But most of it was solid muscle. He wasn't ripped quite like a bodybuilder exactly, where he looked like one of those images in a medical book of what a person looked like without skin. It was more like he was extraordinarily muscular with a layer of softness over it.

Quite honestly, he was glorious to Jett. *If* she could get passed the anger management issues.

Hmm... A man who is physically *perfect for me. He probably only dates women under 5'5". And you're dumb as hell! He just tossed around two dudes like it was nothing. Talk about being attracted to toxic men.* Jett rolled her eyes at herself.

She watched as the two men struggled to get the crazy man back in his hospital bed. The nurse walked back in with restraints. They quickly secured him to the bed.

"I fear I'm going to have to call the psyche floor. He's entirely too much for us to handle down here." Dr. Khatri said.

Jett looked over at the man. Something in her gut told her that he might not be crazy. Something had obviously happened. He was asking for his brothers and she'd found him washed up on the shore dressed in clothes from another time in a ship from another time.

Maybe he and his brothers were on some trip, reenacting Viking voyages or something and he'd been knocked out and his brothers sent overboard. I'd wake up and freak out too if my sis- Well, maybe not her. But if I had brothers and they were lost.

"Wait." Jett reached out and touched the doctor's arm as she turned to leave. "Something obviously happened to him and his brothers that's upset him. It's not his fault he just so happens to be enormous and hard to control when upset. But maybe…maybe I can talk to him and see what happened when he wakes up again. If he goes berserk again, then you can have him sent to the psychiatric floor."

Dr. Khatri looked at her skeptically.

"Please? I kinda feel some type of responsibility for him. We can at least try."

"Fine," the doctor agreed. "But one more outburst and he's going upstairs or to jail. I won't have him endangering my staff."

"Of course, doctor."

The doctor, nurse, security, and orderlies left, leaving Jett alone with the man. She turned and looked down at him. She walked over to the chair they'd turned right side up again. With a sigh she plopped down into it.

"Jesus, Jett. Why do you get yourself into this shit?"

She felt like she was always trying to save world, while everyone she tried to save pushed her head underwater.

"Let someone save you for once."

Chapter 8

Once again, Jerrik's eyes fluttered open slowly. He felt groggy as he blinked until his eyes adjusted to the room. This time only a soft light near the door was glowing. The flat black box thing he'd seen earlier now glowed and had little people inside of it. They were talking and moving around within the box, and his heartrate spiked seeing the magic.

What witchcraft is this?

Jerrik was about to panic once more, but he turned his head and found the dark-skinned beauty he'd been so enthralled by earlier, sitting in a chair. She was covered with a white blanket and he wondered what kind of animal pelt it was covering her. Her head hung slack as she slept.

The need to talk to her made Jerrik move to get up and go to her. But something held him down. He jerked his arms and the bed rattled. Both wrists were strapped to the sides of the bed. His ankles were also strapped to the bed. He began to panic in earnest now.

"Freya!" He called out frantically.

The woman's eyes fluttered open. For a moment, she looked around as if she'd forgotten where she was. Then her eyes landed on Jerrik.

"Please, help me." He yanked on the restraints to show her he was tied down.

"I-I'm not supposed to.

"I will not cause you harm. I swear it," Jerrik said sincerely.

The woman looked at him warily, but finally stood and walked the few steps to the bed. Her trembling fingers worked on the straps. When his arms were free, he reached out and clasped her hand. She jerked back fearfully.

"I told you, I do not wish to harm you." He said as his eyebrows scrunched together still adjusting to the strange language he spoke with ease.

"Then why do you look so angry?" She asked nervously.

"I am new to this language. I do not understand how I have come to know it, as I have never spoken it before."

"Huh?" She said as she untied his legs.

"I am a Norseman. A Northman. A Viking." Jerrik listed off waiting for one title of his people to register on her face.

The word Viking made her eyes light up with recognition. She slid her chair slightly closer and sat back down.

"You know my people?"

"Uh…yeah. Although they haven't exactly walked this earth for centuries. Well, their descendants do."

"I do not understand." Jerrik sat up and swung his legs over the side of the bed to face her.

"The Viking culture died out hundreds of years ago. From my understanding, your people spread across parts of Scandinavia and other European countries and converted to Christianity."

"What trickery is this?" Jerrik raised his voice. "Is this the doing of Loki?"

"Huh? Loki? As in the superhero movies?" The woman looked at him strangely.

"I do not know this superhero movies. I am speaking of the God of Mischief."

She raised her eyebrows, "What century do you think this is?"

"We do not keep track of such things. But it is some time in the 11th century, I believe."

Her eyes widened as she looked at him like he was daft.

"What century do *you* think this is?" He asked.

"Um…the 21st."

"You jest?! Swear it on Thor's hammer!" Jerrik bellowed.

"Shh…" The woman lifted a finger to her lush lips. "Keep your voice down! I had to beg to keep you from being sent up to the psychiatric floor. Although, now I'm reconsidering my choices."

"Freya, why did you bring me here?"

"Why do you keep calling me that? I'm not Freya. And I didn't bring you here."

"Freya is the Goddess of Fate and Destiny. She represents all things beauty and love. I believed you must be her."

The woman blinked at him in shock.

"Why would you think that?" She nearly whispered.

"You are the most beautiful woman I have ever seen. I've never laid my eyes upon anyone who looks like you. I believed you must be Freya and that you brought me here because it was fated."

"I…uh…I… Wow!"

"Who are you?"

"My name is Jett. Well, Jeanette Johnson. But everyone calls me Jett. And trust me, I'm nobody's goddess. Just a regular person. Uh…what's your name?"

"I am Jerrik, Rolf's son." He paused. "May I ask you a question, Jeanette, John's son?"

"It's just Jett. And, of course."

"Who are the little people in that box?" Jerrik pointed to the box in question.

Jett squeezed her lips together.

"That's a television. They're actors who are filmed and then their image is projected onto the TV."

Jerrik stood up and strode over to the box. He easily reached up and tapped the screen. It was hard and his finger didn't go through like he thought it would.

"Witchcraft," he whispered.

"Umm…Jerrik?"

He turned to look back at her. Jett pointed to his back.

"I can see your…uh…behind."

Jerrik twisted to see and realized the long tunic he was wearing had no back. He looked at her and shrugged.

"Is my backside not pleasing to you?" He smirked. "Many a young lass has enjoyed the view of it."

Jett raised her eyebrows and her mouth popped open.

"Tis what I thought." Jerrik turned back to tap and pull on the television some more.

"Could you please quit messing with that before you break it."

Jerrik walked back to the bed and sat down facing her once more.

"I have to get back to my village. Do you think you could help me?"

"Where is your village?

"Tis in Iceland. Have you heard of it?"

"Yes, the name hasn't changed. But if you are who you say you are, you'd probably find it unfamiliar."

Jett reached into her pocket and pulled out a small rectangle and it lit up like the TV. She tapped it several times and then turned it around to show him. Jerrik grabbed the device from her hand and stared at it. She reached over and ran her finger over the screen, magically making the image change.

"That's Iceland today."

"The land is still familiar. But the buildings are not. STOP!" Jerrik burst out when a very familiar place appeared on the screen. "That is my land."

It was a picture of creamy bluish hot springs.

"That's the Blue Lagoon in the city of Reykjavik. I've never been, but I hear it's lovely."

"Reykjavik." He said under his breath. He took another deep breath and expelled it with a huff of determination. "Yes, I must find a way back. Back to Iceland. Back to my time. My village and brothers need me. I am jarl, you see."

"Jarl?" She frowned.

"Laird."

"Oh. You are the ruler of an ancient Viking village?"

"Aye."

"Riiiiight." Jett drew the word out as she nodded her head slowly. Skeptically.

"You do not believe me." He said it as a statement and not a question.

<center>~~~</center>

"No. No, I don't. It's impossible," Jett said.

She looked at the deranged man warily. *It can't be true. There's no way!* Everything she'd seen throughout the day said that he could be telling the truth. The Viking longboat that looked handcrafted from centuries ago. The broadsword that looked strikingly authentic. Even the clothes he'd been in. From the way he spoke to his mannerisms. All of it seemed so real.

But this isn't a movie or a time travel TV show set in the Scottish Highlands. This is real life. And people do NOT time travel. Do they?

"Well, I am here. Am I not?"

"Yeah, but you could be a crazy person telling me anything."

"Why would I lie?"

"Not a clue."

"How did I come to be here. The hospital, I mean."

"I found you."

"And how did you find me?"

"I found you in a boat that had been capsized against some rocks along the coast."

"What else? There has to be something significant you can tell me that gives me a clue as to how I came to be here." Jerrik stroked his hand down his long beard, deep in thought.

"Umm… Oh!" Jett exclaimed. "There was this weird fog. It was creepy and moved like it was alive. As I walked towards the rocks, it moved away and back out to sea. Almost like it knew I'd follow and it wanted me to see. So strange.

"Anyway, once it moved back far enough, it revealed your boat," Jett finished.

~ 52 ~

"Perhaps it was this fog that brought me. If I could find it again, maybe it could take me back."

Jett shrugged, "I have no idea. But you could try."

"What phase of the moon is it?"

"Uh…I don't know. Maybe a new moon. It did seem darker than usual last night."

"I will try to find this fog during the next new moon."

"And where will you stay until then?"

"Can I not stay here?"

"Uh…doubtful. You can't live in the hospital. You'll probably be released later this morning or tomorrow."

"Where do you live?"

"In…in a house a few miles from here."

"Then I shall stay with you." He said matter-of-factly.

"Is that so?"

"Tis."

"And if I say no."

"You will not."

"Oh? And how do you know that?"

"Because you feel the connection between us. And you want to help me."

"Not really."

"Then why are you here? Why do you sleep next to my bed when you could be in your home miles from here?"

Damnit.

"I-I just wanted to make sure you were okay."

"Because you feel the connection." He said with a confident nod.

Jett opened her mouth to contradict him, but then shut it again. It was obvious that the man was stubborn as a mule.

And is he really wrong? Oh, shut up, dummy! You married a hobosexual who only needed a home and to get close to your sister. It makes sense that you'd be drawn to a lunatic claiming to be a Viking chieftain. Just another hobosexual with a better backstory. Although, he does get bonus points for his dedication to his elaborate tale.

A large hand laid gently on her arm, bringing Jett back to the present situation. She felt almost a vibration that radiated between them. Her eyes shot up to his and his ice blue eyes practically stared into her soul.

"Perhaps you have a husband or mate who would not take kindly to me coming to live with you?"

"Uh…not exactly. It's complicated. We're separated and he lives far away."

"So, then in exchange for food and shelter, I can offer you protection. Maybe I can farm your land. Or hunt for food for you. Does this sound agreeable?"

"Technically, in this time, farming isn't something most people do. Or hunt. I mean, people still do it, but not like it once was. We have stores now, where you can buy all those things."

"Ah, like a market?"

"Yes, exactly."

"Protection, then."

"We don't really need that anymore either. Well…that's a lie. Men are still violent bastards. The only thing stopping them from reverting back to caveman behavior are laws."

"I do not understand."

"Never mind." Jett took a deep breath, held it for a few seconds, and then expelled it harshly as she came to a decision. "Fine. You can come stay with me. Whatever."

"This is good. You will not regret it."

"That remains to be seen. I'm an idiot. And deserve to be murdered in my sleep for agreeing to this shit." Jett mumbled to herself and rubbed her temples roughly.

"I would never! Only a coward kills someone while they are sleeping. I look my enemies in the eye when I cut them down."

"That's comforting."

Jerrik placed a finger under her chin and lifted her face up. "Jett, you are not my enemy. Worry not."

An uncontrollable and rather embarrassing shiver ran down Jett's whole body at his touch.

"You see? I affect you," Jerrik smirked.

Jett was beginning to realize that cocky smirk was a regular thing with him.

"You could've ignored that and kept your thoughts to yourself." Jett jerked her chin out of his hand and rolled her eyes.

"I am a forthright man. I do not hide what I see nor feel."

Did this mothertrucker just say he's forthright? Sure thing, Viking Laird, who time traveled to the 21st century. You're the pinnacle of truth and honesty.

"Sure. Whatever you say." Jett said out loud instead.

Chapter 9

Jett drove through the streets of Portland as she made her way back to the hospital. She'd woken up that morning after their late-night conversation, and quietly left the room where the delusional man still slept. She called up a rideshare to take her back home.

She had wanted to take a shower, change clothes, and get her car to bring Jerrik back. And on the way, she picked up some breakfast. She knew the big man would want more than hospital food.

As she walked towards his room, a few minutes later, she heard voices coming from the room. She stopped in the doorway at the sight of an older white man in a white lab coat sitting in the chair she'd slept in talking quietly with Jerrik.

"I believe it was one of Bjorn's men who had coated his axe with poison. Such a minor flesh wound would never bring me down and so quickly." Jerrik said to the man.

"Fascinating."

Jerrik looked up and spotted Jett.

"Ah, Jett. I had wondered where you'd gone." Jerrik smiled at her.

Jett refused to acknowledge the somersault her stomach did when he smiled so brightly at her. Not to mention the sound of her name from the timbre of his deep voice.

"I got you some breakfast. Hospital food usually isn't the greatest." She looked over to the doctor. "Hello."

"Yes, you must be the hero who saved this strapping young man." He stood up and offered his hand. "I'm Dr. Logan. One of the resident psychiatrists."

"Nice to meet you, Dr. Logan. I'm Jett Johnson." She shook his hand.

"I'd like a word with you, if you don't mind," Dr. Logan said.

"Uh…sure."

Jett placed the bag of food on the table. She quickly unloaded the food, pushed the table over Jerrik's bed, and then turned to the doctor. He gestured towards the door.

"I'll be right back," she said to Jerrik.

Jett followed the doctor out into the hall. They walked a few feet before he spoke.

"Jerrik is a fascinating young man."

"That he is."

"So, you found him in a Viking longboat is the rumor."

"It's no rumor. It did appear to be a Viking longboat."

"Huh…fascinating."

That must be his favorite word.

"He spoke to one of the nurses this morning about being an 11th century Viking from Iceland and they called me to come evaluate him."

The plot thickens.

"And your thoughts?" Jett asked.

"I think he has a type of Dissociative Amnesia. But unlike anything I've ever seen before. It's usually brought on by stress or a traumatic event. I'm assuming a shipwreck would be that traumatic event."

"But what is it?"

"It's typically where a person has an inability to recall personal things about their life. But in Jerrik's case, he's created a whole new life. A life where he thinks himself to be a Viking laird."

"Is there anything that can be done?"

"Some people get back their memories within days. Some…it never comes back. The only thing you can do, is to try and get him back to some kind of normalcy. Living life in the 21st century should jog his memory."

"Well, I can't get his life back to normalcy because I don't know what his life was like before this. I don't know him, and I only stuck around to make sure he was okay after I found him," Jett said.

"Unfortunately, my dear, if you don't claim responsibility for him, he will have to be admitted to a psychiatric hospital until he gets better or for the rest of his life if he doesn't." The doctor informed her sadly.

You gotta be fucking kidding me! I found him, so he's my problem. Just fucking perfect! This is what you get for always trying to save someone. For wanting to nurture every damn body. Somebody save me, damnit! Let me be the damsel in distress for once!

Jett raged internally as she nodded and smiled to the doctor.

Always remain agreeable. Never show your anger or you'll be labeled the 'angry Black woman.' Smile through the rage.

"I'd hate to see him in a mental health facility. So, if there's no other recourse, I'll take responsibility for him." Jett smiled but it didn't reach her eyes.

Even though she'd already agreed to take in Jerrik the night before, it still ground her gears that she *had* to take him in or else. That her life had to be turned upside down because she'd decided to help someone in distress. That if he didn't get better or find that fog, if he was really what he said he was, that she'd have to continue to look after him.

I should've called 911 and walked back home.

"Very good, Miss Johnson." The doctor dug in his pocket and pulled out a business card. "But if you need anything or if he gets worse, please do not hesitate to call."

"Thank you, Dr. Logan." Jett took the card and watched as he walked away.

Jett walked back to Jerrik's room. Dr. Khatri was in the room, checking the wound underneath the bandage on his chest. And once again he was talking about his homeland.

"That's very interesting, Mr. Rolfson."

"Good morning, Dr. Khatri." Jett said as she walked in.

"Oh, good morning, Jett. So, it looks like our patient here is doing well. Well enough to leave today. I'll send in one of the nurses to discharge him. Will he be going with you?" The doctor searched her face. "Are you okay with that?"

Jett knew what she was asking.

"It's fine."

Is it really?

"Okay, only if you're sure."

"I'm sure."

The hell you are!

"Alright. Then I'll leave you to it. I glued his wound, which will fall off after about a week or so. So, no need to come back to remove any stitches. If you don't need anything else, good luck to the both of you."

Dr. Khatri left the room and Jett looked over at Jerrik. He was devouring the rest of his breakfast.

"This is delicious," he said around a mouthful of food.

"Look, Jerrik. If you're gonna stay with me, you've gotta stop telling people you're a Viking."

"But that is what I am."

"Yeah, I know." *Uh-huh.* "But they don't need to know that. When you tell people that here in this time, they will absolutely think you're crazy. You need to pretend. You can say you're from Iceland. They'll believe that because of your size and accent. But leave it at that. Tell them you're a farmer or a fisherman. But please refrain from mentioning Vikings, lairds, or the 11th century. Got it?" Jett finished in frustration.

"Understood."

The nurse and two orderlies walked into the room.

"Knock, knock." The nurse said with a muffled voice. "It's release time and we have your belongings."

She carried the clothing Jerrik had been wearing when Jett found him. The clothes and animal pelt were so thick and folded up so high, Jett could only see the top of the nurse's head. And the orderlies carried the broadsword in behind her.

"Perfect." Jerrik said with a smile. "This tunic I am wearing is not very practical."

Everyone else in the room looked at the barbarian looking clothing and sword, and then looked back at the large man incredulously. *And* these *are practical?*

"Uh…do you happen to have any 2X scrubs lying around?" Jett asked hopefully.

I'll be damned if I go anywhere with him in full on Viking regalia!

"I think I could find some. I'll be right back." The nurse turned and left.

The orderlies set the sword down on the table and followed.

A few minutes later the nurse came back with a pair of navy-blue scrubs and handed them to Jett.

"Thank you," Jett said.

"No problem. You're very welcome." The nurse walked to the door and then turned back. "Stop at the nurses' station before you leave. They need to take your information."

"Okay."

Great. I'm assuming I'll be stuck with his medical bills now too. This couldn't get any worse.

"Here, put these on." Jett tossed the scrubs to Jerrik and quickly left the room before he stripped in front of her.

She walked back in a few minutes later and he stood in the middle of the room in the scrubs and his Viking type boots. Any other person would look absolutely ridiculous, but the sight of him once again made Jett's stomach tumble like it was gymnastics practice. It didn't help that the scrubs showed quite a bit of his dick print. A sight that gave her heart palpitations.

"Why must I wear this thin clothing?" Jerrik said looking down at the offensive garments.

"Because you can't walk around in your Vikings' clothes. You'd stand out. And you already stand out enough being all…" Jett gestured up and down at his body. "…*that.*"

"Does everyone in this time wear clothing like this?"

"No, just hospital staff. Now, come on. Let's go home."

Jerrik walked over to the table where his sword lay. Jett blinked as he lifted it like it was a kitchen knife.

The firemen were right.

"I am ready." He grinned at her.

Chapter 10

Jerrik followed Jett down the halls of the hospital. She stepped inside a small empty room when the doors slid open. Jerrik hesitated.

"What are you doing?" She asked.

His only answer was looking at the slots where the doors had disappeared.

"It's perfectly safe. Come on."

As he stepped inside, the doors started to close. He started to lift his broadsword, but the doors slid back once again. He quickly hopped inside the room before the doors could shut on him again.

"Are you done now?" Jett asked.

She pressed the button for the main floor and the doors slid shut. Jerrik's grip tightened on his sword. The room began to move. He stumbled back and pressed one hand against the wall.

"What is this?"

"It's an elevator. It takes you to other floors of a building so you don't have to use the stairs."

The look that Jett gave him made him realize that he should remain quiet and only observe his new surroundings. She already didn't believe anything he said. So, Jerrik tried to remain calm as they stepped out the elevator. But there were several people moving about, different sounds he'd never heard before, and all in a building that made no sense to him.

And then they stepped outside.

"Odin's blood!"

Carts flew by without horse or cattle pulling it. He'd been to England before with his father and had seen some buildings that stood taller than those in his village. But the surrounding buildings that stood over them now were unlike anything Jerrik had seen before. The roads were perfect and smooth. Nothing like the rough dirt roads of his village. And a man ran by with a tiny fluffy creature attached by a tether.

Stranger yet, the signs around the hospital with words he'd never seen before made sense to him. Vikings did not read or write. At least not quite like this. Yet Jerrik could read everything he saw. Words that translated during his time made since to him. And while some words he didn't understand, like ambulance, he could still read them.

Jerrik's mind whirled. He tried to process what was happening, but nothing could explain the phenomena that he was experiencing.

"Come on. My car is over here." Jett waved him to follow her.

Jerrik walked behind her as she wove her way through the parking lot. She stopped at a blue, mid-sized SUV. Jett opened one of the back doors and placed his Viking clothing on the backseat.

"You can put your sword back here," she informed him.

Jerrik placed his father's sword in the back. Jett closed the door, opened the driver-side door, and ducked inside. Jerrik stood next to her door awaiting his turn.

"What are you doing?" She looked at him with eyebrows drawn together. "Go to the passenger side."

Jerrik stood there.

"The other side." She said and touched the seat next to her.

Jerrik walked around and followed what she had done to get inside. His head still didn't clear the top fully and he cracked it hard.

"Thor's hammer!" He cursed and rubbed his head.

Jett squeezed her lips together to keep from laughing.

"You find me amusing, do you?" Jerrik quirked an eyebrow.

"I'm just impressed by your commitment to this act."

"Tis no act, I assure you." Jerrik rubbed his head some more.

"Buckle up!" Jett said as she strapped herself in.

Jerrik looked back at the contraption. He pulled on it, but couldn't really figure it out. Jett unlatched herself and leaned across him. Her arm and side of her breast brushed his chest. Her face was closer to his than she had ever been so far. He could feel her warm breath as she reached for the belt. Jerrik breathed in her scent. She smelled sweet.

"I am fond of your scent. It is pleasing to me." He said as she latched him in.

Her face jerked up and they were almost nose to nose.

"I'm happy you approve." She said sarcastically, and then paused as her eyes locked with his.

Her words were in jest, but her breath came a little quicker. Her soft brown eyes searched his and glanced down at his lips. Finally, her tongue flicked out to wet her soft lips. All clear signs she wanted to be kissed.

In his time, Jerrik would have snatched her up and kissed her soundly. But in this time, his instincts said she wouldn't welcome it. Or that she wouldn't admit she wanted it. She acted prim and proper like many of the Saxon women he'd encountered on his travels to England. Several of them had pretended to be innocent maidens, but behind closed doors they practically ravished him.

Jett finally pulled away from him and strapped herself back in. Jerrik looked around the car. All the buttons and knobs on the dashboard fascinated him. He tapped the windshield and frowned. He opened the door and stuck his head out and then back in again, checking if the image in front of him changed.

"Are you done?"

Jerrik sighed. "I suppose."

"It's a windshield. Clear glass. It's just supposed to stop the wind and debris from hitting you in the face."

She pressed the red start button on the dashboard and the engine came to life. Jerrik pressed back into his seat.

"Alright. So…speaking of scents, yours leaves a lot to be desired. So, we are going to take a trip to the store to get you some manly products and some clothes. Please don't be weird."

Before Jerrik could respond, Jett shifted the car into reverse and backed the car up. Jerrik gripped his seat. She turned the wheel, shifted again, and pressed on the gas. He slammed his hands on the dashboard.

"Odin, Frigg, and Thor!" Jerrik yelped as she took off down the road.

Chapter 11

Jett had no idea that a trip to a corner drugstore could be so dramatic. She'd decided on a smaller store instead of the big behemoths. If he was really telling the truth or more likely really committed to living this lie, places like Wally World would be way too much for him.

They'd walked the aisles and he'd stared in awe at everything. As quickly as she could, Jett filled a basket with masculine soap, deodorant, gray shower pouf, 2-in-1 shampoo/conditioner, and a toothbrush.

The big man had followed behind her, drawing attention down every aisle they'd walked. Whether from his sheer size and attractiveness or the way he acted like a kid in a candy store. Jett found herself smacking his hands on several occasions and scolding him. For someone who called himself a Viking laird, he took it pretty well.

I should've left him in the car. Jett thought as she waited for him.

They were currently in a clothing store. Large & Lanky. A store for tall and/or chunky guys. She heard Jerrik grumble behind the dressing room door.

"Everything okay in there?"

"Aye. I am just unsure of how to close these jeans things. A length of rope could always work, if you have any lying around," Jerrik said.

"Um…no. And we now have something called belts for that. Come out and maybe I can help."

The latch on the door, he'd had difficulties with earlier, scrapped and the door opened. Jerrik walked out, and again Jett's

~ 66 ~

stomach did a gold medal worthy gymnastics tumbling routine. She'd found a navy-blue sweater with a shawl collar and two wooden toggle buttons. The dark blue made his pale, arctic blue eyes stand out even more.

Faded, relaxed fit medium-washed jeans hung from his narrow hips. The fly was opened and folded over, showing off the fair skin of his lower abdomen and the blond happy trail that disappeared within.

Jerrik tugged at the two sides of the jeans. "These will not stay together," he huffed.

"Uh...let me try to show you."

Jett stood with the next pair of jeans she was going to have him try. She didn't dare do it for him, because that would mean getting close and touching him. She unfolded the pair in her hands and demonstrated how to button the jeans. Jerrik did the same. Then she showed him how to pull the tab up on the zipper.

"Wait!" She shouted as she stopped his hand. "Just make sure you pull the fabric away from your..." Jett waved in the general vicinity of his genitalia. "...you know. You don't want to get your skin caught in the teeth of the zipper."

"You mean my cock could get caught in this?!" Jerrik's eyes widened.

"Could you refrain from using that language in public," Jett hissed. "But yeah, *that* could get caught in the zipper."

"Odin's teeth! I would prefer to wear my Viking clothing if clothes in this time are that dangerous."

"You battle entire armies and yet you're scared of a zipper?" Jett raised her eyebrows. "Some Viking you are."

"One does not take injury to one's cock lightly." Jerrik reached inside the jeans and gripped himself as if to check to make sure it was all still there.

Jett's eyes widened. "On that note...you need underwear."

She turned on her heel and she scurried away as quickly as she could.

~~~

Jett unlocked the door to her place and Jerrik followed her in. His arms loaded with bags, his old clothes, and his sword.

I could keep him around simply for unloading the car in one trip.

She swung open the door and he walked inside. She watched as his eyes took in everything.

"I don't know how long it's going to take for you to find this magical mist or come to your senses, but in the meantime, you could definitely find a job. I'm not going to be your mother or your sugar mama. I'm already in the process of getting rid of one hobosexual, I don't need another." Jett said as she shut and locked the door.

"What is this hobosexual?" Jerrik frowned as he looked down at her.

Jesus! Someone who can actually look down *on me.*

"It's someone who only wants to be with a woman for a place to live."

"This is not the Viking way. But if you do not need me to hunt, farm or fight off enemies what shall I do? What is this job you speak of?" Jerrik said with his chest puffed out proudly.

"It's something you do to make money. And money buys food, shelter, and clothes." She explained further at his look of confusion.

"Ah…like gold coin."

"Exactly."

"Then I shall find one of these jobs."

"Great. And I'll help you. But first, let's get you settled…and showered. Follow me."

Jett led him upstairs. She felt self-conscious knowing her ass was probably in his face. And his next words confirmed it.

"I do not believe I have ever seen a backside more lovely than yours. I think I like these jeans on the female form. Shieldmaidens wear pants, but none quite as tight as these. Tis quite pleasing to the eye."

"Could you please keep your eyes to yourself?"

"They are to myself. Who else would they belong to?"

Jett turned on the landing and they stood eye to eye.

"I meant stop looking at my ass or any other parts of my body."

"That would be impossible. Your backside was in my face, there was nowhere else to look. Do women in this time not like compliments?"

"Look Jerrik, if we're to live under the same roof you have to respect me and my space. As temporary roommates, you can't comment on my body. That's for couples. We are not a couple. I'm just helping you out for the time being. If you compliment me like that it'll just make things confusing and uncomfortable. Understand?"

"I think so. The carnal tension between us makes you uncomfortable and you wish to ignore it." Jerrik nodded resolutely. "I will respect your wishes. Just know that I will satisfy your desires if it pleases you. Where I am from, many men rut like mindless beasts. But I was taught a woman's pleasure by a few shieldmaidens who would slit your throat if you ignored their pleasure. All you need to do is ask it of me." Jerrik finished.

Jett could scarcely breathe. She searched his eyes. But there wasn't the slightest hint of a joke. He was completely serious. And if her throbbing clit and wet panties were any indication her body took him seriously too.

It had probably been almost a year since she'd had sex. *And it's no wonder since my husband was busy fucking my sister.* The way Jett's body craved the attention and the way Jerrik offered to sate it, made her want to strip naked and jump in the shower with him.

Crazy person or not.

"I...uh...thanks. If I change my mind, you'll be the first to know. But don't hold your breath," Jett said trying to keep the tremble from her voice.

She turned and walked down the hall.

"So, this will be your bedroom." She stopped at the first room to show him. "And this next room is the bathroom. You can take a shower here."

The look on Jerrik's face told Jett he didn't understand how the shower worked. She sighed deeply. *It's a good thing I'm a teacher and learned patience long ago. But how much further can he take this act?*

She spent the next ten minutes explaining how the shower and hygiene products all worked. He listened intently and watched everything she did. Being in teaching mode helped calm her body after he awakened something within her on the staircase.

"Got it?" She asked when she was done.

"I think so." Jerrik frowned. "But where does the water come from?"

"Honestly, most of us don't really know how it works either. There are pipes underground that lead to a water filtration center. Basically, we just pay for it and turn on the faucet. Voila! Water."

"You *pay* for water?!? Are there no longer lakes, rivers, or hot springs?"

"We pay for the convenience of water coming directly into our homes."

"Ah. There is much to understand and learn here."

"You'll figure it out or come back to your senses first."

"You still do not believe me."

"I'm sorry, but no I don't."

"There is no way I can prove what I am telling you is true. But perhaps one day you will learn that I am an honest man and would never lie to you."

Hmm…maybe there is a way.

Jett dug through her cabinet under the sink. She still had some combs and brushes from before she'd buzzed off all of her hair. She found a detangling brush and handed it to him.

"For after you wash your hair."

"Thank you." He paused as he clasped the brush and her hand. "For everything. You did not have to help me. You have my deepest gratitude."

"Y-You're welcome." Jett stammered. "Let me know if you need anything."

She hurriedly pulled her hand from his scalding touch and closed the bathroom door to get some separation between them. She walked into the spare bedroom where he'd stay. Luckily, in anticipation of Dez coming up to visit, Jett had gotten spare bedroom furniture. But she realized that the queen size bed was probably too small for the enormous man.

"Oh well. It'll have to do."

She set the bags of his new clothes down on the bed and headed down to the kitchen to figure out lunch.

"Jett," Jerrik called out about twenty minutes later.

The sound of his heavy footsteps coming down the stairs reached her ears. She turned just as he reached the living room floor. He was naked as the day he was born as he roughly towel-dried his hair with the towel that should've been wrapped around his hips.

"Do you have my new clothing?" Jerrik asked, although Jett didn't hear it.

She was transfixed.

His shoulders were incredibly broad and sculpted. The muscles in his arms flexed and the veins in them bulged as he moved the towel through his hair. His pectoral muscles were defined with a dusting of blond hair that looked darker because they were still wet and plastered to his chest. His ab muscles rippled with each movement. His legs were practically tree trunks. But what hung between them is what made Jett feel lightheaded. His body was magnificent. His flaccid cock even more so.

It hung long, thick, and heavy. And he wasn't even erect. He was absolutely a shower. At least she hoped he was a shower and not a grower, because how much bigger could it possibly get? He had to be 8 inches soft.

Jerrik pulled the towel back from his face to look at her when she didn't answer. Jett hadn't noticed. She swallowed and licked her lips. She felt parched.

Before her eyes the penis she'd speculated about started to definitely grow. *Well, that answers my question.* It grew about another two inches and even thickened a few centimeters more.

A throat clearing was the only thing to bring Jett out of her stupor.

"Keep your eyes to yourself." Jerrik's deep voice threw her earlier words back in her face. "Especially if you have no plans on satisfying my desires."

Jett's eyes shot up to his and he smirked at her. She quickly looked away.

"First of all, I'm not divorced yet from my husband. We're separated which is still married in my eyes. And secondly, you're not supposed to parade around here naked! That towel is meant to be wrapped around your waist."

"You are tightly bound. I can see why you are divorcing your husband. I would gather that if he satisfied you, you would not be getting a divorce or be so tense."

"That is none of your business. And can you *please* wrap the towel around your waist?!?" Jett pointed at his still hard as a rock cock.

It was beyond distracting and the most tempting thing Jett had ever encountered in her life. Her heart pounded in her clit. Her depths slick with wanting.

Jerrik wrapped the towel around his hips, but the print of his erection still pressed against the plush fabric.

"Is that better?" He asked.

"Barely."

"If you tell me where my clothes are, I can get dressed and stop offending you."

"They're on the bed in your bedroom."

Jerrik turned and started back up the stairs.

"Don't forget to put on the underwear first and pull the zipper away from your skin!" Jett called out to him.

"Aye." He called back.

Jett fell back against the counter and expelled a ragged breath. "Jesus, build a fence…around my vagina." She mumbled low.

I have to resist that *and for how long? He's gotta get a job and get the hell outta here. Or maybe Shawn needs to sign those damn divorce papers. I bet crazy man dick is phenomenal.*

Jett's cellphone rang from within her purse. She ran over and pulled it out.

"Shit! Dez!" She cringed and put it back. "She's just gonna have to wait."

How does one explain to their hard as shit bestie that they've opened their home to a homeless man who claims to be an 11th century Viking?

"Ugh!" Jett groaned as she collapsed onto her couch.

She had changed her entire life to fix the mess that she'd been in. She could only marvel at how her life had ended up even messier than when she left Harlem.

Chapter 12

Later in the evening, Jerrik sat at the kitchen table and watched Jett cook. After his shower, he'd dressed in a plain white t-shirt and a pair of jeans with rips she had gotten for him. He'd thought it was silly to buy something new with holes in it already. But she'd told him it was the fashion. *Whatever that means.*

When he'd come back down to the main living area, Jett had looked him up and down. The attraction that shone in her eyes told him that she approved.

Jerrik liked the new clothes. The fabric was much softer against his skin than the scratchy, roughly hewn clothing of his time. And if wearing them pleased his new hostess, he'd gladly wear them.

She could deny her need, but Jerrik couldn't and wouldn't deny his. She really was the loveliest woman he'd ever seen. He wished they were in his time. For if they were, he'd take her to be his. He'd have to end his betrothal to Sassa and begin a war with her father. But it would be worth it to have the feisty, dark-skinned woman with the icy shell.

Jerrik knew she was soft and pliable underneath the shell of propriety she hid behind. He only wondered what it would take to crack her open.

Perhaps if she knew what I tell her is true. That I am a Viking who has tumbled through time. Maybe then she would soften towards me.

He had no idea how to do that other than to continue to be himself.

"Alright, Jerrik. Dinner is ready. Come fix your plate. There are no Viking lairds or kings or maidservants in this house. You fix your own plate here. And if I cook, you clean the kitchen. Deal?" Jett said.

"Deal." Jerrik stood.

~~~

Jett lowered her fork onto her plate of Spaghetti Bolognese. Eyes wide and blinking incredulously at the man across from her. His fork forgotten or maybe not even considered to begin with.

His blond beard had turned red from the sauce and a few chunks of ground beef had made its way into his long hair that hung forward. He used the garlic bread she'd made to go with it as a shovel of sorts as he gorged himself on the Italian meal. The salad sat untouched, other than when he shoved it away as if it offended him. And Jerrik hadn't spoken, much less come up for air since he sat down.

Well, at least I know it's good.

"That was delicious." Jerrik confirmed her thoughts a moment later.

"I'm glad you liked it. But you really need to eat your salad." Jett looked at the bowl full of veggies.

"You mean the livestock food?" Jerrik scrunched his face.

"Yes."

"Men do not eat horse food."

"It's good for you. Do you see how healthy horses are and how they grow to be so big?"

"Well, aye. But…"

"But nothing. I'm not the pinnacle of a healthy lifestyle, but I do what I can. And studies have told us that eating vegetables are good for your insides. For your heart. So, you can live longer." Jett informed him.

"Is that so?"

"It is." Jett nodded. "How old do people get where you come from that didn't die in battle?"

"Hmm…" Jerrik thought for a few moments. "The village blacksmith my father used when I was young, I believe, died at the age of seven and fifty. And that was the oldest we'd ever seen. Many never make it to fifty. Most die between forty and five and forty."

"Well, in this time, many people live to be one hundred." Jett raised her eyebrows.

"You jest!" Jerrik exclaimed.

"Nope. It's true. And it's because we eat better and doctors have learned a lot about our bodies. So, they can keep us alive longer." Jett grinned at his look of astonishment.

"Incredible."

Jerrik reached for his bowl of salad. Jett pressed her lips together to keep from laughing at his sudden enthusiasm for veggies.

"Here." Jett slid over the bottle of homemade dressing. "Try it with this."

He opened the bottle and was about to dump the entire contents into his bowl.

"Lightly!" Jett blurted out. "You don't want to drown it. That takes away from the nutritional value."

Jerrik added a little dressing, he mixed it up and grabbed some with his hands. Jett shook her head. *Save table etiquette for another time.*

She held her breath as he took the first bite. He chewed vigorously, frowned in thought, and then nodded before grabbing another handful. He quickly ate the whole bowl and then smiled over at her like a little boy.

"Liked it?"

"I did." His voice was filled with surprise. "The sauce you put on it gave the horse food a good flavor."

"The horse food is called salad and the sauce is called salad dressing or just dressing."

"Salad and dressing," he repeated.

Why am I starting to believe him? He can't be lying. Even Daniel Day-Lewis couldn't keep this level of method acting going.

But he could have what the doctor said. Maybe the trauma of being shipwrecked and losing his brothers really did make his brain find a strange way to cope.

Jett knew she had to find out the truth or it would drive her crazy.

~~~

After teaching Jerrik how to wash, dry, and put away the dishes she taught him how to use the TV with a short lesson on the differences between movies, TV shows, fictional, reality, and documentary. By the time she was finished it was time for bed.

Jett headed to the bathroom to brush her teeth and wash her face. She looked down and saw her detangling brush she'd given to Jerrik to use earlier. Several strands of blond hair were wrapped around the bristles. She quickly tipped downstairs, grabbed a sandwich baggie, and crept back up the stairs. She cleaned the brush of his hair and placed the strands into the baggie.

"We shall see who you really are, Viking laird."

Chapter 13

"There's leftover spaghetti in the fridge. And I've made you some sandwiches too." Jett explained the next morning.

Jerrik followed her around as she showed him where things were. She showed him how to use the microwave with explicit warnings against using the stove. He already understood how the television worked. He felt confident that he could be alone without breaking her house. Although, she didn't seem to have the same confidence in him.

"Please, don't break my house. And don't burn it down. If you get cold, just press the up arrow on the thermostat." She pointed to it. "No need to start a fire or anything."

"Do you know who I am?" Jerrik said indignantly. "I am a Viking…from Iceland. These current temperatures are for swimming and lying naked in a field with the sun on your body."

"Thank you for those visuals," Jett whispered under her breath.

"I will keep your home safe."

"Great. When I get back later, we'll discuss how we're going to get you a job."

"Alright." He looked her up and down appreciatively. "You look lovely. Is this how you dress for your job. Are skirts only for work and pants for days off?"

Jett wore a long camel-colored knit skirt that skimmed her hips and thighs, and flared out at the knee to the ankle. A soft, cream cowl neck sweater, paired with brown leather boots complemented the skirt and her skin.

"No, sometimes I wear pants to work. And sometimes I wear skirts or dresses when I'm off. It all depends on the style." She grabbed her purse and brown leather messenger bag. "But I don't have time to explain 21st century fashions to you. We'll talk about it later. Okay?"

"Of course. I shall not keep you any longer."

"Thanks. See ya later, Jerrik."

"Farewell, Jett."

She walked out the door with one last worried glance at him.

Jerrik walked over to the couch, dropped down, and turned on the TV. He scrolled through the guide as Jett had showed him the night before. The show *Vikings* was on and he selected it.

"This should be entertaining."

Chapter 14

"So, I hear you're a hero." Viv said when Jett walked into the teacher's lounge.

"Uh…" Jett said distractedly as she put her lunch in the fridge. "Oh, it was nothing."

"Saving someone's life is never nothing." The principle moved closer to Jett. "I heard he was suffering from a mental break. Thinks he's a Viking or something?"

Jett had wanted to keep her head down about the whole situation. She already felt like an idiot for taking in a stranger. Let alone one who thinks himself a Viking. *But maybe Viv can help.*

"Kinda. The psychiatrist said it was some new form of dissociative amnesia. Not only can he not remember parts of his life, but he's making up new stuff." Jett sighed and leveled her boss with a look. "And because they were going to put him in a mental facility, I may have taken him in."

"Oh wow! Are you sure that's safe?"

"He might have the manners of a barn animal, but he's actually been pretty well-behaved and kind.

"As long as you're sure."

"I am. I think." Jett looked at her boss hopefully. "Actually, I need some advice or help."

"Shoot. I'll do what I can."

"I honestly don't think he's lying. You see, at first, I thought he was lying just to get a place to stay. But this man truly believes he's a Viking. So, either he's totally lost it or…or something that neither of us can explain has happened. But there's one way to find out," Jett said.

She dug into her purse and pulled out the baggie of hair.

"I swear I sound just as crazy as he does. But isn't it possible that I can send this somewhere to get his DNA tested? If he's really an 11th century Viking wouldn't that show up? And if not, at the very least we can see if he's in the police database as some criminal. Or even just finding out who he is, so I can get him back to his family."

"You don't know just how in luck you are. This is crazy and seems destined, but I actually have a friend who's a geneticist. And another friend who is an archaeologist. We all went to school together. They decided to work together after we graduated. The archaeologist goes on digs and when he finds anything like hair, bones, etc. he gives it to her and she analyzes the DNA. They're both brilliant." Viv finished.

"Are you serious?! That would be amazing! And perfect, actually. When I found him, he was dressed in 'Viking' clothing and he has this crazy authentic looking sword." Jett said excitedly. "I could give them the hair and the other items and they could tell me what they come up with."

"I'll text them and let you know by the end of the day." Viv said as she pulled out her phone.

"Thank you so much, Viv. This means a lot. I didn't know who to talk to. And I felt crazy as hell for even considering any of this."

"I got you." Viv winked before her thumbs flew over the screen of her phone.

~~~

"Okay," Viv said breathlessly as she sat next to Jett in the teacher's lounge during lunch. "They messaged me back and they're so excited they could bust."

"Seriously?" Jett asked.

"Seriously." Viv smiled at her. "They said that they'd come by tomorrow morning if you could bring the clothing and sword."

"I'll see what I can do. Hopefully, he won't have a problem with me taking it because I have to ask him to put the dang sword in my car. It's so heavy it takes two people to carry it, unless it's him." Jett rolled her eyes.

"Oh my!" Viv dramatically pressed a hand to her chest. "He's that big and strong? I'd heard but wasn't sure."

"The biggest man I've ever seen."

"And he's living in your house?"

"Yeah. Stupid, right?"

"I wasn't gonna say stupid, per se. More along the lines of why haven't you jumped his bones yet?"

A giggle burst from Jett's lips and she gave her boss an incredulous look.

"I'm older and I might be your boss, but I still have eyes and you're the only other brown face in this little hamlet of Portland." Viv said honestly.

"This is true."

"So, please tell me why you haven't jumped this man's bones."

"Well, for one, it's barely been 24-hours. Also, I'm still married. Well, we're separated, but I still consider that married. And this man might be crazy."

"I have it on good authority that sex with a crazy person is pretty great." Viv laughed. "But I understand your situation. If you don't mind me asking, what happened between you and your husband?"

Normally, Jett would be irritated with how nosy her boss was being. But since she really was the only familiar face and she was helping her out, she decided that she'd open up.

"I caught him cheating…in our bed."

"Girl! If you don't go jump on that big man right now!" Her boss exclaimed. "He deserves not one bit of your loyalty."

"It's not about loyalty. It's about what's morally right."

"Says who?"

"Society. Religion."

"That's all well and good if this was some amicable divorce, but it's not. He broke his vows. So, that gives you the freedom to do as you please with no guilt." Viv reasoned.

"I know. But…"

"But nothing. Be selfish." She laid a hand on Jett's arm. "I can tell you're that selfless to a fault kind of person. You do things for everyone but yourself. I bet moving here took every ounce of strength you had. Am I right?"

"Maybe a little."

"Well, that was the first step in learning to put yourself first. Don't go backwards. And if you were selfless enough to let this man come live in your home. At least let him…take care of your needs too." Viv winked at her.

"I'll think about it."

"I bet you waited for marriage or at the very least married the first man you had sex with, didn't you?"

"Look here, woman. You don't know me!" Jett faked outrage before laughing.

"I think I do. I was you thirty years ago."

"It's that obvious, huh?" Jett said dejectedly.

"There's nothing wrong with taking care of people. Don't ever be ashamed of that. You just gotta take time out to care for yourself too. Other people should be ashamed of themselves for taking advantage of your kindness. Especially that soon-to-be ex-husband of yours.

"You are one *beautiful* young woman. Men should be tripping over themselves to be with you." Viv patted Jett's arm and then stood up.

Memories of her mother flooded Jett's mind. Past one-sided conversations where her mother made her feel small.

"If you lose weight, maybe boys will be interested."

"It's a shame you can't wear heels, but you already tower over these boys."

"I got something for you. It's soap that'll brighten your skin."

Jett couldn't remember the last time her mother complimented her or at least without a following insult. *"You have such a pretty face, if you'd just…"* Insert unnecessary miracle fix here.

Viv's kind words washed over Jett. A much-needed balm from a mother figure to soothe her poorly patchworked esteem.

"Thank you, Viv. But men rarely do what they should." She rolled her eyes.

"Well, they're not the brightest bulbs in the box. I'll give you that. But it sounds like you might have one interested now."

"Possibly."

"Like I thought. Anyway, let me get back to work, the bell is about to ring. See ya later."

"See ya."

Jett watched her boss walk away with a soft smile on her face.

With a heavy sigh she picked up her phone and opened up her text app. She quickly typed out a message.

Jett:
Shawn, would you please sign the papers?

Maybe she wasn't ready to shrug off the rules of morality or society. But she could certainly start applying more pressure on her estranged husband to sign the divorce papers she'd had him served with before she even left for Maine.

Her phone chimed with a new text notification a few minutes later.

Shawn:
Jett, I think we should talk about this.

Ah, yes. 'We should talk about this,' is code for 'I need you to take care of me because your sister is getting tired of me being broke all the time.' No, thank you.

Jett:

__Shawn, there is absolutely nothing to talk about. It's over.__
__Sign the papers.__

Jett turned her phone to silent, threw her trash away, and headed back to her classroom.

Chapter 15

The engine rumbled low as Jett sat in her car out front of her townhouse. She sighed heavily.

"Please Lord, don't let this man have torn up my house." She prayed.

After psyching herself up, Jett finally got out of the car and headed to her front door. She turned the key and opened the door. Her eyebrows raised and eyes widened at what greeted her.

Jerrik sat in sweats and a t-shirt. His eyes had been glued to the TV when she'd walked in. Empty food bags and packaging surrounded him. Along with hundreds of crumb particles.

"I guess it could be worse," Jett said to herself.

Jerrik grinned at her.

"Jett! You're home! What's up?" Jerrik said in a 21st century vernacular.

She didn't think it was possible, but her eyebrows raised even higher.

"Nothing much. Um…what's all this?" Jett gestured around. "It looks like you ate all the food I own. And left nothing for me but crumbs. Although, there are enough crumbs, I could probably fill a plate and have dinner."

"Oh, uh…" Jerrik looked around. "Don't worry about it, girl. I will clean it. Okurrrrrrrrrr!"

Jett's mouth dropped to the floor.

"I left a Viking laird this morning and come home to Cardi B?"

"I think I have learned a lot about your time, today. At first, I tried to watch a show called *Vikings*. I liked it, a great comedy."

"I actually don't think it was meant to be a comedy." Jett said as she walked over to the entry table and put down her purse and messenger bag.

"We grew up with the stories of Ragnar Lothbrok. To see some of those stories on the television was fun." Jerrik smirked. "But I figured watching about the past would not help me learn about now. So, I watched many things. I watched the news and reality shows where women flipped tables. That's common in my time too."

"I can imagine." Jett sat in her recliner chair next to the couch.

"Then I went to that streaming service thing you showed me. There was so much. I watched documentaries, more reality shows about finding love, movies about love. There is a lot of focus on this love notion." Jerrik frowned in thought.

"Do people not love each other where you're from?"

"It is there, but not the only reason why two people would be together. Or even a reason at all. Most marry for duty to one's family."

"Were you...married?" Jett wasn't sure she really wanted to know.

"No, I am betrothed. To a lass who lives on the other side of Iceland. Her father is a powerful man. Almost as powerful as me. I knew if we didn't form an allegiance, he would come to claim my lands. I did not want to risk it. Instead, I asked to marry his daughter. She is a spoiled girl, but life with her would be better than losing the land my father and his father before him had founded. And if it got too bad, I could have always taken a mistress to spend my nights with."

"Oh, so you freely cheat on your wives in your time?" Jett raised a brow.

"It is a normal occurrence. Although, I will admit that the women can divorce us if they wish to do so. And there are those who do so for that very reason."

"Good. It appears I'm not that different from a Viking woman."

"Is this what happened with your husband? He was with another woman?"

The muscles in Jett's jaw flexed.

"Yes, if you must know."

"Ah… Well, that makes your husband daft."

"If you would've cheated on your wife, why would my husband cheating on me make him stupid but not you too?"

"I only would have lain with another woman if my wife made my life unbearable. I would not take a mistress lightly. I saw what my father taking a mistress did to my mother. My parents had a good marriage. They were as close to a love match as one could get where I am from. My betrothed, Sassa, was a difficult girl the last time I saw her. It would not have been a love match."

"But *you*…I would never lay with another woman again if you were mine."

Jett nearly rolled her eyes at the way her heartrate spiked.

"You have no idea if I'd even be any good in bed."

"A blind man could see that. You have fire in you. And you are no delicate flower. You can take a good fuck."

"How romantic."

"Was that offensive?"

"As someone who has been told they're not feminine enough because of their height and size, yeah it is a little insulting."

"I mean no harm. The shieldmaidens I have fought beside and fucked are much like you. In stature. But there is something different about you. They are hardened warriors. You are much softer. I just meant that you aren't weak. That you could handle a man of my size. That I would not need worry about breaking you in the middle of lovemaking." Jerrik gazed at her.

Jett's breathing became a bit ragged. He stared at her unlike any man she'd experienced before. As if he wanted to devour her *and* cherish her.

Just let go, Jett.

Brown eyes stared back at arctic blue. She looked away first.

Jett quickly stood up.

"Welp, I need to clean up this mess."

"No!" Jerrik stood quickly and towered over her.

I don't think I'll ever get used to that. She thought as she looked up at him. *He's just so...so...overwhelming.*

"Do not trouble yourself. It is my mess. I will clean it up."

"Well, let me at least get you the vacuum and show you how it works." Jett quickly scurried away.

It was beginning to get harder and harder to be near him. The virility and masculinity that dripped from his every pore was enough to make Jett pass clean out.

Men just aren't made like that anymore. If he's not the real deal, then maybe they need to bottle whatever made him this way and sell it.

Jett pulled out her handheld vacuum from the hall closet and brought it over to Jerrik.

"Flip the switch, point, and shoot," she instructed.

Jerrik pushed up the switch. The vacuum roared to life and he dropped it like a hot potato. Luckily, it fell safely on the couch.

"Relax. It just sucks up small bits trash." Jett picked it up and demonstrated.

"This time is a revelation." He said with wonder.

Jerrik took it back and started to run it over the couch, coffee table, and floor. Jett walked into the kitchen. She opened her cabinets and the fridge. All of them were pretty much barren. He ate everything that didn't need to be cooked.

"Well, I guess it's pizza tonight because I'm not going to the store."

"I saw this pizza on the TV today. It looks delicious."

"It is."

"Will it help you live longer like those veggies?"

"No. You'll quickly learn that just about everything here that's extra delicious can kill you and/or make you fat."

"Hmm..." Jerrik rubbed his hand down his beard. "This could be a problem."

"Who you telling? It's a battle most of us fight. But if you try to add more healthy things like those veggies, you can meet somewhere in the middle. Oh, and don't forget exercise."

"What is this?"

"Basically, just moving around to get your heartrate up and make your muscles strong."

"Like battle and sparring for battle?"

"Kinda. But please, don't go around killing random people. We don't do that here."

"Then how do you do this exercise?"

"We have places called gyms or you can do it at home. Go for a walk or run. Stuff like that."

"You mean, people run here when no one is chasing them?"

"Uh…yeah."

"This is a strange place indeed."

"I go for evening walks. If you'd like to join me to burn off a smidge of the food you ate today."

"I would like that."

"I'll go change. All you need to do is put on some socks and your sneakers."

Jett hurried up the stairs and changed into her black yoga pants and lightweight buttery yellow sweatshirt. She came down the stairs and Jerrik stared at her for longer than was appropriate.

"What?"

"That color."

"Uh…it's yellow?"

"Aye, I know what it is." He gave her a long-suffering look. "It is just that it is lovely on you. Like the color was made for your skin. You are fairly glowing in it."

"Oh…"

Jett felt heat creep up her face and ears. The rest of her body flushed with warmth. She looked down bashfully. She hated how much he affected her. But it was so rare for a man to compliment her.

"Ahem." Jerrik cleared his throat. "I am ready."

"Uh…great." Jett grabbed her keys and opened the door. "Now, that it's getting darker earlier, I'm kinda glad you're here to walk with me. It's a small town, but a woman can never be too sure."

Says the woman who let a strange massive man who thinks he's a Viking come to stay in her home.

"Then I am glad I am here too." Jerrik said far too close to her as she locked the door.

His breath caressed the back of her neck as he spoke. Jett quickly turned around. That was a mistake too.

Jerrik was so close she could smell his shampoo as a breeze ruffled his hair and see the flecks of silver in his eyes as he gazed down at her.

"Uh…let's go." Jett said, looking away.

Jerrik said nothing. Instead, he turned and followed her.

~~~

After watching TV all day, Jerrik understood better the time he had landed in. They were not only advanced in every way possible; from farming, architecture, transportation, technology to even food. They were far more advanced in human interactions and emotions. But in other ways, they were far behind.

Where the women of this time could wear clothing that were skintight or barely there, they weren't allowed to be open sexually without being called names or treated with disdain. Where Viking women were much freer to explore their sexuality. And the men were happier for it.

In his time, in his country, Jett would have pulled him to her by the neck and taken what she wanted from him. But in her time, in her country, she doused the flames that had reflected in her eyes and walked away.

Jerrik had no choice but to follow.

They walked for a while in silence. He matched her pace and they quickly made their way down the block. The air was cool and damp. The leaves had turned and burned like fire against the setting sun.

Their arms brushed, which seemed to pull Jett from her thoughts.

"So...let's talk about what you want to do for work." Jett started.

"I am fascinated by these planes you ride the sky in. I saw it on TV today. To fly would be extraordinary. I should very much like to captain a plane." Jerrik nodded emphatically.

"Well, that takes years of training. And aren't you looking for that fog to take you back to your time?" Jett rationalized. "I think you need to keep your feet solidly on the ground."

"You have a point."

"What skills do you have?" She asked.

"I can hunt, build homes, I can fish, and farm." Jerrik listed.

"Hmm...I'm assuming all of those are skills specific to your time though. But I bet fishing hasn't changed that much. Boat plus hooks, nets or cages. Does that all sound familiar to you?"

"It does."

"Then maybe we could get you a job on a fishing boat. That would get you on the water where that mist disappeared to. And if all else fails, we could get you a job as a bouncer or security guard," Jett said.

"I am okay with whatever. As long as I can help pay for things while I am here. It is not right that you work and I sit all day. This is not the Viking way. We all work hard."

"Thank you for wanting to help."

"So, you never told me what it is you do for your job," Jerrik said.

"I teach 3rd grade."

Jerrik frowned.

"I teach children at the age of 8 and 9."

"Ah, I see. What do you teach them?"

"Everything. Reading, writing, and math, mostly."

"We do not have books where I am from. I saw them in England. But in my culture, we do not learn such things. For they are not important."

"But you can read. I've seen you read the guide on the TV." Jett looked at him with a frown.

"I do not understand it myself. I didn't know your language nor how to read or write. But when I woke up here in your time, I could speak your language without thought and I could read the words I saw all around me like it were second nature." Jerrik said sincerely.

"Do you think it's something that happened when you came through the fog? It changes you, so that you can communicate here?"

"It would seem so. As if it were fated. You may not be Freya, but she certainly brought me here for a reason." Jerrik looked at Jett pointedly.

Jett stared back.

Jerrik knew that he was bought to the future for a reason. And he was certain it had to do with the woman next to him. He just didn't know exactly in what way. He had some guesses though.

"I think I'm here to protect you. Among other things."

"Why would I need protecting?"

"I know not. But I feel it."

"And what 'other things' are you talking about?"

"I am here to keep you safe and to teach you how to accept and enjoy pleasure."

"Ha!" Jett scoffed. "More like you *want* to take advantage while you have the chance."

Jerrik stopped walking. It took a few steps for Jett to realize she was walking alone. She turned back to look at him. He raised a brow and she reluctantly walked back to him.

"I have not been here long, but I have seen the way other women look at me. If I only wanted my iron wet, there are many a welcoming quim to satisfy it. It is you I desire." Jerrik cupped the side of Jett's face. "All of me, not just my cock. I know not what it means. But I am a man who goes on instinct. It is why I have survived this long. And the gods are telling me that you must be protected and worshiped while I am here. I plan to honor their wishes."

He stroked his thumb across her cheek. His hand covered the entire side of her face from the base of his palm to the tips of his fingers. Jett pressed her face into his hand for only a fleeting moment. It happened so quickly that Jerrik couldn't even be certain she'd shown any vulnerability.

Jett pulled away from him and started walking again. Jerrik quickly caught up to her and they continued on in silence.

~~~

Jett was shaken to her core. Never in her life had a man been so genuinely interested in her. Of course, she'd been catcalled before, she was from New York and had a vagina, after all. But it wasn't the same. Like Jerrik had said, he could have sex with whoever he wanted but he wanted her specifically. She'd always been made to feel like the 'whoever.' The 'might as well.' The last picked.

Being first pick. The sole desire, was a revelation for her. And by someone as ridiculously gorgeous as Jerrik was beyond anything she would've imagined.

The reflection Jett saw in the mirror every day said that she was beautiful. That her skin and its color was nearly flawless. That her curves could be soft and inviting. And she knew what she deserved. But when society tried to tell her she wasn't beautiful or deserving, it was confusing. It made her feel like her eyes were a liar.

But if Jerrik was truly from another time. A time when race wasn't even a thing, let alone colorism. A place where large women were desirable. And he found her to be the most beautiful woman he'd ever seen. Someone unbound to the current standards of beauty. An unbiased eye. Then maybe it really was society who was the liar.

And Jett desperately wanted to take Jerrik up on his offer of teaching her pleasure. She wanted it more than anything she'd ever wanted in her life.

But could she?

Heat radiated from the hand that gently cupped her face as if she were this delicate breakable object. His deep-set blue eyes looked dark denim in the waning light. His dark pink, shapely lips beckoned hers.

Nope. I can't.

Jett turned and walked away as quickly as her feet would carry her. Of course, he was able to catch up to her in a few strides. Fortunately, he remained quiet for the rest of the walk. But unfortunately, the tension was still there.

It was as if there were invisible cords that connected them. That drew her in even when she tried to pull away.

There was no way that she could get close to this man. Only a few outcomes lay out before her:

    a) He's mentally ill.
    b) He's a criminal and/or hobosexual.
    c) He's an 11th century Viking laird.

Absolutely none of those outcomes left her in a good place if she let go and let him in. If he was mentally ill, he'd eventually have to go to a facility. If he was a criminal or hobosexual, he had to get out immediately. And if he was truly what he said he was, he'd be going back the minute he found the fog that brought him to the present.

And I'd be broken…again.

They got back to her townhome and Jett ordered a large supreme pizza and a large pepperoni for him for the next day. She hoped that was enough for the big man. She'd probably only eat two slices and gladly let him have the rest.

Hmm… With him around, he can eat the rest of what I shouldn't. He could keep my calories and carbs down by eating the rest of it.

Once the pizza arrived, Jett watched as Jerrik took his first bite. His teeth bit down and cheese strung between him and the slice. His eyes widened and then closed blissfully. He chewed, while hums of joy emanated from his throat.

"This is sooooo good!" Jerrik mumbled around another bite.

"I told ya. Kill ya or make ya fat." Jett nodded around her own bite.

"Take me to this gym place you mentioned. For I will not deny myself such culinary delights."

"First of all, the gym costs money. Secondly, you need a job. I think jobs on big fishing boats are pretty labor intensive. So, you might not need a gym," Jett said.

"So be it. But it needs to happen soon." Jerrik pat his flat stomach.

Jett rolled her eyes, "Yes, my laird."

Jerrik's eyes brightened and glittered at her words.

"I do not believe that phrase has ever sounded more appealing."

"Don't get used to it. I won't say it again."

"I would not be so sure. I am certain that in the future the words 'Yes, my laird,' will fall from your lips, whilst mine are pressed firmly between your thighs." Jerrik said nonchalantly.

Jett's mouth flapped opened and closed like a fish out of water. Her heart raced. Palms sweaty. And her quim, as he called it, squeezed reflexively as if grabbing at straws.

"I'm done talking to you," Jett said haughtily.

"Do not be cross with me. I am only speaking plainly."

"It is plain that you're talking out your ass," Jett grumbled.

"I have had strong gas, but never so badly that I would talk from my ass."

Jett closed her eyes and sighed heavily.

"Like I said. I'm done talking to you." Jett got up with her plate. "I'm going to take a shower now and then go to bed. I'll see you in the morning."

"Goodnight, Jett."

"Goodnight."

Jett quickly vacated the premises. She couldn't be around the frustratingly sexy man a minute longer.

~~~

Jett laid in her bed unable to fall asleep. She was restless. Her clit thrummed. Her body ached. Everything in her wanted to jump from her bed and head down the hall to the room where Jerrik laid.

As if I've ever been that bold in my life. The one time I initiated sex with Shawn, he turned me down. There's no way in hell I'm going to repeat that mistake.

Jett inwardly groaned. She squeezed her legs together and rolled onto her side as if she were in agony. She blinked at her nightstand and the image of the toy Dez had bought her popped unbidden into her mind.

She'd charged up the thing, but never was brave enough to use it. Her need far surpassed her bashfulness.

She reached the short distance to the drawer and opened it. Her hand blindly searched for what she wanted. The smooth skin of the toy touched her fingers and she grabbed it. It was hot pink and ergonomically designed. There was no fake penis attached to it, like the one's she'd seen before. This one only had a round, hollow tip. The clit sucking feature.

Jett turned on the toy and it came to life. The vibrations were so loud she quickly shoved it under the covers and between her thighs to try and muffle the sound. It definitely went down a few decibels, but to her ears it was still loud enough to wake the neighborhood.

"Make it quick." Jett grumbled to herself.

She placed the stimulator against her clit and almost shot off the bed.

"Holy…shit!" She hissed under her breath.

And that's the lowest setting.

Jett took a deep breath. She was better prepared the next time she placed the toy against her most sensitive place. Her mouth popped open as the pulses sent waves of pleasure through her nub. She licked her lips and small gasps passed them, drying them seconds later.

A sensation built quickly within her. A build-up of something big.

She wasn't ready when she hit the crest and she cried out before she could stop it. Jett slapped a hand over her mouth, but continued to hold the vibrator to her to finish what had begun.

The bedroom door swung open, but it took her a few seconds to register what was happening, seeing as how she was in the middle of her first real orgasm.

"Jett!" Jerrik's voice pulled her from the throes of passion.

Her eyes shot open, she dropped the toy, and she sat up as she pressed the covers against her chest.

Jerrik stood in her doorway an avenging angel with his sword at the ready. In nothing but gray box briefs. His platinum blond hair was a tousled mane around his face and shoulders, like a lion. His chest heaved with adrenaline. His eyes searched her room looking for a perpetrator. When he saw none and his icy eyes came back to her. She watched as they went from defensive mode to realization to barely banked wildfire.

His eyes dropped from her face to the blankets. The toy was still vibrating on the mattress between her legs. Jett quickly fumbled for it and shut it off.

"Do women pleasure themselves with bees in this time?" Jerrik asked.

If it wasn't so mortifying, Jett would've have burst out laughing.

"No. Jerrik, please get out."

"Are you certain?" He asked.

His voice was husky with desire. Jett glanced down as saw that his box briefs were tented in front of him.

Lord, grant me strength.

"I-I'm sure."

"Goodnight, then."

"Goodnight."

Jerrik left her room and closed the door behind him. Jett sunk down into her covers. Everything that the vibrator had released inside of her during her first ever orgasm, had built right back up at the sight of her archangel and his sword. Not the steel one. The sword made of flesh.

"I think this might kill me."

Chapter 16

"So, there's a whole other pizza in the fridge for you. You can heat up however many slices you want in the microwave or you can eat it cold. It's your preference." Jett said all this without looking at Jerrik the next morning.

"Alright," he said.

They stood in the kitchen. Even with the island between them, she could still feel the heat and tension radiating off them in waves.

"Tonight, when I get home, we'll go grocery shopping. So be ready by 5."

"Yes, I would very much like to see how these markets work."

Jett sighed. She knew she had to ask him what she'd been dreading since yesterday.

"I…um…need to ask you a favor."

"Ask it."

"Is it possible for me to borrow your Viking clothing and sword?"

"Why?"

Jett finally looked up at him.

"Well, because I found someone who can analyze them and tell me what century they're from. And if you agree, I'd need you to put the sword in my car."

"The sword was passed down to me from my father. And it was his father's before him. Are you sure it would be safe?"

"I promise. No one can wield it here but you, honestly. It's literally like Thor's hammer."

Jerrik smiled brightly. His surprisingly straight, white teeth gleamed behind the overgrown beard.

"Then it is yours…under one condition."

"Oh boy. And what would that be?"

"When you discover that where and when I'm from is true. That I have been forthright with you, you must allow me to give you and teach you pleasure."

Once again, Jett was left speechless. She blinked rapidly. Her pulse thrummed in her neck. And again, her inner walls flexed for something it longed for.

"I…uh…I don't know if I can do that."

"I will not hurt you. You can trust me."

Yeah, you won't hurt me physically. What about emotionally?

"It's not a question of you hurting me. I don't go around having sex with strange men I barely know." Jett raised her chin proudly.

"I am no longer a stranger to you. And we do not have to have sex for me to show you pleasure. We will not join our bodies in that way until you ask for it."

"I won't ever ask for it."

"You will. But that is neither here nor there." He waved away her rejection. "Do you accept my offer?"

What choice do I have? Let the mystery of this man go, along with the possibility of sating this insane hunger inside of me that I can't seem to shake. Or find out who he is and get mine while I'm at it?

Jett stretched her hand across the island, "Deal."

Jerrik took it, "Deal."

Jett pulled her hand from his. The heat. The itch within her was too much.

She quickly gathered her things and Jerrik followed her out to her car with his old clothing and sword. He placed them in the backseat and then leveled her with a stern look.

"Just be sure to inform them that if my sword is not returned to me, I will kill them." Jerrik said sincerely.

"Duly noted." Jett said with widened eyes.

~~~

"Incredible!" Dr. Balinski said.

Dr. Richard Balinski, the archaeologist and Jett had worked together to heft the sword out the backseat. As they held it between them, he gazed at it lovingly.

He was in his 60s. His hair was all white underneath an old, brown faded wide-brimmed fedora. A face weathered from time spent outside on digs. Classic khakis, button up shirt, and work worn boots. He was basically *Indian Jones*.

"I can already tell that this wasn't made in this time." He informed Jett.

"Really?"

"Absolutely. It's all in the craftsmanship. But what's truly fascinating is that it looks new. As in no evidence of centuries buried under dirt and rock or oxidization from prolonged exposure to oxygen. It's as sharp as it would've been back when it was wielded." Dr. Balinski explained.

"And the hair sample?" Dr. Soo-Yun Jin asked.

"Oh, sorry." Jett said. "Can we get the sword in the car, so I can get it out my purse?"

"Sure," Dr. Balinski said.

They slid the sword into the backseat of his little red Fiat. They had to angle it slightly or it wouldn't have fit. Jett handed the baggie of hair to Dr. Jin after she found it in her purse. The doctor held the baggie up to the sun and looked at it intensely.

Dr. Jin was a pretty Korean woman, also in her 60s. Her black hair with a streak of silver shot through it was pulled back into a neat ponytail. Standard black slacks and a white blouse screamed efficient and sensible.

"Okay, many of the hairs have the follicles attached. Which is good. We'll probably be able to let you know the results in about two weeks. It normally takes longer than that, but this could be the discovery of the century. So, we're going to get right on this. It's our top priority." Dr. Jin said.

"Thank you so much," Jett said.

"No need to thank us. This is the most exciting project we've ever done. Can you imagine the implications if it's true?" Dr. Balinski said with a sparkle in his eyes.

"It would be amazing, but this can't go any further than us," Jett said. "Can *you* imagine what the government would do if they found out there's a time traveling Viking walking amongst us? I can't let that happen to him."

"She's right, Rich," Dr. Jin agreed. "If it turns out he's really from the 11th century, we can't tell anyone."

Dr. Balinski nodded solemnly. "Okay, we'll keep it between us."

"Oh, and he said that if anything happens to his sword, he'll kill you." Jett deadpanned much like Jerrik did earlier.

"Noted," Richard said.

Soo-Yun nodded her agreement.

"Perfect! I'll be awaiting your call," Jett said.

"Thank you, Jett." Dr. Jin said.

"It's good to see you, Viv." Richard said as he turned to Jett's boss.

"It's good to see you both as well."

"We're going to have to get together soon. We're overdue for dinner and drinks." Soo-Yun said.

"Yes, we are. And if things turn out in our favor, maybe we can invite two new dinner guests." Viv looked at Jett.

"I'd have to teach him proper table etiquette first," Jett cringed.

They all laughed before the two doctors said their goodbyes and drove off in Richard's car.

"Welp, nothing to do now but wait," Viv said.

"Yeah." Jett agreed as they walked inside the elementary school.

Yeah, right. Nothing to do but flip the hell out about what this supposed Viking plans to do to my body once the results come back. And whether I'll have enough willpower not to beg him to smash these cakes.

Chapter 17

Jett unlocked the front door and slowly opened it. Jerrik sat on the couch like the day before. But this time he was dressed in the medium-washed ripped jeans, white t-shirt, and brown boots. And the area around him was nice and neat.

Wow! He's a fast learner.

"Ready," Jett said from the open doorway.

She wasn't willing to walk any further into her own home for fear he might change his mind and ravish her on the spot, instead of waiting two weeks.

"Aye," Jerrik said.

He stood up and walked over to her. Jett quickly turned to walk back out.

"How was your day?" He asked as he followed her out.

"Good." Jett said as she locked the door.

"When will you know?"

Jett turned to look up at him. She frowned not understanding the question.

"When will you know if what I say is true?

"Oh! Um...I should know in two weeks."

"Hmm... A fortnight. Not too long then." Jerrik said as he raised a hand to her face.

He stroked his thumb across her cheek. Jett was pretty sure she'd stopped breathing.

"Shall we go?" Jerrik said softly. Deeply.

"Oh...uh...yeah."

Jerrik followed Jett down the aisles of a large store. He was amazed by everything around him. The bright colored packaging, people easily grabbed everything they needed, the mounds of already picked or dug up fresh fruit and vegetables, and so on. He was most amazed by the meat already cut in sections and packaged.

"Where does it all come from?" He asked.

"Honestly, most of us don't even know the full process. There's a farm or ranch somewhere that raises cows, chicken, and pigs. They slaughter them and send the slabs to God only knows where. And it magically arrives here, packaged and priced." Jett tried to explain.

"So, you don't know where your meat is really coming from?"

"Or most food." Jett shrugged. "Most of it comes from processing factories."

"And you trust them?"

"Not always. But we try not to think about it or we go to the super overpriced grocery stores that are deemed organic. But we still don't really know. The only way to really know is to grow all your own food. And most people don't have the talent, the time or the space for that. You're only seeing this small town. If you ever see a big city like New York, you'll understand," Jett said.

"New York is where all those tall buildings are?"

"Yes, some of them. It's where I'm from."

"I have seen it on TV. I think I understand."

"It's very complicated. The world is so much bigger than you know in this time."

Jett chose some packages of meat and placed them in her cart. She moved on and Jerrik followed. As they walked people stared.

The women they passed gazed up at him appreciatively or downright lustful. When they realized he was with Jett, the looks often turned to disbelief, jealousy, and then animosity. The men looked at him first with surprise, then envy, and finally diffidence.

Even in his own time, Jerrik had experienced the looks. He and his brothers had been a formidable trio.

A pang of loss punched him in the stomach at the thought of his brothers. He quickly shook it off. He knew he'd see them again when he found his way back home.

But do I really want to go back? Jerrik thought as he gazed at Jett.

A man passed by and stopped to grab something off the shelf. Jerrik looked into the man's cart and saw a bag of chips Jett had had in her pantry that he'd enjoyed. He shrugged and snatched the bag out of the man's cart and put it in theirs.

"Hey!" The man said before slowly raising his eyes up Jerrik's long body to his finally meet his eyes.

Jerrik was a whole foot taller than the man. Jerrik looked down at him with a raised eyebrow.

"You know what? Never mind. You can have it. I can get another bag." The man said and scurried away.

"What are you doing?!" Jett hissed through her teeth.

"You can't go around snatching items from people's cart. I was gonna go down that aisle. This isn't Iceland back in your time. You don't raid people's lands or carts," Jett scolded.

"I've watched enough TV to know that you do still raid here. Just not as openly. You pick locks or smash windows wearing masks and hope not to get caught by the cops. I watched *Set It Off,*" Jerrik said.

"Yes, people do steal, rob or whatever. But those people are also classified as criminals. And you don't want that classification. Because you'll end up in prison. Understand?"

"I suppose."

"Even though you'd probably thrive in prison. You'd end up laird of the prison yard." Jett rolled her eyes and continued pushing the cart.

They finished collecting all the things Jett thought they needed. Then made their way to the register. As they waited in line, Jerrik noticed that nearly everyone stared at them. A red-faced, middle aged man in a bright red hat to match, glared at Jett with pure malice. She didn't seem to notice any of it.

Jerrik helped her place their items on the conveyor belt when it was their turn. He watched in amazement as it moved towards the cashier.

"Wow! How tall are you?" The cashier asked as she rang them up.

She was a young girl who looked up at him in awe.

"I do not know," Jerrik said.

"Really? That's weird."

"Well, I'm six foot even, if that helps."

"Oh wow! He's like a whole nother head taller than you."

"Exactly." Jett grinned at the girl as she swiped her card.

"You should stick to your own kind." A gravelly voice said from behind them.

An audible gasp could be heard from the cashier and down the line of other people behind them. Before Jerrik looked back, he glanced at Jett and she had an expression on her face he'd never seen before. It was anger, frustration, sadness, and a sort of acceptance.

He turned and looked at the miserable man in the red hat who'd made the remark. The man straightened his back to stand taller. And he raised his weak chin defiantly.

"What was that?" Jerrik asked softly.

He felt Jett's hand on his arm.

"Jerrik, let it go."

"No. I would like to know what he meant."

"You're a big, handsome dude with a pure bloodline. You should be with some little blonde hottie, so you can make pretty blonde babies."

The mouths of the people behind him gapped open in shocked horror.

"Not some giant darkie who will muddy your kids."

"Did he just say that?"

"Oh no he didn't!"

"The hell?!"

"Oh my God! How rude?!"

Everyone in earshot exclaimed at the same time.

Jerrik didn't fully understand, but he'd been watching the news and had started developing a sense of the world around him. And being a Viking, he also understood hostility.

Without a word, Jerrik raised his hand. His fingers balled into a tight and massive fist and thunked the man directly on top of his red hat covered head. The man crumpled to the floor like a deflated accordion.

The crowd that had gathered gasped and then began to clap. Jerrik looked at Jett and her eyes were wide with shock. She blinked and shook off her surprise. She grabbed his arm and pulled.

"Let's go!" She shouted and practically ran as she wheeled the cart towards the door.

Jerrik quickly followed her.

Jett opened the hatch of her car and began to hurriedly load the bags into the back. Jerrik helped. When the cart was empty, she shouted at him to get in the car as she ran the cart to the corral. She jumped back in the car, started it, and took off out of the parking lot just as police cars pulled in.

"Holy shit!" Jett shouted and then burst into laughter. "Jerrik, you can't go around bopping people upside the head when they say something stupid or racist. But damn, that shit was pure perfection!"

"I do not fully understand the extent of how bad the things he said were. But the faces of the others, and how hurt you appeared was enough. Remember, I am here to protect you," Jerrik said.

"I know that's what you believe. But you have to pick your battles. You can't hit someone unless they hit you first. It's called self-defense. He could press charges and you'd be in jail. And then how would you get back home?" Jett asked.

"These rules will take getting used to. Where I'm from, I made the rules and enforced punishment. And if someone insults you or your woman, it is within the bounds of Norse laws to defend her honor as well as your own. Sometimes the men didn't even get the chance to defend their woman's honor for she'd already tossed the man on his arse." Jerrik grinned.

"Well, here we can't necessarily do that. Especially someone like me. I'd be put under the jail. Or worse. Shot and killed."

"Someone like you?"

"Yes, someone Black."

"Oh, you mean your skin?"

"Yes."

"So, this is what they were talking about on the news."

"More than likely. You just got to experience some of it firsthand."

"My father spoke of his travels to Hispania where he met the Moorish peoples. He said they were very intelligent, advanced, but also fierce warriors. He had said that their skin was dark as night. Once my lands were secure, I wanted to travel there. It is in our veins to travel and I wanted to meet all the people my father had. The many cultures he met seemed fascinating. People to learn from and to share my culture with. Mine is a trading village. And I wanted to expand what my father and grandfather had started with people from all the far reaches of the world. Color of the skin mattered not. I do not understand why it matters here." Jerrik spoke candidly.

"Neither do I. But it does. Someone several centuries ago but after your time, made distinctions about people based on skin color. Those with white skin were deemed superior and those with darker skin inferior. It became a system of control. And it's still going on today. Where those of us with darker skin have to fight for the rest of the world to see our humanity," Jett said heavily.

"I see you." Jerrik placed his hand on Jett's that laid on the armrest between them. "You matter."

Her eyes blinked rapidly. She nodded her head once and continued driving. But she quickly flipped her hand over and gave his a tight squeeze before turning it back over.

Chapter 18

The knot in Jett's throat persisted the rest of the evening. She was emotionally exhausted. She'd been worried about Jerrik's behavior out in public and making sure he didn't completely embarrass her. Unexpectedly furious and equally devastated by the verbal assault at the register. Fear, pride, and amusement at the way the Viking defended her. And finally awe, joy, and possibly something else she wasn't ready to start feeling just yet because of his words and affection.

It was all too much in the span of a couple of hours, and especially after a long day of working with a group of high energy 8- and 9-year-olds.

After dinner, Jett sat at the kitchen table. She was supposed to be grading math tests. Instead, she stared off into space. Jerrik dried and put away the last dish after cleaning the kitchen. When he was finished, he walked over and sat at the table with her.

"Are you all right?"

"Oh." Jett blinked back to the present. "Yeah, I'm fine."

"Are you still upset with me for hitting that man?"

Jett looked over at him and he looked almost like a contrite little boy.

"No, it's not that. Even though you can't go around hitting people like that, I'm glad you did. It's what I wanted to do but couldn't. So, thank you for defending me."

"Then why do you look so sad?"

"It just gets tiring is all." Jett breathed in deeply and expelled the breath before smiling brightly. "I'm fine. I promise."

Jerrik reached across the table and squeezed her hand. Warm tingles traveled up her arm. Before either of them could say anything else, Jett's phone chimed. She picked it up and saw that it was a text from Dez.

Dez:
Where are you?!? Why haven't you answered my calls or text me back??? Don't have me come up there. Text me back!

"Shit!" Jett hissed.
"What is it?"
"It's my best friend. I haven't talked to her since I found you in your boat, and we communicate almost every day."
Jett's thumbs flew over the keyboard on her phone.

Jett:
Sorry! Sorry! I'm alive and well. Don't kill me. It's just been crazy here. I'll call you soon to tell you about it.

It killed Jett that she couldn't tell Desiree about all that had happened. But she had to know the truth about Jerrik before she told her anything. She knew her best friend would lose her shit if she found out that Jett had let some strange man into her home. Especially a man who thinks he's a Viking. If the DNA test somehow proved he was what he said he was, she still didn't know how she was going to tell her best friend. It would still sound crazy, but at least she'd have proof.

Even though she hadn't received confirmation on whether he really was a Viking yet, Jett knew it in her gut that it was true. He was the most honest person she'd ever met, next to Desiree. And if he truly was a Viking and couldn't find his way home, what then?

"Jerrik, we need to figure out what story to tell everybody, especially when I take you to see if you can get a job on a fishing boat. You cannot roll up and say you're a Viking laird who traveled through time and now you need a job. That's just not gonna fly." Jett leveled him with a look.

"Then what shall I say? I do not know what works here. So, whatever you decide, I will do." Jerrik conceded.

"Wow. That was easy." Jett squinted at him. "For a Viking, you seem awfully open to a woman calling the shots."

"Norsewomen often have a say in what happens in our village. My mother is very intelligent and my father listened to her before he died. As do I. I also fight alongside shieldmaidens. Yes, men generally rule our towns and villages, but women are often wiser. I am not of this time. I am smart enough to know that you would know better than I."

"An overly confident manly man who doesn't mansplain." Jett said with wonder.

"I will take that as a compliment." Jerrik nodded proudly.

"Of course, you would." Jett rolled her eyes. "Anyway, hmm… As of right now, the only thing I can think of for a backstory is that you're from Iceland, you're looking for work because you want to stay in the US, and… Damnit!"

"What?"

"I'd say you're here illegally and that's why you have no identification. But that's simply not true. You'd at least have identification from Iceland, which they'd want to see in order to give you a job. And I know someone, who knows someone, who can get you a fake proof of identity. I just didn't want to tell my best friend about you yet because she'll kill me that I let a stranger come live with me who thinks he's a Viking." Jett let her head fall back and groaned.

"I do not *think* I'm a Viking. I *know* I am."

"Yes, yes. But that doesn't change the fact that everyone else here will think you're crazy and that I'm crazy for letting you live with me."

"You do have a point."

"Shit." Jett said under her breath.

She grabbed her phone again and shot a text to Dez.

Jett:
Dez, when can you come up? I need your help with something.

~ 113 ~

It only took a minute for Desiree to text back.

Dez:
I'm off tomorrow and Thursday. Just let me know what works.

She needed Jerrik to get a job as soon as possible. The grocery bill alone would've made her pass out if it weren't for the prick Jerrik knocked out cold.

Jett:
Come by tomorrow evening around 5. I'll be home then.

Dez:
Alrighty. I can't wait to see you. I miss you!

Jett:
I miss you too! Can't wait.

Actually, I can wait. But you don't need to know that.
"Okay." Jett expelled a harsh breath. "My best friend will be here tomorrow. I'll ask her if she can contact the guy she knows who can help us out. This is gonna be a total shit show."
"That's a show I would rather not attend." Jerrik flared his nostrils in disgust.
"I meant that figuratively." *Lord, give me strength.*

Chapter 19

Jett heard a car pull up and looked out the window. She saw Dez in a mid-size SUV she'd rented from her car club. Jett had gotten home 30 minutes prior and had been anxiously peeking out the window ever since.

"Stay here. I'll be back in a little bit." She said to Jerrik as she grabbed her purse and jacket and bolted out the door.

Dez was just getting out of her rental and looked up at Jett rushing out.

"Hey, Jett!" Dez greeted her happily.

They hugged warmly and rocked from side to side as they embraced for the first time in weeks.

"I missed you!" Dez cried out.

"Me too!"

Jett realized that she really did miss her best friend as her eyes stung with tears. She'd needed someone to talk to about all that had happened, but was so scared Dez would lose it on her for being so careless.

Dez started to head towards her house. Jett placed a hand on her arm to stop her.

"Let's go to a coffee shop in Portland. It's only about 20 minutes away. It's too lovely an evening to be in the house."

"Oh…okay." Dez frowned slightly.

They got in Jett's car and she drove them to downtown Portland. She stayed silent as Dez told her about the disastrous dates she'd been on.

"…and he tried leaving me with the bill. Girl, I said I had to go to the bathroom and snuck out the side door." Dez finished her story.

Jett chuckled distractedly.

"Did you hear anything I just said?"

"Yeah, uh…I have a lot on my mind. I'm sorry."

"Spill it then!"

"Let's wait till we get to the coffee shop."

They fell silent the rest of the way. Jett was grateful that Dez didn't push it. But her friend did surreptitiously glance over at her with worry.

Once they were inside the quaint shop and had their drinks, Jett led them over to a quiet corner.

"Okay, tell me. You're starting to freak me out." Desiree said after they'd both sat down.

"Do you promise to hear me out and not freak out on me in the middle of this coffee shop?"

"What are you talking about?"

"Do you promise?"

"Yes, yes. I promise." Dez rolled her eyes.

"Okay." Jett took a huge fortifying breath. "Saturday morning, I took my daily walk. I went to my favorite spot."

"The lighthouse."

"Right. Anyway, there was this super creepy fog. It was unlike anything I'd ever seen before. It was like…*alive*. Well, as I walked closer it moved back until it revealed this boat. But it wasn't any boat, it was a Viking longboat. Capsized against the rocks."

Dez sat forward, completely engrossed in Jett's story.

"So, I started climbing down the rocks towards it. It looked all burnt up, which seemed weird. Anyway, I walked around to the side of the boat and a man was in it. And he was straight up dressed like a Viking."

"Say what?!"

"Right?!?" Jett sat forward. "I couldn't tell if he was dead or just passed out. So, I climbed over the side of the boat to feel his pulse. I was terrified, but I didn't wanna leave him there. He had a pulse, but it was faint. His eyes shot open and he called me Freya and asked if he was in Valhalla."

"Like the Viking heaven?"

"Yes! It was crazy. Then he passed out again. I called 911 and the fire department came. He's this big ass dude, so it took five guys to lift him onto the stretcher. And then they lifted him up the rocks with a pulley or something. I rode with him to the hospital to make sure he was alright. The man had been poisoned from a wound on his chest. It was poison from a pufferfish."

"This is literally the craziest shit I've ever heard." Dez leaned forward to hiss under her breath.

"And it gets crazier. So, the doctor runs to the waiting room for me to come with. Turns out the man has lost it when he regained consciousness. He's throwing shit and breaking hospital equipment and screaming for his brothers. To make a long story short, he believes himself to be an 11th century Viking from Iceland. He's completely committed to this story.

"Now this is where you're gonna get pissed at me. But just chill, okay?"

"Okay."

"So, the psychiatrist comes and says the guy has some type of amnesia. The kind that you forget important information about your life. But his is unlike anything the doctor had seen before. He said this guy's is rare, where not only does he not remember, but he's made up a whole new life for himself.

The doctor said the guy has to be placed in a facility unless I claim responsibility for him." Jett takes a deep breath. "So…I did."

"What?!" Dez screeched.

Everyone in the coffee shop turned to look at them. Jett shushed her best friend.

"Keep your voice down!" She hissed.

"Sorry. Go on."

"Anyway, I claim responsibility for him and now he's living with me. Wait," Jett held up her hands to silence Dez as she opened her mouth to say something. "I swear, he's not lying. The fog. The clothes he arrived in. The sword that was with him. Even down to the way he talks and looks. I swear he's telling the truth. And to be sure, I took some of his hair from my brush I let him borrow as well as his clothes and sword, and gave them to a geneticist and an archaeologist team who are going to let me know what they discover about him."

"Shit! Jett, I know you're fucking lying." Dez collapsed back in her chair. "Please tell me that you didn't take in some delusional man and that you actually *believe* him?!"

"I know it sounds crazy, but I'm telling you it's all true and I do believe him. But I swear, if they tell me that he's just some regular dude, then he's gone. I'll call the cops and have him physically removed." Jett tried to reassure her friend.

"So, there's a crazy dude sitting in your house as we speak?"

"Yes."

"Let's go! I wanna see him." Dez started to rise.

Jett reached out and grasped her arm. "Finish your coffee first. It's not like he's going anywhere. And, of course, you're gonna meet him. You are staying the night, right?"

"Of course, I am. I gotta make sure my bestie is safe. I gotta feel this dude out."

~~~

Jett unlocked the front door and stepped inside. Jerrik wasn't on the couch like usual. She spied him in the kitchen over the stove and a pan of something cooking that smelled heavenly. Her eyebrows shot up as Dez stepped around her to find the man in question.

Jerrik turned with a smile. He was in relaxed fit jeans and a white tee that hugged his body. His hair was loose around his shoulders and back and his long beard was clean and brushed, if not a smidge in need of a trim. His feet were bare and strangely sexy.

He looked gorgeous.

The way that her friend faltered made Jett smile. *Exactly!*

"Oh wow." Dez whispered under her breath.

"Jerrik, this is my best friend, Desiree. Dez this is Jerrik."

Jerrik wiped his hands with a towel as he walked over to them. His gait was easy and confident. He politely held out his hand. Dez took it. She shook his hand as she looked up at him in complete awe. Jett was shocked herself.

Since when did he learn manners and *to cook?!?*

"It is a pleasure to make your acquaintance." Jerrik finally spoke. His voice deep and colored with his ancient Scandinavian accent.

"Well…shit."

"Uh huh," Jett said knowingly.

"You're fucking beautiful!" Dez said dropping his hand and looking him up and down.

"You'll have to excuse my friend. She has no home training." Jett moved past him over to the stove. "But since when did *you* get training in the culinary arts?"

"I watched that cooking channel all day today. It seemed easy enough and you had all the ingredients to a recipe someone cooked today. I simply followed it." Jerrik shrugged.

"'Simply.' Right. It takes most people years and several baby steps along the way to learn how to cook." Jett breathed in the steam coming from the shrimp sauté he'd made. "But it smells amazing. Thank you so much for cooking."

"You are welcome. I wanted to help. It did not feel right sitting all day as you work and then come home to cook." He said as he briefly stroked her cheek with his thumb. "I only need to boil the pasta and it will be ready."

He walked back to the stove and Jett turned to Dez. She found her friend's eyes still on the large man as he moved about her kitchen. Jett smiled at her.

"Earth to Dez." She waved her hand in front of Desiree's face.

"Oh, sorry. Girl!" Dez pulled Jett over to the living room. "You didn't tell me he looked like *that*! Like Thor's even bigger, older brother."

"I figured you'd see for yourself."

"I can see why you let him come live with you. Hell, I'd let him live inside my womb if he'd fit."

Jett choked on her laughter. "I can't deal with you."

"And the way he touched you." Dez fell dramatically to the couch. "Are y'all fucking?!"

"Shut. Up!" Jett gritted out.

"Have you?!" Dez asked less loudly but just as passionate.

"No." Jett collapsed to the cushion next to her friend. "But he's made no bones about wanting to."

"Are you gonna let him." Dez looked back at him. "I'd let him fuck me every which way from Sunday."

"It's complicated."

"What's complicated? You just jump on and ride."

"You know I've only been with Shawn. And you know how I feel about infidelity."

"Shawn was unfaithful to you first. The gloves are off now, girl. Hell, the only reason you're not officially divorced is because that fucker won't sign the papers. Fuck that beautiful man in there. And don't feel one bit guilty about it."

"But you know I also don't have sex with anyone lightly. And I genuinely like him. So, what happens if he is mentally unstable? Or a criminal? Or really is a Viking and has to go back?" Jett looked at her friend sadly. "What would I do then? I've already been hurt enough this year."

"If he's mentally unstable, it'll be one wild ride before he has to go to the facility. If he's a criminal, then the sex will be extra good and maybe a little dirty. If he's really a Viking, he'll fuck you barbarian style and you'll be happy for the experience you can take with you for the rest of your life." Dez reached out and took Jett's hand. "Not everything has to be so serious. Life or death. Or so black and white. Not to be trite, but you've got one life. *Live* it!"

"We'll see. We already made a deal." Jett sighed heavily. "Apparently, my prudish schoolmarm nature has proven just as obvious to him too. So, in exchange for letting the scientists study his clothing and sword, if the results come back that he is, in fact, a Viking, I have to let him show me pleasure."

"Yass!!! This is gonna be so good!" Dez clapped joyfully.

"How do you know the results will come back that he's a Viking?" Jett crossed her arms.

"You were right. That dude is absolutely a Viking. You couldn't convince me otherwise. I mean, it's crazy as hell, but I believe it. And when the DNA test says he's one-hundred percent that barbarian, he's gonna beat up that pussy like you stole something. And I'm so here for it."

"You suck! I'm nervous as hell." Jett wrung her hands.

"You just better call and give me all the juicy details."

"Anyway, let's change the subject before I vomit. Can I get to the actual reason I asked you to come up here?"

"Oh, yeah. I completely forgot. Go ahead, I'm ready."

"I was hoping you wouldn't mind contacting James," Jett cringed. "We need to get Jerrik some identification. If not an ID, definitely a passport."

"You want me to call James? James Grimes, who I fondly nicknamed Jay-Jay Crimes? As in, my ex with the criminal record?"

"It's not like it was for murder or armed robbery. It was just a little fraud." Jett smiled sweetly.

"Ah, yes. A little white-collar crime never hurt anybody. Nobody but the old ladies he pilfered money from." Dez shook her head. "The one time I break my rule and date a white dude."

"You know I wouldn't ask under normal circumstances. But in order for Jerrik to get a job, he has to have some kind of documentation." Jett said hopefully.

"I hate you."

"You love me."

"Ladies, dinner is ready." Jerrik interrupted them.

They both looked over at him and smiled brightly.

"Damn." Dez eyeballed the big man. "I think I'mma move to Maine. Maybe a Viking can roll through for me too."

The two friends got up and walked into the dining area. Jett's mouth gaped open.

"I have prepared for you a tomato, spinach, and shrimp with penne pasta dish. As well as a cucumber and feta cheese salad."

Jerrik said as if he were on an episode of *Chopped* and pulled back Jett's chair.

"Who are you and what have you done with Jerrik?" Jett asked as she sat in the chair.

"TV. Lots and lots of TV. I have learned much about this time."

"I see that."

"But I must admit, I am not a man of leisure. I would very much like to find work."

"Whoa. He is *so* not Shawn." Dez said impressed. "You couldn't get that dude to work to save his life."

"But do you see why he needs identification?"

"Yeah, yeah. I'll talk to James. I'll probably have to give him some in exchange." Dez sighed. "But the D is good, so it's a win-win."

Jett palmed her face and shook her head.

"What?" Dez asked.

"Nothing. I just missed you."

Dez grinned at her as they dug into their food. Jett ate a couple of forkfuls of the salad. Her eyes shot up to Jerrik as she chewed.

"What all is in this salad?"

"It has cucumber, tomato, avocado, watermelon, and crumbled feta cheese with fresh cracked pepper," Jerrik said.

"I never would've guessed that those ingredients, especially with the watermelon would be so damn good!" Jett groaned around another mouthful.

"It was on the show I watched."

"You're a genius."

"It was fun to cook for you."

Jett looked over at him bashfully as she slowed her chewing.

Dez looked between the two of them and grinned.

"Oh, yeah. This is gonna be so good. The sex between you two is gonna be straight fire," Dez said.

"Aye, I would agree." Jerrik nodded to Dez.

Jett would've dissolved into a puddle of embarrassment under the table if she could have.

"That is not an appropriate discussion to have at the dinner table."

"That's her teacher's voice."

"She has used it on me before."

"We'll let her think that it works."

"I think that would be wise."

Jett blinked at them with a frown as they talked conspiratorially together. *Just when I thought my best friend would give me a hard time for letting a stranger come live in my house, she turns on me and joins teams with him.*

"I'm still sitting right here."

"Aye, we know," he said.

Dez winked and grinned.

They continued eating. Throughout dinner, Jett's head swiveled back and forth as Dez and Jerrik bantered. Unfortunately, most of their banter was at her expense.

"Ugh! I'm gonna wash the dishes and then take a shower. You two do whatever." Jett said after she ate her last bite.

Jett got up, took all their dirty dishes and put them in the dishwasher. She put a dishwashing pod in the washer. Then she hit start.

"You jest!" Jerrik bellowed.

Jett looked over at him. Astonishment was written all over his face.

"This whole time I have been washing dishes, you had that dishwashing machine I have seen on TV?"

"You had to earn your keep somehow." Jett grinned, glad to get him back after his teasing all evening. "Also, everyone should learn how to clean dishes properly before learning how to use a dishwasher. Builds character and dishwashers break."

"Hmm…I suppose so."

"Alrighty. I'm off to take a shower. Behave yourselves." Jett squinted and gave them the 'I'm watching you' point.

She turned on her heel and headed upstairs.

~~~

Jerrik's eyes followed Jett's retreating back as she went upstairs. He turned back with a soft smile. His smile faltered as he looked at her friend. She gave him the evil eye his mother sometimes did when he was small.

"You've got one time to hurt her, big man, and I'll kill you." Desiree threatened.

"I would not. I am certain I am here to protect her."

"I'm not just talking physically. Don't hurt her heart either."

"I fear mine is not safe either." Jerrik said earnestly. "If hers is hurt, so will mine. Alas, I believe it is destined to be so. For I cannot stay. I am laird of my village. It is my duty to care for my people. And I do not believe Jett would leave all of this to come with me." He gestured around the room.

"I appreciate your honesty. Even if it sounds crazy."

"I know."

"So, then, what's your plan?"

"Protect her while I am here. And show her that her husband was a fool."

"That'll be easy."

"Convincing her that she deserves better will not."

"True."

"It is strange to me, for she is the most beautiful woman I have ever seen."

"That you are right, my friend. But the standards of beautiful are a strange thing here."

"Aye. They aren't what is, but what someone else tells you it is."

"Exactly!" Dez looked at him impressed. "I really dig you, Jerrik."

"Thank you…I think."

"Don't worry, it's a compliment." Dez pulled out her cellphone and sighed deeply. "Alright, I gotta call my ex. You're really lucky I like you."

Jerrik raised his brows as she tapped her phone.

"James? Hey, it's Desiree." She paused while the man spoke. She smiled and flushed. "Aww…thanks. Look, Jay. I have a favor to ask. I need a passport for a man from Iceland."

Jerrik didn't know exactly what was happening, but Dez winked at him and continued talking.

Chapter 20

The next morning, Jett came downstairs dressed in a soft, cream cowl neck sweater dress and her brown knee-high boots. Jerrik looked back at her, as was becoming his daily routine. It was as if he liked to see what she was wearing for the day. He smiled brightly.

Dez sat in the chair next to the couch. She grinned as she watched Jerrik smile hard at Jett. Jett could only roll her eyes at her friend.

"Morning, sunshine!" Dez sang out.

"Morning," Jett replied.

"You look lovely, Jett," Jerrik said.

"Thanks," Jett replied bashfully.

"So, we've got a busy day today, and I've got it all covered." Dez assured her. "I talked to Jay-Jay Crimes. He moved to Boston after his probation ended. I guess he started over and moved his life of crime to where the cops don't know him. Anyway, he's already getting the passport ready. Rik and I are gonna get some passport pictures taken, and then we're gonna take a ride to Beantown."

"Rik?" Jett mouthed to Jerrik.

He shrugged.

"We're gonna give Jay the photos, and while he's finishing the passport, I have some plans for big man over here as a surprise for you. Then we'll roll back up here, and if we have enough time, go to the docks and see if we can't see about getting him a job. You have to work Monday through Friday, so getting him to the docks to find a job during the week is impossible. So, I got you."

"Why are you so good to me?" Jett asked.

"Because you helped me through school and convinced me I was smart enough to be a nurse." Dez stood up, walked over to Jett, and clasped her arms. "Because you make people feel like they can accomplish anything, so you deserve the same."

"That's because I knew you could do it."

"Aaaaah!" Dez fake cried as she pulled Jett into a hug. "Come back! I miss not having you a few minutes away."

"I know!" Jett hugged her back just as tightly.

Jett felt a warm chest and strong arms band around her. Arms so long, they were able to also encircle her friend. She turned her head to the side. A curtain of blond hair covered her face as Jerrik laid the side of his face against the top of her head. Jett blew his hair out of her mouth.

"Um…Jerrik?"

"Aye?"

"What are you doing?"

"Embracing you both."

"Because?"

"It looked so comforting."

Dez pulled away and Jerrik took the opening. He wrapped his arms fully around Jett and hugged her from behind with a deep rumble in his chest as he hummed happily. Jett could feel his heart beat against her back. His heat enveloped her like a comforting blanket. His masculine scent mixed with his shampoo and something else she couldn't put her finger on, filled her nostrils. Whatever it was made an almost unbearable ache radiate within her sex.

It's gotta be his pheromones.

"Uh…I gotta go." Jett shrugged out of his embrace.

"Have a good day at work," Jerrik said.

"Thanks." She looked over at Dez. "Watch him. He's…a handful out in public."

"Got it."

Jett looked back one more time before she walked out the door.

Lord only knows what those two are going to get in to.

Chapter 21

As they drove into Boston, Jerrik was overwhelmed with all there was to see. The buildings that stretched out to touch the sky. Hundreds of cars moved in relative order, when he thought they'd all crash into each other eventually. And thousands of people in all shapes, sizes, and colors. All headed in different directions. So many not knowing who the person next to them was. In his village, everyone knew everyone. Jerrik couldn't imagine being in a place filled with so many people that at any given moment, you knew absolutely no one around you.

"Who governs all these people here?" Jerrik asked.

"The government. The president is in charge of the whole country, senators and governors each state, and the mayors are in charge of each city. And they all work together…most of the time, to make sure everything runs smoothly," Dez explained.

Jerrik turned and looked out the window once more at all the people. He couldn't imagine living in the city if he were to stay. But where he was with Jett. In Maine. He could see life there, if he couldn't find his way back.

They met with Dez's ex in a coffee shop. The man had dark hair and green eyes. Of average height, slim build, and a handsome countenance. Jerrik watched as they hugged longer than was appropriate. Her ex gazed at her appreciatively. Once seated, she slid across his passport pictures in an envelope like she was in one of those mob movies he'd watched.

"So, who is this guy?" James asked with tinge of jealousy as he looked over Jerrik's impressive form.

"My best friend's man." Dez answered.

The tension in James's shoulders immediately eased and the scowl between his eyebrows smoothed out.

"What's your name?"

"Jerrik Rolf's son."

"Jerrik Rolfson." James repeated as he wrote it down.

"Date of birth?"

"Late summer. I am seven and twenty."

James stared at Jerrik as if he'd grown another head. Dez reached across the table and laid a hand on her ex's to draw his attention.

"He's twenty-seven. And he was born August, 15th 1994." Dez quickly lied. "And he's from Reykjavík, Iceland."

James wrote it all down.

"Alright, I'll have it to you in a couple of hours." James started to rise. "So, dinner tonight?"

"Okay, that should work?" Dez smiled. "I gotta go back up to Maine after you give us the stuff. But I should be able to get back here for a late dinner."

"Okay, I'm holding you to it."

"I'm sure you are." Dez touched his arm.

She turned and walked out as Jerrik followed.

"You dig him." Jerrik stated as he used the vernacular, he'd picked up from Dez.

"He's bad news."

"You still dig him."

"Yeah, yeah. I make poor choices. Sue me."

Jerrik chuckled.

"Come on. There's somewhere I wanna take you.

~~~

"I need you to hook up my guy here if you're free," Dez said.

They'd walked into a Black barbershop. Dez spoke to the barber who'd just finished up a client.

"Absolutely, ma." The handsome barber in a dark denim smock said flirtatiously.

He glanced at Jerrik and his eyes widened.

"Damn! This dude is big as hell!" The barber looked Jerrik up and down. "Is this your man?"

"No, he's my best friend's man. She's at work and I thought I'd get him hooked up for her." Dez grinned.

"Alright, bet. Come take a seat, my man. I'm Bryan." He said as he dusted the hairs off his chair and turned it towards Jerrik.

The big Viking walked over and sat down.

"Just his beard," Dez said.

"What would you like? A trim and clean up?"

"Aye. I wish to look like the modern man."

"Say no more, my dude. I got you."

Jerrik closed his eyes as the man went to work on his beard.

The man used a straight razor to shave the hairs that had grown up Jerrik's cheeks. He cleaned up the hairs on his neck. He expertly wielded scissors to cut off several inches of Jerrik's long shaggy beard. He slathered what was left of his beard with a delicious smelling product and then wrapped Jerrik's face with a wet, steaming towel.

Jerrik had never felt more relaxed in his entire life.

After about fifteen minutes under the towel, Bryan removed it. He ran a comb through Jerrik's beard, and then ran aftershave on the parts of his skin where he'd used the straight razor. Bryan spun the chair around for Jerrik to see himself in the mirror.

Jerrik leaned forward to get a good look at himself. His beard now only hung an inch or two longer than his chin. He smoothed a hand over the blond hairs. It was soft and fragrant. Jerrik smirked and with the hair cleaned from his cheeks, a dimple appeared.

"Wait! Hold up." Dez blurted out. "Smile, Rik."

Jerrik smiled and two deep dimples appeared in his cheeks.

"Oh shit! You've got dimples too?!? Jett is gonna fall out for sure."

"These are good things here?" Jerrik asked.

"Absolutely. Why? They weren't where you're from?"

"No. I grew my beard to cover them. They made my face look too kind. Too soft."

"Makes sense. Well, you should definitely flaunt them here." Dez turned to the barber. "Thank you, Bryan. You hooked it up."

Dez paid the man and she guided Jerrik back out onto the busy sidewalk. She'd looked up directions to their next destination and they walked down to the subway. Dez tapped her debit card at the turnstile for her and Jerrik to go through.

"Okay, Rik. We're taking the subway because it's easier than finding parking everywhere we go. But just a heads up. Whatever you do, don't manspread."

"What is this?"

"It's where you sit and spread your legs apart really far making it uncomfortable for other people, particularly women, to sit next to you. There's usually limited space on the train and manspreading makes it worse. Men do it all the time, and we hate it. Got it?"

"Got it."

They got on the train and headed towards the only two empty seats. Immediately, Jerrik noticed a man with his legs spread wide, just as Dez sighed heavily in frustration.

"See what I mean?" She asked.

"Hmm…" Jerrik grunted.

The Viking moved around her to stand in front of the man.

"Close your legs," Jerrik commanded.

The man looked up. Jerrik's size and height didn't seem to faze the man.

"Fuck you."

"Close your legs and make room for the lady." Jerrik said softly.

Everyone pretended to mind their business, but many began to glance over to see what would happen next.

"And if I don't? What the fuck are you gonna do about it?"

In a blur of movement, Jerrik reached down. He grasped the man by his jacket, gripped it tightly, and proceeded to toss him onto the floor of the train. He nodded his head to the empty seat and Dez took it with a satisfied smirk on her face. The man crawled away and moved to another car. Others around them clapped boisterously as he left. Jerrik bowed his head before he sat next to Dez.

"I need to take you everywhere with me. You'd make a great bodyguard."

"That is what Jett said if I cannot get a job on a fishing boat."

"You'd be good at it. You tossed that dude like a ragdoll and he was not small. That shit was hilarious." Dez wheezed.

"Where are we going now?" Jerrik asked.

"Just a place for you to get those split ends taken care of. And for someone to show you the power of the top knot."

Thirty minutes later, Jerrik sat in another swivel chair. This time a white guy with a stylish haircut and black smock worked on cutting off Jerrik's split ends after he'd gotten his hair washed.

"You have such beautiful hair." The man said with a soft voice. "Honestly, it goes with the whole gorgeous package. My goodness."

Jerrik looked at the man curiously. He then looked over at Dez. She gave him a nervous look.

"Honey, is he yours?" The stylist asked Dez.

"Uh no. He's my best friend's man."

"Well, I tried. But oh, to find a man like you for myself."

Jerrik turned slightly to look at the man.

"You are with other men?"

"Oh, yes, sweetie."

"Rik, I'll explain later." Dez quickly jumped in.

Jerrik frowned in thought but didn't say anything more.

"Okay, all done with your trim. Now, you said you wanted him to learn how to tie up his own hair?"

"Yes. I think my friend would lose her mind."

The hairstylist demonstrated all the ways Jerrik could tie up his hair. All of it up in a top knot. Half up, half down. And a ponytail at the nape of his neck. Before they left the salon, on his own, Jerrik put his pale blond locks up into a messy bun. An extra black hair tie around his thick wrist as a backup.

He looked at himself in the mirror and nodded in approval. His beard was cleaned and trimmed. His hair gleamed and the messy bun suited the whole look.

"Damn, Rik! Jett is gonna lose her shit."

Everyone in the salon, from the stylists, shampoo girls, and customers, all stared at him appreciatively.

"We've got one last stop. After that, James should be ready with your stuff," Dez said.

They started down the sidewalk. Several eyes followed Jerrik as he passed.

"So, there are men who are with men here?" Jerrik asked curiously.

"And women with women. Some who date both. Some who were born one sex, but feel like another. Basically, things are getting pretty fluid these days. If that makes sense?" Dez said.

"Sex between men happen where I am from, but it must not get in the way of marriage and procreation. It is quite complicated in my time. It is acceptable to be the dominant male during such and act. But those in the submissive role are shunned." Jerrik said thoughtfully.

"Have you been with a man?" Dez asked.

"I have not. And as laird, I have not come across anyone who has." Jerrik thought for a moment. "But with the world as it is today. The population as it is and no need for children to help farm. It is good that people are free to be themselves."

"Dude, there are people born and raised in present times who aren't as enlightened as you are. Are you sure you're a Viking?" Dez asked as she looked at him impressed.

"I am." Jerrik raised his chin.

"Well, you're good people either way, Rik."

Jerrik nodded matter-of-factly as they continued on.

Last, she took him to a nail salon. She spoke with the tiny Vietnamese woman and the woman guided Jerrik over to a table, while Dez sat in a chair to get a pedicure.

"I saw something on social media that I think will look so good on you. Trust me." Dez said to him as he looked at her curiously.

Jerrik had no idea what was happening. But he sat and let the woman start snipping and clipping at his nails. His hands were massive compared to hers, but she handled him like it was nothing.

After she cleaned up the rough skin around his nails, clipped and filed his nails short and even, and pushed back his cuticles; she took matte black paint and added a couple thin lines and tiny dots on each nail. Each line razor thin. Some horizontal, most vertical with accompanying dots. Until each finger had a simple design, but every nail was different. The minimalistic design looked tribal. Almost Viking. And she finished off the look with a clear matte coat to protect the masculine design.

"Lemme see!" Dez said from her spot in the pedicure chair.

Jerrik walked over and held out his hands to her.

"Yassss!!! You look like a fucking rock star! So hot!"

Her phone chimed with a notification. She opened it and her fingers flew across the screen.

"James is done. I told him we'd be there in about twenty."

Once they were finally done, and Jerrik had his new passport in hand with a few random stamps from around the world for authenticity, they were back in the car and on their way back to Maine.

"Alright, last stop the docks! Let's see if we can't get you a j-o-b." Dez said.

~~~

"Well, son." Mr. Murdock said looking Jerrik up and down. "You certainly are a big strapping young fellow. But have you worked a day in your life? You look like one of those social media people. What do they call it?"

They stood on one of the several docks at the marina in Portland. Desiree had purposefully walked to every fishing boat, large or small, she could find. They'd finally found Mr. Murdock as he'd just come in after 48 hours at sea. His was a lobstering boat. He wasn't one of the big commercial fishing boats, which was good in order to get Jerrik a job under the table. But he wasn't small time either, so Jerrik had potential to make good money.

Mr. Murdock was a tall man himself. His face was weathered from a rough life at sea. White stubble covered half of his leathery face. And his blue eyes were faded. But he had a head full of pure white hair that curled out from under his hat and against his collar.

"You mean, Insta model or social media influencer," Dez chimed in.

"Yeah, one of those."

"Sir, I do not even own a phone. Will this be proof enough?" Jerrik held out his hands palms up to show the side that hadn't been pampered earlier.

Mr. Murdock grabbed Jerrik's hands and turned them this way and that.

"How old are you again?"

"He's twenty-seven," Dez blurted out before Jerrik could say 'seven and twenty' again.

"Your hands almost look as rough as mine and I'm three times your age. What did you do in Iceland?"

"I fished, farmed, hunted, and fought."

"What kind of fighting did ya do?"

"He fought with those big fish he's gonna help you catch." Dez stepped in again.

"We're lobstermen, sweetheart."

"Yeah, that." Dez shrugged.

"Well, son, you're actually in luck. I had a sternman just quit after a few months. He said it was too hard and getting too cold, so ya can see why I asked if you'd done hard labor before. If hard work and a little cold weather doesn't scare ya, can you start Monday?"

"Yes, sir."

"We leave out before dawn. We get here around 3:30 in the morning and are out on the water by 4. Some trips out, we come back by evening. Other times, we might be out for four days. It all depends on how full the traps are. It'll be a two-man crew. Just you and me. As big and strong as you look, you'll definitely be pulling in the lobster traps, baiting them again, and getting 'em back out there. They weigh about 40lbs each. But I think you could handle that. Would that work for ya?"

"Aye, it would."

"He doesn't have a car and it would be hard for anyone to take him at that time." Dez added.

"That's okay. The address you gave, I pass by on my way to the docks. I can pick you up at 3am." Mr. Murdock offered.

"I will be ready." Jerrik nodded.

"Perfect, Jerrik. Then I'll see ya on Monday at 3am sharp. I'll give ya a one-week trial period. If ya work out, you can stay through to the end of the season in December."

Mr. Murdock held out his hand and Jerrik took it. They shook hands firmly. Jerrik was excited to have something to do again. And being out on the water always made him happy. Although he didn't have the heart to tell the old man that if he found the fog, he'd be leaving long before the end of the season.

And if there was any where he'd find the mysterious fog that had brought him to the 21st century, it would be out on the open sea.

Jerrik and Dez bid their goodbyes to the lobsterman and headed back to the car. Once back in the car, Jerrik's heart pounded a little faster as they got closer to home. Excitement at the thought of seeing Jett prickled his skin. He'd had an entertaining day with her best friend, but throughout the day all he could think was how Jett felt about the things he'd seen and discovered. He wanted to know her thoughts. And he didn't want to admit it, but he was nervous about how she'd like his new look.

He was a confident man, but this new place and this new woman had him a little out of sorts. Nothing the arrogant man had ever experienced before. When a woman was attracted to him and he returned her desire, he'd toss her skirts and fuck her anywhere he chose. He knew Jett wanted him just as much as he wanted her, but she had more control than anyone he'd ever known. Jerrik was positive his balls had swelled to twice their size and ached constantly. His dick would permanently turn to stone if he didn't find relief soon. His hand was certainly not enough.

Hopefully, work would be a welcome distraction.

Odin give me strength.

Chapter 22

As Jett pulled into her usual parking space, Dez and Jerrik pulled in right next to her. Jett quickly got out of her car. She was excited to see how everything went and prayed Jerrik didn't do anything too crazy.

Well, he is with her. So, at least he's not in jail somewhere.

Jerrik unfolded himself from within the car and turned to face Jett. Her mouth popped open in shock. His hair was pulled back into a messy knot. His beard was nice and even and much shorter than when he'd left. And when he smiled at the sight of her, Jett's stomach did a somersault at the appearance of dimples she didn't know he had.

Jerrik walked around the car and towards Jett.

"So…what do you think?" Dez asked.

Jerrik stroked his beard. Jett reached out and quickly grabbed his hand. She examined his nails and looked up at Dez questioningly.

"I needed to go get my toes done and figured he could get the new Manly Mani that's getting popular." Dez explained.

The design on each nail of his enormous manly fingers, somehow made his hands look all the more virile. If that were possible.

"I never would've even thought of it, but it suits you perfectly. Very masculine. Very…*Viking*." Jett smiled up at him.

Jerrik turned over his hand and clasped hers warmly.

"I am pleased you like it."

Jett felt heat flush her face. She quickly removed her hand and started towards the front door. She missed the look of disappointment and sigh of resignation from Jerrik. Her best friend did not.

Jett unlocked the door, but Dez stopped her from walking in.

"Hey, Jerrik, could you give us a minute?" Dez asked.

"Aye." He said as he walked inside.

Dez closed the door.

"I gotta roll out because Jay wants to take me to dinner and it's a two-hour drive back to Boston."

"Oh, okay." Jett said as she pulled Dez in for a big hug. "Thank you so much for everything."

"I'll let Jerrik fill you in on the job front." Dez pulled back to look at Jett. "But please, give him a shot. He cares for you more than you know. He knows there's a possibility of hurting you and he doesn't take that lightly, because he knows that it'll hurt him as well. And he let me play 'dress up the Ken doll' with him today in the hopes that you'd be receptive of it. Open up and let him treat you the way you deserve. If nothing else, it'll teach you what you deserve and should demand of any man who wants to be in your life."

"You're right. You're right." Jett breathed in deeply and blew it out quickly. "I know I should let him in. I'm just so scared."

"Of what?"

"Of *everything*!" Jett cried out in frustration. "What if I won't be enough, like I wasn't enough for Shawn? What if he thinks I'm just as lame in bed? What if it is so great that I'll be heartbroken and can't find someone else as good when he's gone?"

"You'll 'what if' yourself to death if you keep going like this." Dez rubbed up and down Jett's arms. "But *what if* you just go for it? Because you may never get a chance to be with someone as crazy beautiful as he is. They don't make 'em like that anymore. Besides, he's obviously smitten with you. I know for a fact that you've been waiting for that your whole damn life. Girl, you better jump on that dick!"

Jett laughed and hugged her friend.

"I love you, Dez."

"I love you too, Jett." Dez pulled away. "Alright. I'm outta here. I got my own dick to attend to. If nothing else, that criminal can lay some pipe. And my plumbing certainly needs some unclogging."

"You're disgusting." Jett joked.

"I know. Toodles!" She wiggled her fingers before she turned and headed to her rental.

Jett watched as her friend pulled out and drove off. A fat drop of rain fell on her head and she looked up. The patter of more drops followed. Jett took a deep breath and walked inside her home just as the sky opened up. Her eyes landed on Jerrik sitting on the couch. Her heart raced again at the sight of him.

"How about some chicken noodle soup and grilled cheese sandwiches? It's a perfect night for it." Jett suggested.

"I don't know what that is, but I am sure it will be wonderful." Jerrik stood. "Can I assist you?"

"Uh…if you'd like. Even though there's not much to it."

Jett busied herself with grabbing four cans of traditional condensed chicken noodle soup from her childhood. Jerrik stood next to her as she instructed him.

"Pop the cans and pour them into this pot." She handed him the pot. "Fill up one can with water twice and pour the water in with the soup."

Jett heated the skillet on the stove as she grabbed the bread, cheese, and butter. They stood arm pressed to arm as she showed him her way to make grilled cheese. Her body ached to be closer to him. Instead, she focused on the food.

"I butter the outside of each slice of bread, put the cheese in the middle and put it in the hot skillet. And I flip when one side is toasted. That's it."

"That seems simple enough."

"It is."

"Back during my time, as laird, I always had my mother, a servant or thrall make my meals. I did not know how soothing cooking could be. I enjoy it."

"Thrall?"

~ 141 ~

"A slave. Usually, a villager captured from a rival Viking settlement. I didn't keep many. I usually set them free once they'd gained my trust. And they often stayed because life in my village was preferable to where they'd come." Jerrik explained.

"Ah, okay. Um…do you miss your family?"

"I do." Jerrik turned to look down at her. "But not as much as I think I should. Does that make sense?"

"It does." Jett paused as her gaze was held captive by his intensity. "I…uh…miss my dad. But other than that, I don't miss my mother or my sister."

"Why?"

"My mother has always made me feel self-conscious of my body, height, and skin color. And…well, my sister is the woman I caught my husband with. She's always had a habit of taking what was mine." Jett finally looked away.

"Your mother is blind. I find your body most appealing. Welcoming." Jerrik said as he turned to face her fully. "You skin color is extraordinary. Rich and smooth. It draws my eye."

He cupped the side of Jett's face and added the slightest pressure to make her turn to him.

"And your height is preferable for me. Your lips are within kissing distance to mine."

Jerrik's lips slowly descended to hers. He gave her plenty of time to turn away. Jett didn't want to. Not this time.

His soft, pink shapely lips brushed gently against hers. Jett was ready to open up fully to him and Jerrik pulled away.

"I apologize. I said I would wait until you receive confirmation that I am who I say I am." Jerrik turned back to the stove and flipped the sandwich in the skillet.

For the first time, Jett wanted to say 'Fuck the food and fuck that DNA test.' But she didn't know how to initiate intimacy. Or maybe she was too afraid to after being rejected by Shawn. Instead, she bit her lip and continued cooking beside Jerrik.

They sat down to eat when the food was ready. Jerrik moaned with delight over the flavor of one of her childhood favorites.

"Good right?"

"Tis." Jerrik hummed happily. "I do not believe there has been one meal I have not enjoyed here."

"The culinary arts have evolved I'm assuming."

"Aye, they have."

"Tell me about your village."

"Well, it is nestled in an inlet surrounded by mountains. It is a trading village, but also has some of the best soil in Iceland, which is why I often had to battle off others who sought to take what was mine."

Jett listened as he continued talking about his lands and the feuds there had been. There were no signs of artifice. He was a great storyteller and Jett was enthralled. It was then that she realized that it didn't matter what the test results said, because she knew what they would say.

He is what he says he is.

Jett knew it in her gut that he really was a Viking who had somehow jumped through time. She believed him. And that changed *everything*.

She no longer wanted to hold back. Jett wanted him with every fiber of her being. But she was no seductress. It felt impossible, but she was more nervous than she had been in days previous. Now that she knew there was nothing there to hold her back from being with him, her hands shook and her stomach twisted into knots. Jett placed her spoon in her bowl. She couldn't eat another bite.

Jerrik ate another bowl of soup and grilled cheese sandwich as he told her about his new job. All while Jett had an existential crisis internally.

After he finished, Jerrik looked at her curiously. She'd been quiet for the last half hour.

"Are you alright?"

"Yeah, I'm fine."

"Would you like to watch a movie after I clean the kitchen?"

"Uh…sure. That sounds good."

Should I sit on the couch next to him? Or maybe that would be too obvious. But if I don't sit next to him, how will I ever find the

~ 143 ~

opening to be more intimate? Ugh! This sucks. Wine! Wine will help loosen me up.

Jett got up and went to the fridge. She found an unopened bottle of her favorite sweet wine. She quickly poured herself a very large glass. She took the opportunity while Jerrik was cleaning the kitchen to sit on the couch. It would be less awkward if she was already there when he came over. She removed her brown knee-high boots and tried her best to relax back on the couch cushions.

Once Jerrik was finished, he walked over and sat next to her. Jett internally sighed. *That part was easy.*

"What would you like to watch?" Jerrik asked.

He picked up the remote and turned on a streaming service.

"It doesn't matter. Pick whatever you'd like."

"Well, I have been wanting to watch this." Jerrik said as he scrolled to *365 Days.*

Oh, dear God!

"Um, sure. That works."

Yes, let's watch this movie where these two people have incredible chemistry and have some of the hottest love scenes ever created for a non-pornographic movie. And all when I'm already on the verge of combusting because I have to watch it while sitting next to an Adonis, who, for reasons unknown to me wants to fuck me senseless.

Jerrik selected the movie and it began to play. Jett quickly downed the rest of her glass of wine, jumped up to get more, and came back with a full glass and the rest of the bottle. She sat next to Jerrik once more.

Jett couldn't have sat straighter if she tried. Her back was stiff as a board. Her thick, deep dark chocolate thighs pressed together. Her feet were planted flat and firmly on the floor. She tried to pull down her sweater dress to cover her knees, but it only slid back up when she moved even slightly. So, instead, she primly laid her left hand across the top of her thighs and held her wineglass in her right hand.

You're such a prude!

Jett took several more giant sips of wine. The first glass slowly began to do its work. Just not fast enough for her nerves.

"This man is very much like Norsemen. He takes what he wants." Jerrik said as the main character on screen grabbed his captive and shoved her up against a wall.

Maybe you should do the same. Because I'm certainly not brave enough to make the first move.

As the movie progressed and the tension grew on-screen and in her living room, Jerrik's hand moved closer to Jett's leg. She kept one eye on the screen and one eye on his sexy manicured hand. Once his hand got close enough, Jett spread her thighs ever so slightly, so that her right leg moved a little closer to his hand. Jerrik's pinky finger lightly stroked the side of her thigh. At first contact, Jett's back straightened even further than she knew was possible.

When she didn't pull away, Jerrik's exploration became bolder. His rough palm slid up her soft skin. Jett's breath became more ragged. Jerrik paused to let her catch her breath. It was no use. The scene when the couple on-screen has sex for the first time on a yacht had begun. Jett's clit thrummed. She felt her sticky arousal coat her inner walls in preparation and anticipation.

Without thought Jett leaned over and kissed his cheek. His beard smelled woodsy. Masculine.

"I believe you." Jett whispered after the chaste peck.

It was all she could do. It was her only opening.

"I do not understand." Jerrik turned to look at her.

Their faces were only inches apart.

"I-I don't need a test to tell me. I believe you."

Blue fire practically shot from his eyes. He understood without her saying it word for word that she was ready for him to teach her passion and pleasure.

Jerrik reached over and clasped her left arm and tugged her up. She parted her legs and placed her knees on either side of his hips to straddle him but refused to sit fully on his lap.

"No, I can't."

"Aye, you can."

"I-I'm too heavy."

Jerrik gave her a long-suffering look.

This isn't Shawn. This is a big ass Viking.

Jett took a deep breath and began to lower herself. Jerrik's huge hands braced the sides of her thighs that were exposed from her dress that hiked up in the intimate position. A shiver ran down her spine at the heat that radiated from his rough palms. His hands slid up and around to her rump and continued up her back as she sunk down to his lap.

As Jerrik guided her towards the hard ridge of his jeans, Jett wondered if her intuition had told her not to change out of her dress and into sweats just yet. The ease in which the warm apex of her legs fit snuggly against his contained erection she was sure of it.

Jerrik raised his hands to her face and cupped it gently. She looked at him and his eyes caressed her every feature.

"Norsemen do not often use soft words. But you are so achingly lovely," he said gruffly.

Jett could no more stop her eyes from welling with tears than she could stop the rain from falling outside. Jerrik's thumbs were there to catch them as they fell. He wiped them away as he pulled her towards him.

First, he bent her head and gently kissed the top of her closely buzzed hair. Then his lips and the soft hairs of his beard found and brushed over her mouth. He kissed her tenderly. It was all the coaxing she needed. Jett's lips opened for him willingly.

Permitted access, Jerrik's tongue plundered her awaiting mouth. He gripped the back of her head tightly, holding her to him as he tongue-fucked her mouth. With every foray into her depths he went, her clit pulsed with need for the same affection.

Of their own accord, Jett's hips rocked forward. Her body shuddered at the friction. Her fingers found their way into his hair. She found the hair tie and unwound it. His long locks spilled into her hands and onto his broad shoulders.

A soft hiccup of emotion jerked her body. Jerrik pulled back and looked at her still watery expression. He lifted his lips slightly and kissed the tip of Jett's nose. Still more tears came. He kissed them away as he gently kissed each cheek. He turned her head this way and that to pay respect to her forehead, jawline, and chin. Her eyes fluttered closed and Jerrik kissed each lid as well.

He reclaimed her mouth and Jett opened eagerly. His massive hands moved to her breasts as he cupped them. His thumbs stroked over her nipples still covered by her bra and the cloth of her dress. But they still hardened to little nubs. His greedy hands moved to the cowl neck of her dress and he easily pulled the fabric down her ebony shoulders. The rough pads of his fingers slid back up her arms to her bra straps. He bent his fingers into claws and let his nails gently rake her tender skin as he pulled the straps down.

Jerrik's lips kissed a path down to Jett's neck. He licked and sucked the highly sensitive skin there. He kissed a path down her clavicle to the swells of her breasts. He tugged the right cup of her bra down and a tiny pebbled nipple with large dark areola popped out. Jerrik's pink lips wrapped around the peak and his hot wet tongue flicked the nub. Jett's head fell back and she cried out as her hips rocked against his tucked away erection.

One of his hands trailed down her soft tummy and disappeared under her dress. His hand reached the apex of her thighs and stopped. He moved around to her ass and Jett felt a sharp tug. The sound of cloth ripping followed. A moment later, Jerrik lifted her ruined lacy briefs.

"What are these?" He asked huskily.

"P-Panties."

"What are they for?"

"To cover our private parts, like the boxer briefs I got you."

"Women don't wear such things where I'm from. There is nothing to tossing up the skirts of a lass and taking your relief from her behind a barn or against a tree. These would get in the way. Perhaps you should not wear them anymore."

"Some women don't wear them. But it kinda feels immodest to wear a dress, especially knee-length or shorter and not wear them," Jett said.

"Then wear something longer. But I would advise you not to wear them again," Jerrik ordered.

"W-Why?"

"I will destroy every pair I find you in."

Sweet baby Jesus! I think my vagina purred.

Jerrik lifted the ripped pair of lacy underwear to his nose. Arctic blue fire stared at her before his eyes closed as he inhaled deeply.

Yep. Definitely purred.

Jerrik tossed her panties and rubbed his nose against hers. His lips brushed slightly over hers.

"I-I guess that could get expensive." Jett whispered against his lips.

"No. Not if you do not buy anymore."

"There's that too." Jett said breathlessly as his fingers slid up her thigh.

Her stomach muscles tightened and quivered at the anticipation of his fingers reaching her aching sex.

A large, single digit stroked down between her slick folds. Jett sharply inhaled just as Jerrik hissed through his teeth.

"Thor's blood! You're so wet." He panted against her lips.

"Yes," she said on a gasp.

Their foreheads pressed together. His finger, slick with her arousal, swirled around her clit. Jett cried out. Her damp breath fanned his mouth. Jerrik pulled his fingers away.

"No!" Jett huffed, feeling the loss.

He brought his hand up to this mouth and sucked on the finger that glistened with her slickness. He groaned deep in his throat and his eyes closed. As if she tasted better than any food he'd ever sampled.

"You taste like the finest meal served in Valhalla."

Jett looked away bashfully. Jerrik placed a finger under her chin and lifted her face. His eyes caught hers and he stared at her. She saw the barely contained lust in his eyes. But there was more. So much more that she wasn't ready to address. But her heart stumbled and then started back faster than before.

Jerrik raised his hand up to show Jett his fore and middle fingers.

"Ride them."

He dropped his hand and it disappeared under her dress once more. His fingers swirled around her entrance, coating them. Once they were saturated, he stroked them inside her as his thumb slid over her clit. Jett shuddered. Jerrik hissed through his teeth.

"You are so tight. Your quim is going to squeeze my cock empty of every drop." Jerrik flicked his tongue against her lips. "Now, ride them."

Her fingers gripped his shoulders. Her white teeth bit down on a plump, ebony lip. Curly lashed lids fluttered closed. She rose up to his fingertips. Only to sink back down to his palm. His thumb stayed stationary as her clit slipped up and down its length.

"Look at me," he commanded.

Jett's eyes slowly opened.

"I want to watch you come undone."

Her body involuntarily shuddered.

Fuck!

Jett felt his words in her clit. The walls of her pussy contracted convulsively around his fingers. She continued to ride his thick, long fingers. She lifted and slid back down, adding a roll of her hips on the way down. It created added friction against his thumb.

A decade worth of pent-up sexual frustration swiftly brought Jett to the peak.

"Aah…aah…unh!" She cried out as she held eye contact with Jerrik.

Jett's sheath squeezed his fingers as she flexed around them and rode out her climax. She felt the rush of feminine cum drip from her onto his hand.

He brought his fingers to her mouth. They were coated with her cream. He traced her lips with his wet digits. Jett's tongue peeked out to taste her own cum as he licked his fingers clean while he watched her. His eyes lit with icy flames.

"Breathtaking."

Passionately, he gripped the sides of her face and pulled her towards him. His tongue licked the rest of the spicy salve from her lips and dipped into her mouth. He devoured her until her lips were swollen and her taste was gone. Jett shuddered and melted onto his chest. Jerrik wrapped his strong arms around her.

The attention, comfort, and affection he'd lavished on her as he brought her to the first orgasm ever bestowed upon her by another person, finally broke the carefully constructed dam she'd built around her emotions the last few months. Maybe years.

Ignored by her husband.

So little affection by men outside of her father.

No protection from her own mother.

How her father always deferred to her mother when he knew she was wrong.

The way her twin absorbed everything that was Jett's or what Jett wanted like a parasite.

She'd never truly been loved properly.

All of it crashed down as she'd come hard on his hand and she couldn't hold back any longer as his arms embraced her. Jett sobbed like a baby as he cradled her tenderly.

For the first time since she was five, Jett felt small. She'd been bigger than her sister. Bigger than the kids in the neighborhood. Bigger than all the girls in school and even most of the boys. She hadn't realized it, until this very moment. But in every space, she found herself in Jett tried to make herself smaller. Until Jerrik... He made her feel tiny. She forgot to shrink. She didn't need to.

His hands rubbed her back soothingly. She felt his lips on the top of her head. She sucked in a shaky breath.

A Viking barbarian has more tenderness and love within him than the modern men in my life.

But he can't stay. He'll eventually find that fog and disappear from my life as quickly as he'd come into it. Which means I can't keep him. How can I experience something like this, and then let it go?

~~~

Jett felt warm and soft within the circle of Jerrik's arms. The spicy scent of her sex floated around them. Her tears dampened his chest. Jerrik's cock ached with need, but he dismissed it as he comforted the woman in his arms. He also tried to ignore how his heart that thumped thickly in his chest ached as well.

I cannot feel such things. I must go back. To my village. My brothers. And my mother. They must know I still live.

Her tears subsided and she slowly rose up. Her big, expressive brown eyes looked at him sweetly. He could tell Jett tried to hide her bashfulness by bravely looking him in the eye. But it was no use. Her shy smile and innocent look said everything.

"So…um…what about you?" She asked.

"What about me?"

Jett's eyes dropped to his lap and back up again.

"Oh. That." Jerrik grinned at her and inhaled deeply. "Well, I suppose that depends on you."

"Me?"

"Aye." He stretched and put his hands behind his head. "Are you ready to ask me inside?"

"If by inside, you mean sex…then, no."

"Suit yourself." He expelled a breath and dropped his arms. "I will be fine."

He moved to get up, but Jett placed her hands on his chest.

"I-I…c-could…you know. Do to you what you did to me." Jett shrugged shyly.

"Aye. You could."

Jerrik stretched his arms out across the back of the couch. He fought the smile that tugged at the edges of his mouth. He wanted to ravish every inch of her. He wanted to feel her hands on his skin. But he wanted her to want to do it too. So, he had no plans to help her.

If she wants it, she knows what to do.

Jett hesitated for a moment. Then her hands slowly slid down his chest. Jerrik's cock jumped within his jeans at the thought of her hands around him. She made her way to the button. Her fingers trembled as they fumbled with the zipper. Jett peeled back the sides of his jeans once they were undone. She bit down on her bottom lip as she pulled down the elastic band of his boxer briefs.

Jerrik's erection sprang out from under the cloth. Jett's breath hitched as she gazed at him. A pearl of clear fluid leaked from him. Jett dabbed her finger in the liquid. She brought it to her mouth and her tongue flicked out to lick the pad of her finger clean. His cock jerked.

"Odin's blood!" Jerrik shouted out. "I nearly spilt my seed."

He gripped the side of Jett's head and pulled her mouth towards his. He attacked her lips and tongue with a ferocity he'd never felt before. Her fingers slid around his length. Soft, warm hands stroked him. Each caress of her hands down his shaft matched every dip of his tongue into her mouth. Jerrik's testicles drew up and his spine tingled.

Jett wasn't masterful in her handling of him. She fumbled often. Her hold was too gentle when he could handle a much firmer grip, the way many a shieldmaiden would handle him. But her touch alone was enough to make him lose himself. Her eagerness aroused him more than he could have imagined. And the feelings within him that had been building since he opened his eyes in his boat and thought her the Goddess of fate and destiny, made Jerrik bark out a shout of pleasure as cum shot from him.

"Aaah! Aaah! Jett." He panted against her lips.

Semen spurted onto his shirt up to his chest in torrents. As if he hadn't relieved himself a few nights before after catching Jett pleasuring herself. She made him feel like a boy still wet behind the ears.

"You steal my very breath," Jerrik said.

He pressed his forehead against hers.

"Same." She said softly.

He pulled back and looked at her. Her expressive eyes were more open than they'd been since she'd saved him. The wall she'd built up had crumbled in the space of time it took them to both orgasm.

Jerrik kissed her nose and smiled, his dimples deepening. He looked down at himself and the mess he'd made.

"I think I shall shower. Would you like to join me?"

Jett scrunched her face and pulled up her sweater to hide behind. She shook her head vigorously.

"I'm not ready for that just yet."

"It is okay. Tonight, was the first step."

~~~

Jett rolled off Jerrik's lap. He jumped up and headed for the bathroom. Once the door closed, Jett buried her face into the couch cushion and screamed into it. She fell back and sprawled across the couch.

Never in all my life…

Her phone chimed that she had a text message. She got up and grabbed it out of her purse. It was an unknown message.

Unknown:
Hello, Jett. This is Soo-Yun Jin. Viv gave me your number. I hope that's alright. I was wondering if it were possible for me to come to your place or for you to bring Jerrik to my lab? I've discovered some interesting findings. But I'd like to get a blood sample and inner cheek swab to be sure.

Jett:
Hello, Dr. Jin! That would be fine. If you could come to my place either before 7:30am or after 5pm, that would work.

Dr. Jin:
I could do the morning. Also, Richard would love to come with to meet the owner of the sword and clothing. If that's okay?

An idea crossed Jett's mind and she smiled brightly before she texted back.

Jett:
That will be fine. I actually have a favor. I was wondering if we could have the clothes and sword back for the day. I could bring them back to Dr. Balinski Saturday.

Dr. Jin:
Perfect. And I'll let Richard know. I just need your address and we'll see you tomorrow morning.

Jett texted her address to the doctor. Her mind wondered what the doctor had found. She also prayed that Jerrik wouldn't mind.

Fifteen minutes later, the door opened to the bathroom.

"Jerrik, I need to ask you a question when you get a chance." Jett called up to him.

Moments later, Jett heard his heavy footsteps on the stairs and she looked back.

Heavenly father!

Water droplets glistened across his bare, broad shoulders. His wet hair hung around them and dripped down his chest and abs, and disappeared into the towel wrapped around his waist. The scar across his chest from the wound that had poisoned him, along with other old scars gave his already masculine body an even more virile look.

"Don't look at me like that, woman." Jerrik growled. "It already takes every bit of strength I have not to fuck you into delirium."

Jett couldn't be sure, but she was fairly positive that she squeaked.

"Now, what is it that you needed to ask me?"

"I...um..." Jett closed her eyes and shook her head. "The doctor who is testing your DNA would like to come by in the morning to take a sample of your blood and a swab of your mouth."

Jerrik's brows drew together. "That does not sound pleasant in the least. And I thought you believed me."

"I do. It's just that now I'm curious as to what she found."

"Hmm... I will do it for you."

"Thank you. I swear it'll be painless and quick."

"Woman, I am a Norseman. Pain does little to scare me."

Chapter 23

"Ow! Thor's hammer!" Jerrik bellowed.

"Where's that tough Norseman you mentioned last night?" Jett teased. "And I'm surprised you didn't say Odin's blood, since you are getting blood drawn."

Drs. Jin and Balinski had arrived right on time. And Jerrik scowled down at the needle in his arm she'd stuck him with to draw his blood. Richard just stared on in complete fascination.

When Jett had first opened the door and the doctors had walked through, the look on both their faces the moment they'd laid eyes on Jerrik had been priceless. He was an impressive sight to behold. He took Jett's breath away every...single...time.

Richard had watched in awe as Jerrik pulled the sword from the backseat of Dr. Jin's car and lifted it as if it were a child's plastic sword.

"I said I do not fear pain. Not that I do not *feel* pain." Jerrik lifted his chin proudly. "Besides, I was not expecting such a small weapon to hurt as it did."

"It's a needle, not a weapon." Dr. Jin said.

"Says you," Jerrik said.

Jett squeezed her lips together and nearly choked on her coffee.

Jerrik was in a black t-shirt that had no business fitting as well as it did. And a pair of charcoal sweatpants. And the way God had gifted him, it was also sinful the way they hugged all the right and wrong places. Right because Jett enjoyed the show. Wrong because her lady bits sat at attention.

Dr. Jin quickly pulled the needle from his arm and gave him a bandage.

"There. You can relax now. The swab won't be nearly as bad." Soo-Yun held up a cotton swab. "Open wide."

Jerrik opened his mouth and the doctor expertly swabbed both cheeks. She put the sample in a sterile container and packed everything away.

"All done." She smiled and stood up. "I'll be calling you in about a week with the results. It was truly a pleasure and an honor to meet you Jerrik."

She held out her hand. Jerrik shook it firmly. Dr. Jin turned to Jett and gave her a look as she walked the doctor to the door while Richard said his goodbyes to Jerrik.

"You're a good woman. Having all that living with you." She waved in Jerrik's general direction. "He's a beautiful man to be sure. A rare find. And I can see why you're at least curious to see if his story is true. He certainly looks like he fell through time."

"I'm glad I'm not the only one who sees it. Almost everyone who's met him sees it."

"Well, just look at Richard."

They both looked over at Dr. Balinski who smiled brightly up at Jerrik as he asked him a few more questions about 11th century Iceland.

"If what I've discovered so far is true..." Dr. Jin left it at that.

Jett's eyes widened. She nodded her head. She knew Dr. Jin didn't want to say too much without knowing for sure. So, she didn't push the issue.

"Well, I can't wait to hear what you find out."

"It was good seeing you again. Talk to you soon."

"You too. Have a good one."

"Let's go, Richard. Stop ogling the Viking."

Jett watched as Soo-Yun and Richard got in her car and took off around the corner. Jett turned back to Jerrik and he was standing directly behind her. She jumped back and hit the door.

"Jesu-!"

The rest of Jett's words were caught in Jerrik's mouth as he crushed his lips to hers. She gasped into his mouth. His hands gripped her ass and she found her feet lifted off the floor. Jett wrapped her legs around his waist.

Jerrik's strong arms held her firmly against the door as he rocked his erection against the crotch of her black 'Casual Friday' leggings. The ridge of his clothed cock slid easily over her covered clit. And although they had a few layers of clothing between them, Jett felt every inch of him.

She pulled her lips away from his hungry mouth with a gasp and cried out.

"Aah! Aah!"

Every cry fell from her lips at the upward stroke of his hardened length. Her feet pressed into his ass to pull him closer. And she felt the ridge of his cock head. It only took a few more strokes and his mouth sucking at her neck for her to crumble into pieces.

"Aaaaaaaah! Jerrik!"

His hips jerked at his name on her lips.

"Grrrr!" He growled in her ear as he came.

He slowly lowered her feet back to the ground and she started to collapse on shaky legs. Jerrik's arms quickly shot out to catch her before she fell in a heap on the floor. Jett pretended to tuck an imaginary lock of hair behind her ear, as if she still had hair to tuck. She pressed her hands to his chest as she got her bearings.

"I'm okay. I'm okay."

Jerrik slowly released her and she looked down. His pants were drenched in the front. And in all honesty, Jett wasn't sure if it was all him or not. Her pants and panties beneath were ruined.

"Welp. I guess I better find something else to wear to work." Jett started quickly towards the stairs. "You better not have made me late to work."

"I'm sorry."

"No, you're not."

"Aye, you are right. I'm not." Jerrik smirked.

An adorable dimple appeared in his cheek, and Jett nearly called in to work just so she could sit on his face all day.

She quickly changed into a pair of jeans for 'Casual Friday' instead. Then she ran back downstairs.

"I need you to be ready at noon. I'll be back to get you and I need you to bring the Viking clothing and your sword with you. There's something I need you to do if you don't mind." Jett said as she made her way to the door, he held opened.

"I will be ready."

"Great. Bye!"

Jerrik grasped the back of her head and pulled her in for a deep kiss.

"Goodbye, Jett."

It took a moment before Jett realized that she had been standing still with her face raised up and eyes closed for a few beats too long after he'd released her lips.

"Oh, yeah. Um...bye," she said.

Jett quickly shook off her trance and closed the door behind her. She was certain she heard Jerrik's deep chuckle.

He sucks!

Chapter 24

"Alright, everyone." Jett called out to the classroom. "Get out your book reports on your favorite book. It's time to hand them in."

The sounds of backpack zippers and papers shuffling filled the room.

Once all the kids settled down and they had their reports out, in an orderly fashion they passed their papers to the desks in the front of each row. Jett walked to each row and collected them. She'd moved their desks back into rows because certain students weren't mature enough to sit in a circle like she'd set up the first week.

The children buzzed with excitement. It was the day most of them had been waiting weeks for. Many could barely sit still in their seats.

"Okay, ladies and gentlemen. Before we get started, let me lay down some ground rules. There will be no laughing or teasing *anyone* who is up speaking. *None*. Do you understand me?"

"Yes, Ms. Johnson." The class said in unison.

"It is hard enough to get up in front of people to speak, you don't need to also worry about someone making fun of you. For some people it's easier to speak in public. For others, it's their worst nightmare. So, keep that in mind. Just remember to be kind."

Even with her speech, she knew Caleb, the king of mean boys, would find a way to make fun of his classmates, especially Mason. Jett really tried to be patient with him, but it wasn't easy. She'd dealt with people like him her entire life. Some never grew out of being bullies.

"Well, as long as you all know the rules…" The class leaned forward and practically held their breath. "…it's time for Show & Tell!"

Cheers went up throughout the room. Jett smiled. Like most people, the children couldn't wait to showoff and talk about their favorite things. And it was a chance not to do any schoolwork the rest of the day if it took each person long enough to talk.

One by one, her students came up to speak about their favorite toy. Several kids held demonstrations. Some in the classroom, one outside. Caleb's chest stuck out as far as it could go, as he demonstrated how his drone worked. It flew through the air and he controlled it like an expert drone pilot.

"I'm gonna be a drone pilot for the military when I grow up." Caleb said with a smirk.

He soaked up the attention all his classmates gave him.

"Can I fly it?"

"Let me fly it?"

"Come on, Caleb! I wanna fly it!"

Several boys shouted out.

"Guys, it's Caleb's drone." Jett interjected. "I'm sure it's expensive and he's had a lot of practice. I'm sure he doesn't want it to get broken."

"My dad has a drone at home. I know how to fly a drone. Caleb isn't the only one." A boy named Danny said.

"Yeah, right." Caleb scoffed. "If you had a drone, you would've brought it to Show & Tell."

"It's my dad's. He wouldn't let me." Danny said as he tried reaching for the control to the drone.

"Yeah, sure." Caleb said and pushed Danny back.

Jett saw that it was about to escalate into a fight.

"Boys! That's enough. Caleb, bring the drone back. It's time to go back inside."

Caleb was about to open his mouth to protest, but he looked at Jett and she gave him the Black mama stink eye. He immediately brought the drone back without another word.

Once they were all back in the classroom, Jett called Mason up for his turn. The sweet boy slowly stood up from his desk in the first row. He used his brace to assist his walk to the front of the class. It was the reason Jett had placed him in the front. She didn't want him to have to walk down one of the aisles and accidently trip or purposely be tripped by one of the class bullies on his way. Jett also didn't want him to fade into the back and get lost, which was so easy for a child to do if they wanted to melt away into the background.

"And what have you brought to show us today, Mason?" Jett asked.

"I-I b-brought my wand a-and some pics from my vacation." Mason said with a crooked smile.

He pulled several photos out from his cargo pants pocket. Mason handed them to Sophia, the girl in the first desk across from his. One of the only students who was nice to him. If Jett wasn't mistaken, she was sure that Sophia was kind of smitten with Mason.

He held up a long, rectangular box. He slid the top off and nestled inside was a tan colored wand with a carved handle that looked like a dragon's wing. The kids who were into the famous young wizard leaned forward and buzzed with excitement. Mason smiled brightly.

"I got it from the real wand shop where Harry got his wand." Mason said flawlessly without a single stammer. "There were boxes and boxes of wands stacked all the way to the ceiling on shelves. It was so cool."

Mason pulled out the wand from its place of importance within the box. He recited a spell and waved the wand. It thrilled with a magical sound. Fans of the book chattered excitedly.

"It didn't even do anything." Caleb sneered.

This child. He can't let Mason have anything.

"It's c-called using your imagination. H-How about you g-get one?" Mason rolled his eyes.

Yes! Way to tell 'em, Mason! Jett mentally high-fived the little boy.

"H-How about y-you speak like a normal p-person?" Caleb mocked.

"That's enough, Caleb." Jett warned.

"B-Better to speak with a st-stutter than th-think with one."

BOOYAH! Stick that in your pipe and smoke it, Caleb.

The class burst out laughing. Sophia high-fived Mason. Caleb crossed his arms and sunk down in his chair. He gave Mason a dirty look. Jett sighed internally. She knew that Caleb would find a way to get back at Mason. She hoped she could catch him before he did anything too horrible.

Mason sat back down. And Sophia leaned over.

"I hope my parents will take me next summer. It sounds so fun."

"It was." Mason smiled brightly at her.

They softly talked more about their favorite books as the next student made her way to the front of the class.

Jett could see that Caleb's anger was building by the second.

Sophia was a pretty little girl. A kind and sweet personality to match. It was obvious that Caleb was smitten with her. It was also obvious that a boy like Caleb would turn her off and a sweet boy like Mason would attract her.

This is gonna be a long year.

As the last student finished showing his favorite toy, the bell rang for lunch. Jett walked over to Mason's desk just as Caleb was about to pass. She gave him a knowing look and he changed course and ran out the room with his friends.

"Mason, would you like to read in Miss Arthur's room while you eat? You can stay in there for recess too," Jett said.

"Can I come too?" Sophia asked.

"Sure," Jett smiled at her.

She walked the two students to the 2nd grade teacher's room.

"Hey, Julie." Jett said from the doorway. "Could Mason and Sophia eat lunch in here and read during recess."

"Absolutely!" The petite brunette said.

As the two kids walked into the room, Jett mouthed the word 'Caleb.' Julie nodded solemnly. She'd had the same group of children the year before. She knew exactly what was up.

"Thank you."

"Any time."

Jett turned on her heel and hurried out to the parking lot to head home to get Jerrik.

~~~

"If any adults ask don't forget your backstory. You're from Iceland, your family is gone, and so you're looking to live here permanently. Easy and not far from the truth, which is the key to remembering." Jett coached him after they'd finished eating sandwiches and chips in the car. "To the kids, you can tell the truth of where you're from. They'll believe it. To the adults, stick to the story we made up."

"I am ready."

"Alright, let's go."

They walked towards the entrance to the school. Jerrik had to duck his head to get inside. He carried his Viking clothing and sword with him. Jett was glad none of the students had seen him as they walked in. She wanted him to be a surprise.

Jett guided him to the principal's office, so that Viv could finally meet him and to make sure it was okay that he was on school property. The school secretary looked up and her eyes widened to the size of golf balls, which wasn't too hard to do considering the thick lenses on her eyeglasses that already made her eyes look twice as big.

"Is Mrs. Pennyman in?"

"Uh, yes. Just knock."

"Come in." Viv called from the other side of the door when Jett knocked.

Jett opened the door and peeked inside.

"Hey, Viv. I have someone I want you to meet."

Jett swung the door all the way open. Viv's eyes did the same as everyone who caught sight of Jerrik. She stood up and came around the desk.

"Well, my my my. It's as if you fell straight from the pages of a history book." Viv looked up at Jerrik.

"Jerrik this is my boss, Vivian. Viv, this is Jerrik."

"It is my pleasure." Jerrik held out his hand.

Viv looked at Jett as she shook his hand. The older woman's face was filled with wonder.

"You have more willpower than anyone I've ever met, my dear."

Jett knew exactly what her boss meant.

You have no idea.

"I just wanted you to know that he's a surprise for the kids, if that's okay with you?" Jett said instead.

"Oh, sure! They'll love it." Viv looked down at the sword. "Just make sure Caleb doesn't poke his eye out with that. That kid is some work."

"Already on high alert."

They nodded knowingly to each other.

Jett turned and headed to the men's bathroom for the male teachers. She gestured to the door.

"You can change in there." Jerrik started inside and Jett placed a hand on his arm. "Thank you for doing this."

"You are most welcome, Jett." He gave her a heart-melting grin.

A few minutes later, Jerrik emerged in full Viking regalia. Loose-fitting, soft brown leather pants. Off white tunic. Thick, dark leather armor. And a gray, fur animal pelt to cover his shoulders. He'd tied his hair half up half down to complete the look.

Jett was ready to risk it all and don a fur bikini like Raquel Welch in *One Million Years B.C.* and be his captive.

"I have warned you about looking at me like that." Jerrik said huskily as he stepped closer.

"Sorry. Sorry. Don't do anything crazy, there are children present." Jett pressed her hands against his chest.

"You are lucky it is your time. In my time, children learned the ways between a man and a woman very early."

"Lucky, indeed. Okay, let's focus." Jett gave him her best stern teacher's face. "The bell is about to ring at any second. Go back in the bathroom and wait until the halls are clear. Once they are, come to that door right there."

Jett pointed to the door across the hall.

"You should be able to hear me from the hallway. Come in when I introduce you. Got it?"

"Got it."

"Fantastic. The kids are gonna love it."

The bell rang and Jett pushed Jerrik back into the bathroom. She walked over to her classroom door and greeted her students as they all ran inside, still energized from recess. She kept an eye on Caleb as he entered and looked for Mason.

Mason walked in slowly on his brace with Sophia at his side. Jett squeezed her lips together to keep from grinning ear to ear. The pair held hands as they walked in. Sophia smiled shyly at him as their hands separated so they could take their seats.

My heart! Jett internally pressed a hand to her chest.

She glanced at Caleb and his face was so red, she was sure he would pop.

"Alright, everyone. Settle in." Jett looked over at the window of the closed door and saw movement. "I have my very own Show & Tell surprise for you all."

The kids stopped talking and focused on Jett.

"He's come a very long way to meet you all. So, I want everyone to be on their best behavior and welcome Jerrik the Viking."

The door opened and as if in slow motion, Jerrik ducked down to fit through the doorway. Then he stood to his full 6'6" height, menacing Viking sword in hand.

"Whoa!" The class burst out excitedly.

"Góðan aptan!" Jerrik said with his fist against his chest and a polite bow.

Jett's mouth popped open at him speaking his native tongue.

"What?!" Several of the children said with a giggle.

"Good afternoon." Jerrik translated.

"Good afternoon!" they said.

"Are you really a Viking?" Danny asked.

"Aye, I am." Jerrik nodded. "I come from Iceland. I believe sometime between the years 1050 to 1053. We do not keep track of such things."

"Wow!"

"Is that sword real?" Caleb asked.

Of course, he would.

"Tis." Jerrik inclined his head. "Would you like to touch it?"

Jett cringed slightly. "Please…be careful! And one at a time."

The kids got up and formed a semi-orderly line. Jett watched as Caleb got behind Mason. She breathed heavily and gritted her teeth.

Each student approached Jerrik and his sword. The girls a little more cautiously than the boys. Most of the boys looked up at him with awe and pure adoration on their faces. He was what they hoped to be when they grew up. Big and strong.

They touched, tapped, and stroked the sword away from the sharp edges. They giggled when they felt that it was real, and then ran back to their desks to chatter enthusiastically.

As Mason stepped forward, Caleb stuck out his foot. Before Jett could stop him, Mason stumbled forward. With the reflexes of a viper, Jerrik's arm shot out and caught Mason before he fell. He straightened the little boy and handed him his brace back that had fallen to the floor.

Mason's chin trembled and his eyes began to well with tears. Jerrik knelt in front of him, coming down to his level. Or at least as close to his level as he could.

"Hmm…" Jerrik looked the boy over like he was deep in thought. "You seem like a strong lad. My brother Dag was our fiercest warrior and trained all our men and women."

"Women?!" The boys scoffed.

"Women!" The girls said with newfound interest.

"Aye, women. They are called shieldmaidens. Many of them were our best fighters." Jerrik looked back to Mason. "I bet if my brother could have trained you, you would be one of our best warriors."

"Really?!" Mason asked hopeful. His embarrassment of a moment ago forgotten.

"Aye, really." Jerrik pulled his sword over for the boy to see. "I am sure you could help me lift it. Want to try?"

"Yeah!"

Jerrik turned Mason around. He brought the sword around in front of his little pupil.

"Wrap your hand around the grip."

Mason wrapped his good hand around the handle of the sword. Jerrik enfolded Mason's hand and the hilt with one hand. Together they lifted the heavy sword. Jett wasn't sure Mason had smiled so hard in his entire life.

"See, I told you," Jerrik said.

"You did!"

Jerrik let the sword back down. He glanced up at Jett before he stood back up to his full height. The band that had been tightening around Jett's heart tightened further. The way Jerrik treated the little differently-abled boy with care broke down whatever walls she had left. And she was left defenseless against the feelings that flooded her.

Jett's hands trembled as she wiped the sweat from her palms on her jeans. She smiled at Jerrik and nodded her thanks for what he'd done for Mason.

He patted Mason on the back before the little boy made his way back to his desk. Jerrik then looked down at Caleb. His face turned stern and the little boy shrunk before Jett's eyes.

The Viking knelt down once more and crooked his finger at the boy. Caleb stepped forward and Jerrik whispered in his ear. The 8-year-old nodded his head and blinked rapidly as if he was trying to hold back tears. Jerrik then held out his sword for the boy to touch. He touched it morosely and then headed back to his desk. He quickly dragged his arm across his damp eyes.

Jett looked at Jerrik curiously but put her question away to ask him later.

"If you have any questions for Jerrik, raise your hand and do not speak unless he picks you." Jett instructed them.

Nine hands shot up in the air. All but Caleb.

~~~

"What did you say to Caleb? The mean kid who tripped the boy with the brace?" Jett asked.

Jerrik sat on the edge of her desk as she packed up her things for the weekend after all the kids had gone. He'd changed back into his jeans and charcoal gray thermal shirt that hugged his body sinfully.

"I told him that being cruel to people weaker than him only made him look weak. A true warrior protects those who cannot protect themselves. And that he would never be a part of my Viking clan acting as such," Jerrik said.

"You really said that?"

"Aye." Jerrik sighed. "In my time, unfortunately, the little boy with the cane would be left to die in the wilderness shortly after birth."

"My God! Seriously?"

"Aye. It is our way. No one has time to care for one like him. The days are long and the work is hard."

"Then why defend him today?"

"Well, since he is here and alive, someone stronger should not take advantage of his weaknesses. It is nice that children such as he, are able to live life here in your time." Jerrik paused and continued quietly. "And because I knew it meant something to you."

Jett fell silent.

The band that tightened on her heart, practically choked it.

"Uh...come on. My weekend started ten minutes ago. Let's get outta here." Jett jerked her chin towards the door.

Jerrik placed his hand at the small of her back. Jett tried to play it cool and pulled away from his touch. The frown on Jerrik's face told her she hadn't fooled him.

They rode home in silence. Jett tried to process her feelings on the short ride. All she knew was that she was now afraid to be alone with him. She feared he'd try to be intimate with her. Lusting after him had been one thing. But the affection, and dare she say *love*, that was pumping thickly through her already ravaged heart terrified her.

I can't. I can't be broken again.

She'd only just begun to heal after her summer heartbreak. She didn't believe that she'd ever truly loved Shawn. She'd simply settled because she feared she'd never find anyone. Jett only felt betrayed by him. After all she'd done to take care of him and support his pipe dreams.

No, it was Nic. Nic was the true heartbreak for Jett. She'd always known that Nic wanted whatever she had. Being their mother's favorite. Being the favorite at school and in the neighborhood wasn't enough for Nic. She wanted it all. But Jett had never thought Nic would stoop so low as to take her husband. She was her twin. She realized now that she'd been extremely naive.

Either way, she couldn't handle any more heart break. So, when Jerrik tried to pull her in for kiss when they walked into her house, she did the only thing she could think of. Run.

"I have been wanting to kiss you all afternoon." Jerrik whispered in her ear right before he flicked the shell with his tongue.

"I...uh...wanna get outta these jeans and get comfortable." Jett untangled her body from his.

She fled up the stairs and into her bedroom. She leaned against the door and thudded her head against it a few times in frustration. Jett shoved off the door with a groan. Quickly, she changed into a comfy, gray off-the-shoulder sweater dress with pockets that she adored. Jett debated with herself for at least ten minutes on whether she should leave her bra on or not.

This is my house damnit! And if I want to go braless, I can without some big ass Viking ogling me.

Jett whipped the bra off.

She grabbed her laundry hamper and headed to Jerrik's room. She wanted to get at least part of the laundry done, so she could relax on Saturday. Her head poked in half expecting his room to be a disaster. It was surprisingly neat. He'd refolded all the clothes he'd worn. She wondered how many times a Viking wore their clothes before they washed them. She quickly gathered them and added his clothes to her hamper.

Quietly, she walked down the stairs. She hoped he was watching TV and wouldn't pay her much attention. Jett wasn't ready to have the argument she was sure they were going to have.

She rounded the corner and there he stood. He leaned against the kitchen counter facing the stairs. As if he'd been waiting for her. He had a glass of water in his hands that he set down before speaking.

"Jett, what is wrong?" He asked.

"Nothing," she said and continued walking.

He followed her into the laundry room around the corner.

"Do not lie. I never lie to you."

"Nothing is wrong, Jerrik." Jett said as she began to sort through the clothes.

"Last night and this morning you were open to experiencing pleasure. Now, you can barely lay your eyes upon me. What happened between then and now?"

"*Nothing!* Drop it."

"Why will you not submit to me?!?" Jerrik bellowed as he spun her around to face him.

His patience had finally snapped. Blue eyes burned with anger, lust, and possibly hurt.

"Because I'm not some easy shieldmaiden who will fuck you behind a barn or in a field because she's impressed by your title." Jett shot back.

"Maybe you would still be with your husband if you did!" Jerrik hit below the belt.

Before Jett could process what she was doing, she drew back her hand and slapped Jerrik as hard as she could across his cheek. His head snapped to the side. He slowly turned back to her and his icy blue eyes scorched her as if she'd touched dry ice. There was the Viking laird.

Jerrik's hand shot out and gripped her neck. Not enough to truly choke her, but enough that her breath was snatched away. He stepped closer to her. So close that their hips and thighs were flush against each other and she bent back over the washer. She could feel his erection against her abdomen.

"You do not fool me, Jett. Let me guess. You push my patience and strike out at me so that I will lose my temper and become the barbarian you claim me to be? So that you can blame me and say I forced you, just so you won't have to feel the guilt and shame of enjoying me fucking you." Jerrik squeezed her throat a little tighter. "It's true. Isn't it?!"

"Y-Yes."

Jerrik's eyes flashed. "Yes, what?"

"Yes, my laird."

An animalistic growl emitted from his throat as his mouth crushed hers. Jerrik's tight grip moved up to grasp her throat and jaw. Jett was held captive. Helpless. It was what she desperately wanted. Yet she hated him for it.

She balled her hands into fists and pummeled his chest. Jerrik released her, reached down to grasp the bottom of his shirt, and pulled it up over his head. His broad shoulders, thickly roped arms, flexing chest, and sculpted abs made Jett's fingers itch to touch him.

"You want to scratch me too? Go ahead."

"I hate you!"

"Whatever makes you feel better as I fuck you, sweet lass."

~ 172 ~

Jett tried to slap him again. This time Jerrik caught her by the wrist. He gripped the other and pulled both her hands behind her back. He held them together with one of his massive hands. His free hand tugged the neckline of her already off-the-shoulder sweater dress. Jett squeezed her lips together to keep from moaning as the fabric slid over her hardened nipples.

Once freed, Jerrik palmed her left breast and held it up to give better access to her nipple for his hungry mouth. His lips closed around the sensitive peak and Jett couldn't help but cry out. Her fingers tangled in the loose hair around his shoulders. She got a good grip and pulled back as hard as she could. Jerrik's mouth ripped away from her flesh with a grunt of pain.

"You do not want to play this game, Jett." He warned. "I can show you rough."

Jett couldn't speak. If she parted her lips to say a word, she'd beg for it. She was embarrassed enough by her wanton behavior. Furious at herself for falling so hard so quickly. Enraged at him for making her feel so much only to leave her as soon as he was able. The only way she could cope. The only way she could accept pleasure from him. A hate fuck. Because if he was soft. If he dared to be gentle, her heart would be lost. She didn't think she'd recover.

So, even though she knew she should put an end to their battle of wills. Even though she knew she should've asked him to make love to her. Instead, Jett tried to knee him in the groin.

Jerrik caught her knee between his powerful thighs. The dimpled smile that spread across his face, should've given her comfort. It did not. For it held the promise of complete devastation and destruction. It was more sneer than smile.

He'd been sweet. He'd been soft. He'd been patient. The latter had finally snapped and the former were gone.

Jett should've been frightened. Well, she was. But certainly not enough. No. She was more aroused than she'd ever been in her life.

Jerrik's calloused hand slid up the leg he'd caught between his. It slipped under her dress. His eyes lit up at what he found.

"No, panties." His nostrils flared. "You wanted this like a bitch in heat."

"Fuck. You!" Jett fairly spat in his face.

"Aye, I'm about to." He said as he unfastened his jeans.

Jerrik painfully gripped her ass and lifted her off her feet and onto the washer. His hips were at the perfect height. Jett had only a split second to see his erection up close. It was 10-inches of perfectly veined, upwardly curved flesh covered steel. The fat, angry purple tip disappeared into her slick opening and slammed deep within her depths.

The first strike stole her very breath. The second ripped a scream from Jett's throat. And an orgasm she hadn't expected, shot through her and her pussy gushed on his outward stroke.

"OH MY GOD! Ohmygod!" Jett cried over and over.

Jerrik didn't let up. He gripped her ass tighter and pummeled her tender flesh. The washer rocked like it was on a spin cycle and she hadn't even turned it on. Jett reached back for the wall. Her hands couldn't find purchase. The washer. They slipped back. Finally, her nails dug into his back. It only spurred him on.

His greedy cock glistened with her cream and feminine cum on every outward stroke. On every deep plunge back in, Jerrik vocalized his pleasure. He wasn't silent like Shawn. Or like the men Dez had complained to Jett about. This Viking had no years of societal brainwashing that convinced men it was unmanly to vocalize their pleasure.

"Fuck, Jett! Aaaaah!" Jerrik cried out.

It was as if his very verbal desire vibrated directly through Jett's clit. Her pussy fluttered with the stirrings of another orgasm. Jerrik slowed. He wrapped his arms around her waist and buried his face in her neck. Her hands clutched his back and her teeth bit into his shoulder. This time he punctuated each deep thrust with a sharp roll of his hips. Jett fell apart.

Her nails raked his back. She released his shoulder with a cry of ecstasy.

"Jerriiiiiiiiiiik!"

She felt his cock ripple within her and he growled in her ear as he came.

He pulled her down from the washer. He spun her around and bent her over. His hand firmly gripped the nape of her neck. His legs shook as he slid within her from behind. His erection never waned.

Jett gasped at the feel of him from a different... A deeper angle. Jerrik hissed. The fingers at her nape, slid around to the front of her neck. He clutched her neck tightly and pulled back. Jett's back bowed.

"Ah fuck!" Jerrik moaned. "That is so good."

The slap of their skin reverberated against the walls in the tiny room. Jett could barely catch her breath. His hand choked her seductively, his cock stroked deeply, and the fingers on his other hand played her clit expertly. She was raw, exposed nerve.

Jett's ass rippled. Her breasts bounced. Her skin glistened. She felt like the goddess Jerrik first thought her to be.

The tingle of another orgasm built. Jett was energized at the same time exhausted. She didn't think she could take another, but Jerrik wasn't letting up. He was all beast. Mindless with his need to have her. Own her. Break her.

He applied pressure on her jaw and she raised up. His teeth scraped against her ear as he bit her lightly. His tongue flicked against the bite to sooth it.

"Cum on my cock." He growled.

Her third orgasm ripped through her almost painfully.

"AAAAARRRRGGGGHHH!!!" She screamed.

Jerrik continued to pump into her. Jett's entire body was wracked by tremors. She tried to pull away.

"ENOUGH!" She cried out.

"I will say when I have had enough." Jerrik snarled in her ear.

"Jerrik, please!" Jett begged.

Something in her voice must have brought him back to the man he had been. His hands relaxed his hold on her. His strokes slowed. He rolled his hips smoothly. And Jett's orgasm rolled into one more.

"F…uuuuu…ck!" Jett hissed.

Her pussy squeezed tightly around his thick shaft. It rippled and a roar ripped from his throat as he spilled his seed within her depths once more.

Jerrik pulled out and spun her around. He gripped either side of her neck and pressed his thumbs against her jaw to lift her face up to his. His cock pressed between them. Still hard. Still throbbed and leaked out onto her sweater covered tummy.

His arctic blue eyes searched hers before his mouth captured hers. His kiss was passionate and desperate. He released her mouth and pressed his forehead to hers. His breath fanned against her lips as he panted.

"Forgive me," he whispered.

Jett's legs could no longer hold her up. They buckled and she collapsed to the floor. Strong arms caught her before she hurt herself.

Chapter 25

Jerrik gently scooped Jett up into his arms. He gingerly carried her out of the laundry room and into the living room. He laid her on the couch.

"I will be right back."

He jogged up the stairs. First, he found a pair of clean boxer briefs to pull on. Then he went into her bedroom to find her a change of clothing. He found a short satin and lace nightgown in her drawers. He didn't know if it was something she'd want to wear but shrugged and brought it back down.

Jerrik walked around the couch and found Jett fast asleep. He looked down at her with the love he'd dared not show her radiating from his eyes.

She'd wounded his pride earlier. Everything he'd done since he'd woken up in this strange time was for her. He wanted to make her happy. He wanted to pleasure her. He wanted to please her. Even if it were only for a little while. If he were being honest with himself, he knew he hoped that she would decide she wanted to go back to his time with him. That life with him would be preferable to staying here in her own time.

So, after all he'd tried to do, the fact that she tried to shut him out, sparked a rage within him that he hadn't been able to control. He'd wanted to fuck her into submission. Jett was a strong, stubborn woman. If anything, he'd only fucked her into exhaustion.

Jerrik sighed heavily and guiltily.

He slid his arms under her neck and knees and lifted her off the couch.

"Mm...what are you doing?" Jett asked groggily.

"Taking you to bed."

"I'm too heavy."

"I have lifted grown men larger than you. Now, go back to sleep."

Jerrik carried her up the stairs and placed her in her bed. He tugged at her sweater dress until he was able to drag it over her head. Her inner thighs were covered in the evidence of their lovemaking. The sight of his markings on her made Jerrik's chest swell with pride and possession.

He strode to the bathroom, dampened a washcloth, and came back to sit next to her hip. Jerrik cleaned her thighs methodically and with care. He took the towel back to the bathroom and cleaned off his own body. His manhood still partially erect. He'd barely been able to tamp down his desire for this remarkable woman.

Once he was done, he returned to her room to cover her prostate body with her comforter. He turned to walk from her room, when fingers lightly touched his forearm. He looked back down to find Jett looking up at him.

"Stay."

"Aye, okay." He said without hesitation.

Jerrik slipped between the covers. He reached over and wrapped an arm around her waist. He slid her to the middle of the bed and flush against him. Her warmth and softness quickly lulled him to sleep.

~~~

Jerrik's eyes blinked open. The soft light from Jett's nightstand illuminated the darkness. He laid on his side facing her. Her eyes blinked at him as she faced him as well. He wasn't sure how long she'd been awake. And he couldn't read her face.

"Are you cross with me?" Jerrik asked softly.

Jett shook her head. "No."

He reached across and wrapped his hand behind her neck and head. He pulled her close and kissed her first on her nose and then her soft lips.

"I pushed you to lash out at me." Jett looked away bashfully. "I wanted you to lash out at me. It made it easier."

"It made what easier?"

"Easier to want you."

"You could have just told me. It is not like I didn't want you as well." Jerrik stroked his thumb over the soft skin of her cheek.

"It's not that. You make me *feel* things."

Jerrik's heart raced.

"Then *feel* them," he urged.

"Will you stay?"

He looked away.

"I didn't think so." Jett rolled onto her back and sighed heavily. "You can't expect me to let go. To open up my heart. And then you leave without a care in the world and take my heart with you."

"It would be okay. Because I would be leaving you mine in exchange."

Jett's head whipped around to look at him. Her warm brown eyes searched his for any falsehoods. He doubted she'd find any.

"It was fated that I come here. To find you. Or you find me, as it were." Jerrik reached out to pull her close once more. "To love you."

Her eyes immediately turned glassy. "It's too much. Too soon." She shook her head.

Jerrik placed his hand under her chin and lifted her face up. "Says who?"

Jett shrugged.

"Time and space do not apply to us. Obviously. I was sent to your time. You moved here and was the one to find me." Jerrik grasped her hand and placed it over his aching heart. "You think that a coincidence?"

"No." Jett whispered.

"We were meant to love each other."

"And then what? Break each other's hearts when you leave? I'd rather be numb, than to be part of some tragedy." Jett said.

She tried to pull away from him. Jerrik held on tighter.

"Then come with me!" He blurted out as he rolled on top of her.

"Come with you?" She searched his eyes.

"Yes." He reached down, parted her thighs, and settled between them. "Come with me."

"Jer-"

He pressed his lips to hers to silence the refusal he knew would come. If he couldn't convince her with words, he hoped he could with his body.

Jett's lips parted and Jerrik dipped his tongue inside slowly. The flick of his tongue against hers made her hips reflexively pump towards his already rock hard cock.

"Not yet." Jerrik said against her lips.

He kissed down her jaw to her neck. Passed her clavicle. He stopped at her breasts to show them love. His tongue swirled around each nipple. Her small cries made his cock drip with precum. He continued down her soft tummy, kissing a pathway to her mound.

The black, springy curls there were soft and smelled of her. Her scent aroused him beyond any others and he nuzzled his nose against her.

"Jerrik, I haven't showered after we had sex." Jett tried to push his face away from her sex.

"So?"

"So, I probably stink." She whispered the last word.

Jerrik's head popped up to look at her incredulously.

"You smell amazing! I was just thinking that your scent is more arousing than any other woman's I have smelt before."

"Oh."

"What is a quim supposed to smell like?"

"Um…according to feminine hygiene companies and some men…flowers?"

Jerrik's head jerked back.

"Pssh! I have never heard of such a thing."

Jett squeezed her lips together in an attempt not to laugh.

"You think I jest?"

"No, I believe you. I just forget sometimes that you're not like the men of this time."

"Then I shall just have to remind you."

Jerrik growled. In one swift move he jerked her knees up, wrapped his hands around her thighs, and jerked the apex of her legs towards him. Jett fell back with a yelp. He buried his nose between her labia and stroked it up to her clit, nuzzling it. She gasped and her hand grasped the back of his head.

Jerrik crooked his tongue and stroked it upward. He gathered her slick arousal on the tip and used it to swirl around her hardened nub. Jett's back arched. Her hips rolled up to meet his tongue.

"Oh, God! Jerrik!"

He bathed, sucked, and slathered her clit. His saliva and her heady nectar combined and slid through her nether lips to her ass. Jerrik followed it, swirled his tongue around her rosette and back to her clit again.

He was a messy eater. His beard was saturated. His nose and lips glistened with it. He loved it. And so, did his passionate lover.

Jett rose up on one elbow. She gripped the back of his head. Her hips bucked wildly against his mouth. She fucked his face with abandon.

Jerrik gazed up at her. Her long, curly lashes fanned across the tops of her cheeks. Her ebony skin glowed in the lamplight. Her nostrils flared. And her plump lips were opened in an O as she panted through her lips. She was resplendent. The most beautiful woman he'd ever seen.

His hips pumped against the mattress as he pleasured her. His testicles tingled and his cock throbbed.

"Jerrik! Jerrik! I'm gonna come. I'm gonna c…Aaaaaaaah!" Jett sobbed.

Her hips shuddered and pumped erratically. Her quim flexed reflexively. Jerrik moaned against her clit as he spilled his seed onto the sheet under him. The beauty of her orgasm had sent him over the edge.

Jerrik quickly crawled up her body and stroked deeply into her. His hardened flesh unable to get enough of her. He lowered himself over her body. Jett raised up to kiss his still wet lips. She licked her cum from his lips.

"I cannot let you go. You are mine." Jerrik raised her leg up and stroked in deep. "Come with me."

"Yes." She said breathlessly.

Jerrik claimed her lips in a fiercely possessive kiss. His thrusts came faster. Desperate. Urgent. He raised up, lifted her other leg to her chest, and held onto the backs of her knees as he pumped into her warm, wet quim. Jett's hands reached for his chest. Her fingers traced the battle scars that covered his torso.

"You're beautiful," she breathed.

Her hands then slid around to his backside. She gripped his ass cheeks and pulled him towards her.

"Ah…shit!" Jerrik hissed.

His powerful strokes slid Jett across the sheets. Her head reached the headboard. She had to release his backside to press her hands against the headboard. Jerrik felt the flutter of her pussy around him. He knew she was close and he was almost there with her. He slowed and rolled his hips. At the end of every inward thrust, he rapidly hit the top of her cervix. Then he slowly pulled back out to do it again.

Jett's cries became louder and faster. Jerrik stroked his thumb over her clit. Jett's body bowed, tensed, and her voice was snatched from her for a few beats as she crested. Right before she came apart.

"UNGH!" She cried out.

Her hands tore at the sheets. Her hips bucked wildly. Her pussy milked him.

"Jett! Grrrrrr…aaaaaah!" Jerrik shouted as his cock burst and showered her womb with his seed.

He released her legs and they flopped next to his hips and thighs. Jerrik melted onto her chest in exhaustion. Their chests heaved together as they slowly calmed.

Jett sweetly stroked his hair back from his face, that had come loose during their lovemaking. Her fingers combed through the strands. Jerrik relaxed further at her gentle ministrations.

Suddenly a loud growl ripped through the silence. It was his stomach. Jerrik felt Jett's body shake with laughter. And another growl followed shortly thereafter. This time from her stomach.

"We skipped dinner."

"I am famished. You exhaust me, woman." Jerrik groaned.

"It's like one in the morning. *Way* too late to eat."

"Says who?"

"Says the inches around my waist."

"I like your waist."

Jerrik scooted down, wrapped his arms around said waist, and nestled warmly against her tummy.

"You are perfect."

"Well, since you put it that way… Let's go find something to eat."

~~~

"Ow!" Jerrik yelped and jumped back. "What kind of torturous food is this?"

"It's bacon." Jett laughed. "And you'll feel differently once you eat it."

Jerrik scowled at the skillet as he rubbed his abs where he'd been popped.

"Sorry, I should've warned you to wear clothes when cooking bacon. Move over. I'll finish." Jett brushed him out of the way.

She'd decided that eggs, bacon, and waffles would be the perfect middle of the night meal to replenish them. Jerrik tried to help but the man dressed in nothing but his boxer briefs was more distracting than anything.

"Go sit down. I can't concentrate looking at all that." Jett gestured up and down with her spatula.

"I affect you, do I?" Jerrik sauntered up behind her and kissed her neck as he caressed her ass through her nightie.

"You already know you do." Jett flinched away playfully. "Now, get outta here. Before you make me burn everything."

Jerrik finally let her cook in peace and sat at the kitchen table. But even though he was a few feet away, she could still feel him. Jett glanced over and he was watching her appreciatively.

The negligee that she wore, she'd purchased for Shawn a little over a year ago. It was black lace and deep purple satin. The satin panel started under her breasts and stopped at about mid-thigh in the front. The peekaboo black lace covered, or maybe not so much, her breasts, sides, and back. She'd bought it for Shawn's birthday, in the hopes that he'd want to have sex. It was the one time she'd initiated sex and he'd brutally turned her down.

"You're too big for that."

It was probably more along the lines that he'd just finished screwing her sister.

The way Jerrik stared at her now, washed away the pain of that moment and put a salve on her battered self-esteem. When she'd tried on the nightie that first time, she'd felt beautiful and sexy. It was her husband who hadn't seen the same thing and made her question her own eyesight. Made her doubt her own views on the way she looked. Jerrik saw her in the same way she saw and felt about herself.

"The women of my time either sleep naked or wear white woolen shifts." Jerrik remarked. "Is this the shift in current times?"

"Not exactly. This is mostly used to arouse a woman's lover. It's meant to be taken off." Jett smirked at him.

"I like this very much." He bit his lip as he stared at her ass.

Jett grabbed a piece of bacon that had been draining on a paper towel on the counter. She slowly walked towards him with the slice. Jerrik's eyes devoured her. Once she reached him, she straddled his thighs and gradually lowered herself to his lap. His very hard erection between them.

"I do not recall a time until I met you that my cock was at full staff almost all the time. Odin's blood, woman. You make me insane with lust." Jerrik growled and nipped at her chin.

"Wait until you taste this." Jett held up the piece of bacon to his lips.

Jerrik bit down in the middle of the strip. The moment the flavor hit his tastebuds his eyes widened. He quickly chewed and then snatched the rest of the bacon from her hand with his teeth. He closed his eyes as he chewed the rest.

"I have decided. You are a witch."

Jett choked and then laughed happily.

"Am I?"

"You are. You lead me by the cock and fill my belly with delicious foods. I am your captive." Jerrik held his arms outstretched. "Do with me as you will."

Jett pulled down the waistband of his briefs, releasing his erection. She wrapped her fingers around him.

"Like this?"

"Aye. Just like that." Jerrik panted.

Jett raised up on her tiptoes and then lowered herself onto his stiff mast.

"Ah! Thor's hammer!" Jerrik gasped.

"Aaah!" Jett breathed onto his lips.

The food forgotten, Jett rode his cock until they both came hard.

Later, they had to open the windows to let out the smoke and Jett started their late-night meal over again.

Chapter 26

"Hi, Dad." Jett spoke into her cellphone.

Jerrik looked over at her on the couch. It was a lazy Sunday afternoon. He rubbed her feet as they watched a movie in between lovemaking sessions. Jett held up her finger and pulled her feet away from him. She got up and walked into the kitchen.

Her father had called multiple times a week every week since she'd been in Maine. He texted her on the days he didn't call. His only source to know she was okay was Dez. It was his text the day before that made her finally pick up.

Dad:
If you don't answer my calls, I'm coming up to Maine to make sure you're okay. I got your address from Desiree.

The last thing Jett needed was her father to find Jerrik. The large man was not easy to explain.

"Hey, sweetie. I guess it took threatening you with a visit to get you to pick up the phone." Morris accused.

"I'm sorry, Dad. I've been busy. And honestly, I wasn't ready."

"I know, Nette. I know I hurt you. But if you'd have answered my calls, you would've found out that I finally gave Nicky a deadline."

"And what deadline was that?"

"I told her that she had three months to get a job and save up before I cut her off. If she's bold enough to take your man, she's bold enough to get a job, keep one, and pay her own bills."

Jett raised her brows in surprise. Her parents never held her twin responsible for anything she did.

"Really?"

"Yeah."

"And what did mom have to say about that?"

The other line was quiet for a few beats.

"That's what I thought."

"You know your mom can't say no to your sister. But as long as I'm breathing, I can't let her get away with what she did." Morris sighed. "I know I let your mother talk me into being lenient. But not this time. What she did was wrong. And I promise you, if she hasn't gotten her life together by the first of December, then I'm selling her apartment and she'll have to find her own way."

"If I know Nic, she'll find a way to get around it. Whether it's going through mom behind your back or finding a man to take care of her. Although, good luck if she's still with Shawn. He's just as lazy as her."

"Ain't that the truth." Morris chuckled. "But your sister is not the only reason I'm calling you."

"Okay." Jett said warily. "Why else are you calling me?"

"I'm calling because, as you know, your mother and my anniversary is coming up at the end of the month. And if your sister doesn't cause us to divorce first, we're having a party. A big one. It's our 30th and your mother wants to do it up big."

"She always wants to do it up big."

"Well, since our anniversary is Halloween, she wants to do a masquerade ball with all the high society elites. And I'd love for you to be there." Morris said hopefully.

"And I'm assuming my sister and her new man will be there?"

"Nette, of course, your sister will be there. I'd prefer it if Shawn was banned from attending, but I can't stop her from bringing who she wants without causing a scene. I'm hoping by then, she'll realize he can't take care of her and will have broken up with him."

"Maybe."

Jett looked over at Jerrik. He looked back at her and winked with a dimpled grin. His hair was pulled back into a sexy, messy top knot.

I'm not above showing off myself.

"I'll be there. And I'm bringing a date." Jett decided.

"Oh ho! Did my daughter find herself a man up there?" Morris said with delight.

"Possibly."

"Well, if it means anything, I'm happy for you."

"Thanks, Dad. I gotta go, but send me the invite with all the details. I'll be there."

"Alright. Bye, sweetie."

"Bye."

Jett tapped the end button on her phone. She looked at Jerrik and he looked at her curiously. She walked back over to the couch and sat on her knees facing him.

"So...I know I said I'd go back with you. But first you have to find that fog. If it's really during the new moon like we think it might be, that would be around the 24th or 25th of October. I...um...just found out that my parents are having a wedding anniversary party on the 31st. So, what if we waited?" Jerrik turned to look at her and she rushed on. "Only one more month. You could see if you can find the fog on those days when you're working. If you do, then I get a chance to say goodbye to my family and they can meet you. And then we can go the following month."

Jett hadn't really examined her decision to go back with him. She'd blurted it out in the middle of a passionate moment. And she was too afraid that the cons would far outweigh the pros. But for now, if she could wait a little longer. To prepare. To get her mind right. It would be a good thing.

"Alright." Jerrik said easily.

"Really? You'd wait for me?"

"I said that I am yours and you are mine. Where you go, I go. Where I go, you go. Simple as that." Jerrik said.

"Okay."

"So, you would like for me to meet your family?"

"Uh…yeah." Jett looked down and picked at her fleece pajama pants. "If I'm going to disappear from their lives, I'd like for them to know that I'd finally found love."

Jerrik clasped her arm and pulled her onto his lap. He kissed the top of her buzzed head and then her nose. It had become his thing. And her heart swelled to ten times its normal size when he did.

"Then I shall gladly meet them."

"Thanks."

Jerrik raised her chin and kissed her deeply.

Per usual, the world fell away, leaving nothing but her and this man.

Chapter 27

The beep of the bedside alarm Jett had lent Jerrik jarred him from a pleasant dream. He'd been introducing Jett to Thorin, Dag, and his mother Gyda. The presence of his family in his dream squeezed at his heart. He missed them, but he was enjoying his new life with Jett. Maybe a little too much. He'd been more than happy to stay another month when she'd suggested it.

Jerrik slid slowly out from beneath the covers. He crept out of Jett's bedroom and into the bathroom to get ready for his first day on the job.

After his shower, he brushed his teeth and tied up his hair in a top knot to keep it out of his face while he worked. He walked into the spare bedroom to dress for the day. He slid into a pair of jeans and a thermal shirt. He threw on a black and red, buffalo plaid button-up over it. He stepped into his boots and headed back into Jett's bedroom.

He walked quietly to her side of the bed. Jerrik bent over and kissed her softly on the lips.

"Mm..." she stretched. "You're leaving?"

"I did not mean to wake you. Go back to sleep."

"It's okay. I'll live. I wanted to say goodbye to you on your first day of work." Jett said groggily.

She smiled sleepily and puckered her lips for another kiss.

Jerrik's throat constricted. He tried to clear it as he bent over to kiss her. Jett wrapped her arms around his neck and pulled him down onto her. Jerrik chuckled before dipping his tongue into her warm mouth.

"Alright, woman." Jerrik pulled back. "I want to be outside when Mr. Murdock arrives."

"Okay. Bye, Jerrik. Have a good day."

"It could be longer than a day."

"Oh, yeah." Jett's brow furrowed with a cute pouty frown. "Well, have a good work trip. However long that might be. But I'll miss you if it's longer."

"Aye, I will miss you too." He leaned forward and kissed her nose. "Have a good day at work. And tell Mason I said hello."

"Oh, he'll love that." Jett pushed at his arm. "Okay, go. I don't wanna get you in trouble your first day."

Jerrik grinned down at her and stood. He headed down the stairs and grabbed his jacket off the hook by the door. He walked out into the cool early morning air. He locked the door and by the time he turned to walk down the front steps, an old pickup truck pulled up. He walked up to the passenger side and saw Mr. Murdock inside.

"Jump on in, Jerrik."

Jerrik slid inside.

"Good morning, Mr. Murdock."

"Mornin', son. You might as well call me Sam, now."

"Alright, Sam."

"Well, ya ready for a hard day's work?"

"Yes, sir."

"Good man. Let's get after it."

Sam put the truck in drive and they rumbled down the street.

~~~

Sam worked the hydraulic hauler, and a lobster trap broke the surface of the open ocean. Jerrik dressed in waterproof bibs, gloves, boots, and jacket lifted the 40-pound trap onto the hull. He flipped the trap open and started to toss starfish, small lobsters, and other sea life that had gotten into the trap back into the icy waters.

~ 191 ~

The lobsters that looked close to 'keeper' size he tossed into a crate on the boat.

When the trap was empty, he lifted it and sat it on top of the other traps that he'd stacked so far on the platform. He replaced the empty bait bag with fresh bait bags filled with herring. By the time he was done, the next trap was ready to be emptied.

Sam wanted to pull up 300 of his 600 traps in that section of the ocean marked with his buoy. They were halfway through.

It was back breaking work, and Jerrik loved every minute of it. He'd been too idle. In his village, he woke early and went to bed late almost every day. There was always work to do or his people to help. And if he wasn't working in his village, they were at sea headed to a new destination to conquer. Or battles to wage.

Before he'd been cut down with poison, Jerrik had grown tired of battle. He'd wanted peace. And he'd wanted travel in between.

Work on the lobster boat was good work. And with cars and airplanes, travel was more possible than he'd ever imagined. But he knew he couldn't hope to stay. He had a village to lead. It was his duty. It was what he'd been born for. What would his father think if he stayed and left his world behind?

"Now, son, this is the most dangerous part of the job." They stood by the stacked traps after they'd finished one trawl. "Sending the traps back out to sea. If your foot or anything else gets caught up in the trawl, it'll rip you right off the boat and into the water. And it'll pull you on down to Davy Jones' Locker. As in, to your death. But as sternman, it's also your job to keep the line from tangling. So, watch your footing. Keep clear of the rope and get the traps back out there.

"I'll show you this time. After that, the rest is up to you."

"Alright, Sam."

After Sam demonstrated how to get the traps back out to sea, he led Jerrik over to the lobsters they'd kept. They measured them, threw out what was too small or females carrying eggs back into the ocean, and tossed those they'd keep in another bin. Once done there, Sam taught Jerrik how to rubber band the lobsters' claws and send them down below to the stored saltwater lobster tank to await their fate.

Lunch was a brief fifteen minutes to scarf down a sandwich before they got back at it. Jerrik didn't complain or slow down. It was dark by the time they pulled into the dock, where Sam pulled in his haul to be weighed by his usual lobster dealer.

It was an okay day according to Sam. Some of the traps had been full, but not nearly enough. Their haul weighed in at about 500-pounds, which brought in nearly $1400. But after fuel and the cost for more bait for tomorrow and Jerrik getting cut twenty percent, his first payday was $200.

It might as well have been $200,000 with the way Jerrik grinned. He'd earned an honest day's salary and was able to contribute to the things Jett needed to pay for.

"Thank you, Sam." Jerrik said as he folded the money and placed it in his pocket.

"Get yourself a good wallet, young man. You can't walk around with loose cash in your pockets." Sam scolded him.

"I will make sure I do that."

"You worked hard, kid. Harder than anyone I've worked with in my life. Not a single complaint outta ya." Sam looked Jerrik up and down, obviously revising his first impression of the younger man. "If ya continue to work like that, you can be my apprentice. And when I retire, I just might pass my boat down to you. My own kids didn't want to have anything to do with the lobster business."

"You would do that?" Jerrik asked.

"I sure would. So, keep that in mind." Sam slapped a hand on Jerrik's back and guided him towards the parking lot. "Now, let's get ya home. You deserve the rest. And I can't guarantee a short, day trip tomorrow."

"I will be ready."

~~~

"Honey, I am home!" Jerrik called out as he walked through the door.

Jett graded papers at the kitchen table as she usually did in the evenings. Her head immediately shot up. Jerrik grinned at her brightly.

It was 7 in the evening, so she'd been worried that it would be days before she saw him again. In a week's time, he'd become so much a part of her everyday life that she couldn't see him not being there. In her excitement, Jett shot out of her chair and ran to him as he closed and locked the door. She launched herself at him. And with his Viking reflexes, he caught her just in time.

Jett hugged him tightly. Jerrik's strong arms held her gently, his hand rubbed her back calmingly.

"Oh, I'm sorry." Jett yelped and unwrapped herself from his body. "You've been lifting stuff all day. You do not need to be lifting my heavy butt."

"Hmm…I beg to differ."

Jerrik crouched, banded his arms around her, and lifted her off her feet. Jett gasped and then giggled as he carried her to the couch. Her giggles quickly died as he laid her down and proceed to make love to her like he hadn't seen her in months.

"I guess you should work more often." Jett said after she caught her breath.

She was sure if she had hair, it would be a nest on top of her head.

Jerrik hummed contentedly.

"It was a good day."

"So, you like it?"

"I did. Oh…" Jerrik pulled up his jeans that had been around his ankles. He reached into the pocket and pulled out money. "I made $200 today."

"That's fantastic!" Jett wrapped her arms around his neck.

"You can have it. For all the things you have bought me." Jerrik held out the money.

Jett looked at the money. *Don't be a pushover. You care, but he still owes you for clothes and food. Don't repeat what you did with Shawn.*

"How about I only take half for now. Just in case you need money for anything when I'm not around. How's that?"

Baby steps.

"It will work." Jerrik nodded.

Jett quickly counted out $100 and gave him back the rest.

"Alright, it's late. You need to eat and get to bed. You have to be up in a couple of hours." Jett got up and pulled him off the couch towards the kitchen table.

She'd made a big pot of beef stew for him to eat. Something hearty to fill him up and give him some energy the next day. And he ate it like he hadn't eaten in a week.

She pushed him upstairs to shower and go to bed while she continued to grade her papers. Once she was finished, she headed up to shower and get in bed too.

Jett smiled softly at him in her bed. He snuffled softly. He was all Viking, yet he had started to fit into the present world with more ease than she'd believed.

She slid into bed next to him. She tried not to disturb him, but he must have still sensed her presence. His strong arm wrapped around her waist and tucked her backside against his front.

Jerrik was hard as a rock and quickly slipped between her folds. Over the weekend she'd learned not to wear panties to bed and to leave a few clean hand towels for cleanup in her nightstand.

His big, calloused hands caressed her body lazily. His skillful fingers found her sensitive nub. He strummed her clit as he languidly pumped into her. He expertly brought her to her climax and he followed quickly behind. His arms squeezed her tightly as his hips shuddered.

"Ek elska pik," Jerrik whispered in her ear before falling asleep.

Jett drifted off to sleep, her thoughts swirling around the meaning of the ancient words he'd spoken.

Chapter 28

"Jett is coming to the party. But my dad says she's coming with a date." Nic said to Shawn as he played video games on her TV. "So, now what?"

"Don't worry about it. I got it covered." He said as his thumbs flew over the controller.

"Did you not hear what I said." Nic shoved Shawn with her foot. "She won't be alone."

"Get off me!" Shawn smacked her foot away. "Like it matters. Whoever she brings ain't gonna be shit anyway."

"Oh? Like you?" Nic asked.

"Fuck you, Nic. I was the best Jett was ever gonna get."

"My point exactly." Nic rolled her eyes.

"You talk all this shit now. Just wait till my business gets off the ground."

"Just make sure it doesn't go wrong. I wasn't made for prison life." Nic flipped the hair of her new wig.

She'd finally gotten up the guts to buzz her hair like her sister. She hated it. She'd immediately bought several different types of wigs to cover her head, while her hair grew back.

"I'm not trying to go to prison either. Just calm down and stop nagging me, woman!" Shawn growled and continued playing his game.

"Ugh!"

I wonder if Jett found someone better than him. Nic looked at Shawn as he shouted at the TV. *Doubtful. But I can't wait to meet him.*

Chapter 29

The rest of Jerrik's first week at work passed quickly, but at the same time dragged at a snail's pace for Jett. His next trip out took three days. Jerrik still didn't have a phone and even if he did, it was doubtful that there would be service out at sea.

At the beginning of the third day, Jett had been sure he'd found the fog and went back to his own time without her. She could barely breathe. Her heart had constricted. Tears continually stung the backs of her eyes.

When she'd heard the key turn in the lock Thursday night, she'd jumped up from the couch. Jerrik had walked through the door, and for the first time he'd looked tired. But he'd still had enough energy to catch and lift her in his arms when she ran to him.

It was finally his day off. The Sabbath. And it hadn't even crossed their minds to leave the bed. Especially since Jett's period had ended the day before, and they'd taken full advantage.

They laid temple to temple on a shared pillow. Jerrik held up his hand, fingers splayed. Jett gently slid her fingers through his as they chatted.

"You know, it never even crossed my mind to get you tested for an STI. You could have some ancient disease I don't even know about." Jett joked.

"STI?"

"Sexually Transmitted Infection."

"We do not have those where I'm from."

"Oh, I'm sure you do. They just haven't been diagnosed yet. Vikings probably died from them all the time but you didn't know what it was."

Jett's phone chimed before he could respond. She rolled over to grab it from her nightstand. It was the text she'd been waiting for. It was Dr. Jin.

Dr. Jin:
Hello, Jett. The results are finally in and we'd love to meet up with you.

"The results of your DNA test are finally in." Jett told Jerrik.

Jett:
Let's meet today, if that's okay?

Dr. Jin:
We'll be at your place by 3.

Jett:
Perfect. See you then.

~~~

"So, what's the verdict, doctors?" Jett asked.

They all sat at the kitchen table. Jett already knew the answer. She believed Jerrik wholeheartedly. But she was curious to know what the tests said.

"Well," Richard began, "I found that the craftsmanship of the sword is ancient. The way the sword was forged is a lost skill. We tried to replicate the sword with all the known ways to make a sword. But none of them produced the same sword as Jerrik's.

"The clothing could have been replicated, but the animal pelt is from a type of fox or wolf that has long since been extinct. And there's simply no way for these ancient items to be in such an impeccable condition in the 21st century." Richard finished.

Jett turned her attention to Dr. Jin.

"And in laymen's terms, Jerrik's DNA *is* found in this century. *But...*" Soo-Yun paused. "...it is found in people from Scandinavia as *part* of their DNA strand. There are other ancestral DNA markers that are in a Scandinavian individual's DNA. Like Anglo-Saxon, Germanic, etc. Jerrik's DNA is only Norse. Nothing else. That's not possible in this century. Unless..."

Dr. Jin let the rest of her words and their implications drop like a bomb in the room.

"Unless, he is not of this time." Jett finished for her.

"Precisely." Dr. Jin agreed.

Three sets of eyes looked at Jerrik.

"In other news, water is wet." Jerrik said.

Jett choked on her spit. They all laughed.

"He's watched entirely too much TV. He's picked up on our sarcasm." Jett said when she could finally speak again.

She wiped the tears of mirth from her eyes and smiled over at Jerrik. She reached over and clutched his hand.

"And now you know... Officially," he said.

"I do."

Chapter 30

The water was still as Sam's lobster boat cut through it. The sun peeked over the surface of the ocean. It painted the sky in brushstrokes of orange, pink, and magenta. A clear autumn morning.

Jerrik enjoyed these moments as he stood at the doorway to the helm of the boat. The wind on his face. Only the sound of the engine and the water.

As they approached one of Sam's buoy marked zones, a mist appeared on the horizon. It hung low. Tendrils like fingers crawled across the water. Jerrik's heart rate spiked and he squinted to see better.

"Well, that's a strange sight." Sam scratched his head. "I've been doing this job my whole life, and I don't believe I've ever seen anything like that fog before."

Jerrik counted the days in his head. Being wrapped up in Jett and simply enjoying his work, he hadn't even thought about searching for the fog. But if his count was right, it was the new moon.

"Sam," Jerrik said and laid a hand on his boss's shoulder. "I would not go further. Try one of your other zones. Trust me."

Jerrik felt a shiver pass over Sam's body.

"Being a part of the fishing community, we have our superstitions. And that gut feeling I have is agreeing with you, son. We'll come back tomorrow." Sam said as he turned the wheel of the boat in the opposite direction.

~~~

"You're home early," Jett said when Jerrik walked through the door.

She was in the middle of fixing fried chicken. When he didn't say anything, she turned back to look at him. His face was whiter than usual.

"What's wrong?"

"I found it."

Jett's eyes widened. Her stomach dropped and then shot back up and into her throat.

"Aye." Jerrik answered her unspoken thoughts. "I found the fog."

"Did you…" She let the question hang between them.

"No. I told Sam to steer clear of it. It made the hair on the back of our necks stand on end."

"That's what I felt when I saw it and found you." Jett nodded. "So…now we know. Do you think it'll be there next month too?"

"I think so." Jerrik walked over to her and covered her hand that pressed against the counter. "It felt like it was beckoning me."

Jett swallowed.

"You must prepare for next month. Spend time with your family and Dez." He cupped her face. "The party is this weekend. It could be a start.

Jett pulled her face away from his hands.

"Okay."

She said okay, but she found it hard to look him in the eye as she said it.

Chapter 31

"It's yrup winnit rint fran ya."

Jett choked and coughed as she looked at herself in the mirror. She tried to stifle the giggle that bubbled up and squeezed her lips together to stop the smile that wanted to spread across her face.

Music played through her Bluetooth speaker as they got ready for her parents' party. She was in the bathroom as she applied her makeup. Jerrik was in the main room of their hotel room. Missy Elliot's *Work It* blared through the speaker.

Jett walked to the doorway and peeked out at him. Jerrik was shirtless and barefoot in a pair of tuxedo pants. He shook his backside to the beat of the music. His muscled and scarred back flexed as he body-rolled.

"It's yrup winnit rint fran ya." He tried to mimic the backwards lyrics.

At the part where she raps about nails, pedis, and hair, Jerrik wiggled his newly Manly Mani nails and patted his man bun. Jett collapsed against the doorframe and slid down in a fit of laughter. Jerrik's head whipped around. She could barely see him through the tears of laughter that streamed down her face. He grinned at her, but his face still turned a few shades of red.

"What? I know how to work it." Jerrik lifted his chin proudly.

"You actually can. In more ways than one." Jett finally said after catching her breath. "You've got rhythm for sure."

Jerrik walked over and helped her off the floor.

"But I'm gonna need to confiscate your new phone. It's obvious that you've been watching *way* too many music videos."

"There is no such thing as too many music videos. Besides, I like the music of this time."

"I noticed." Jett grinned.

Jerrik leaned down to kiss the top of her head. She lifted up her nose for him to kiss next. Then he kissed her lips softly before he smacked her butt. She yelped and scurried back into the bathroom.

Over the last few weeks, they'd fallen into a coupledom that left them both relaxed and happy. Jerrik's job kept him busy most days. It took Jett a little while to adjust, but in the end, she liked their schedule. His job kept him away so often that when he got home, when he wasn't sleeping or eating, they were fucking on every available surface they could find.

Jett liked being able to miss him.

There was only one thing that marred their little protective bubble of happiness. Going back to his time. Jerrik often talked about his time to prepare Jett for what was to come and how life would be. She hadn't told him, but she was terrified.

Is our love enough to give up everything here?

~~~

"Ready?" Jett asked after she took a deep breath.

"Aye." Jerrik looked down at her with a grin.

They stood at the entrance of The Mill. A beautiful 19th century building of brick, steel beams, glass ceilings, and creeping green ivy restored as an event center in Queens. The party was held in the mezzanine that was romantically lit with string Edison bulbs. Above on the wraparound terrace were tables that overlooked the dance floor below. More tables were set against the brick walls below, surrounding the dance floor. Soft music played from hidden speakers as people milled about during cocktail hour.

Jett wore a shimmering Prussian blue gown that made her deep mahogany skin glow. It cinched in her thick waist. The neckline left her collarbones and her shoulders bare, and plunged into a deep slit. The slit stopped just above where her stomach began, leaving a delectable peek at her plentiful cleavage within. The full skirt reached the floor in ripples of fabric. A nearly hip-high split exposed one lush, shapely ebony leg. And for the first time in five years, Jett was able to wear matching blue and silver glittering heels. Four-inch heels and Jerrik still stood two-inches taller next to her.

He was resplendent in a black tux. It made his shoulders appear even broader and his long frame even taller. A sliver of black satin on the inner side of either lapel gave the suit a modern flare. His white shirt was crisp, and made his Prussian blue necktie pop. His nails were painted with a slightly new masculine design that reminded Jett of ancient Norse runes. His beard was freshly trimmed and conditioned. And his blond locks were pulled back into a neat top knot.

They wore matching masquerade masks. Jerrik's was a matte metallic blue to match his tie and her dress. The style was *The Phantom of the Opera* inspired, hiding both eyes and half of his face. The deep blue made his piercing, icy eyes stand out more than usual. And his pink, shapely lips looked even more inviting.

Jett's mask was matte silver with blue swirl accents and a blue orchid on one side. Her eyes underneath were smokey and mysterious. And her plump lips were painted a deep red that popped against the blue and silver and deep ebony of her skin.

They made such a striking pair that all eyes were on them as they walked inside. Jett took a shaky breath.

Remember. You don't have to shrink yourself for anyone anymore.

Jerrik wrapped his hand around Jett's and slid his fingers between hers. He squeezed gently.

"I know you are nervous." He leaned into her to whisper. "I know your mother and sister often say unkind things to you. But I can assure you, you take my breath away. And will do the same to anyone who sees you tonight. And they cannot take that away from you."

"Thank you, Jerrik."

"Jeanette Mother-effing Johnson!" A familiar voice screeched across the room.

"Desiree." Jerrik said with a partially pained expression.

"The one and only." Jett whispered and turned to her friend.

Dez ran on her tippy toes towards the couple in a slinky floor length black dress and matching lacy mask. When Dez reached her, she clutched Jett's hands and raised her arms out to her sides to get a better look at her.

"Maine, and dare I say, this handsome specimen has been *good* for you. Because you look so beautiful my heart hurts." Dez's eyes shimmered with tears.

"If you make me cry…" Jett choked out.

Dez breathed deeply and blew it out through pierced lips. "I'm trying to hold it together. But damn, Jett! You look fucking stunning. It's like I got to witness the shedding of your cocoon. And now, you're standing here in your truth. The truth that you're a motherfucking *god-DESS*!"

"Freya," Jerrik whispered with a nod of pride.

"Thank you, Dez. You look beautiful too."

"No! This night ain't about me. You're about to light up this whole event. Who are we celebrating?" Dez looked around comically. "Because I'm pretty sure we're celebrating *you*."

"Okay. Okay." Jett felt her face heat. "People are starting to look."

"Let 'em! And they already were." Dez finally focused on Jerrik. "And Rik! You are killing the game in that tux."

Jerrik clasped his lapels and tugged them sharply. "Thank you."

"Oop. Your Moms and Pops are heading over. I was gonna go get a drink, but I can't miss this." Dez stepped to the side.

"I can't stand you." Jett grumbled and tried not to laugh at her friend.

"Nette!" Morris said looking her up and down. "You look gorgeous, sweetie!"

"Thanks, Dad. You look handsome too. Happy anniversary!"

He was in a classic tux. His sandy brown hair was faded and lined to perfection. His hazel eyes sparkled behind his black mask. He was as handsome as ever.

Her mother was in a cream-colored ensemble. It was a sleek pant with a jacket that turned dress in the back and dusted the floor. Perfect for a bride 30 years later. Her eyes behind her white lace mask looked at Jett in shock.

"Jett, you…" She placed her hands on Jett's arms.

Jett held her breath.

"You are dazzling."

"Happy anniversary. Thank you, mom." Jett's voice held the slightest chill.

"H-How are you doing? How's Maine?" Gloria glanced at Jerrik. "It looks like you're enjoying yourself."

"It's been wonderful." Jett pulled Jerrik's hand over to clasp it with both of hers, silently bringing him into the conversation. "Mom. Dad. I'd like to introduce you to my…boyfriend, Jerrik. Jerrik, this is my mom and dad, Gloria and Morris Johnson."

Jett realized that they hadn't talked about an official title for their relationship. Jerrik felt like more than a boyfriend. But that was hard to explain.

"It is an honor to meet you, Dr. and Mrs. Johnson." Jerrik said perfectly the way Jett had coached him.

"It's nice to meet you, Jerrik." Morris greeted and shook hands with Jerrik. "Wow, you've got a strong grip and hands rough from hard work. Nice."

Jett's father really looked at Jerrik, impressed by the large man.

"It's nice to meet you, Derrick," Gloria said.

"It's Jerrik, Mom."

"Oh, sorry, Jerrik. My apologies."

"It is okay."

"Is that an accent I hear?" Morris asked. "Doesn't sound like something from Maine."

"I am from Iceland."

"Oh wow! What are you doing here?"

Jett looked at Dez and her best friend cringed.

"He came to visit and loved it so much he decided to stay. He's become a lobstermen apprentice." Jett interjected before Jerrik said something seemingly off the wall.

"That's fantastic, young man." Morris put his hand on Jerrik's back and started to lead him away. "Tell me, is there good money in lobstering?"

Jerrik's fingers slipped from Jett's as he was led away.

Please God, don't let him say anything crazy.

"Well, he's certainly a handsome young man." Gloria's eyes followed them as they walked away. "How did you meet?"

"Um…at the lighthouse in my little town. His boat was trapped on the rocks when I was there for a morning walk," Jett said.

She'd decided to take the same advice that she'd given to Jerrik. Keep it simple and as close to the truth as possible.

"So…were there no Black men up there?" Gloria asked.

Here we go.

"Mom, don't start."

"Have you heard of Maine?!" Dez chimed in, her comedic timing always impeccable.

"I don't appreciate your sarcasm, Desiree." Gloria gave Dez a withering look.

"Sorry, Mrs. J." Dez cringed at Jett.

"Just make sure he's not some good ole boy."

"Mom, he's from Iceland. I don't think they have that there." Jett rolled her eyes.

"I just wanna make sure you're protected."

"Like you protected me from Shawn or my parasite of a sister?"

"Don't be disrespectful, Jeanette."

"It's not disrespectful to ask your own mother to care for and protect you. But that's okay mom. You don't have to worry about Jerrik. I've never felt more protected and cared for in my entire life. I've found my family."

Jett turned in a flurry of blue skirts and walked away from her toxic mother.

"Jett. Jeanette Johnson!" Gloria called after her.

Jett continued to walk towards the bartender.

"A whiskey, please." Jett order.

"Oh, shit! You plan on getting lit," Dez said.

"Are you following me?"

"Of course, I am. Who else am I gonna talk to here?" Dez leaned against the bar. "Besides, I'm here for the fireworks. I knew it was gonna be telenovela level drama the minute I saw how gorgeous you look and how striking you both look together."

"I can't take you anywhere." Jett rolled her eyes and grinned.

She took a sip of her drink. It burned a path down her throat and into her stomach. She felt a flash of warmth spread through her body moments later.

"Now, I'm just waiting for the finale." Dez smirked.

"And that would be?"

"Your sister and the hobosexual." Dez looked at something over Jett's shoulder. "Speak of the devil and she shall emerge with her lapdog. The audacity."

Jett turned. As her eyes landed on her sister, Nic's eyes widened in shock. Shawn walked beside her and stumbled when he realized it was Jett. Nic tried to school her features as her grip tightened on Shawn's arm.

Oh, please! The last thing I want is your man. And how soon we forget you stole him from me.

Nic wore a red mermaid style dress that hugged her petite curves. Jett internally frowned at the blonde lace front wig her twin wore. When it came to any event they attended together, Nic tried to wear her hair similar to Jett's. Her wig was lovely and looked good on her, but it was a change of habit for her sister.

Either she's growing up or... Oh my God! She buzzed her hair and it looked horrible.

Jett internally rolled her eyes so hard she was surprised no one saw it. She glanced at Dez and her bestie gave her a knowing look.

Shawn wore an ill-fitting tux. It was a few sizes too big to hide the weight he'd gained. His mouth gaped open as they stopped in front of Jett and Dez. Jett also noted that he had to look up at her from his 5'9" vantage point. She did tower over him in her heels that he'd never let her wear when they were together.

"Wow, Jett! You never looked like this when you were with me. Maybe things could've been different if you did," Shawn said.

Nic elbowed him in his side.

"Well, you'd have to be a better man first. So…" Jett shrugged.

"Yeah, right." Shawn scoffed and then looked around the room. "Speaking of, where's this new man you were supposed to be bringing? Lemme guess. He had to back out?"

"Yeah, where is he?" Nic asked smugly.

Jett sighed. "Why do I threaten you so much?"

"Ha!" Nic laughed nervously. "You don't."

"I must. All you ever do is try to put me down, yet always trying to copy me. I mean, I get why he does it." Jett gestured to Shawn with her chin. "He's mediocre in every way. Average at best. But you've always had everything, including what's mine. Why do you need more? Why must you try to crush me while you're at it?"

"Fuck you, bitch!" Shawn stepped towards her with fist clenched.

"You lay one hand on her and I will snap your neck like a twig." Jerrik stepped in front of Jett.

Shawn craned his neck back to look up at Jerrik. Nic's mouth flapped open and closed as she gazed in awe at the Viking.

"Who are *you*?" Shawn said indignantly.

"Jett's future. Am I to guess you are her regrettable past?"

"Oh shit!" Dez hissed under her breath.

Nic slipped her arm free from around Shawn's and tried to discreetly step away from him. She cleared her throat. Jett looked down at her sister incredulously.

"Jett, don't be rude," Nic said. "Introduce me to this handsome man of yours."

"Did you have a stroke when I was talking to you a few moments ago?" Jett scrunched her face in disbelief. "Like, I can legit see the wheels in your brain working to figure out a way to drop Shawn and dig your claws into my new man."

"Ha! I have no idea what you're talking about." Nic defended herself as pure lust practically shot from her eyes like laser beams.

She didn't even look at Jett as she said it. Her eyes hadn't left Jerrik's person since he walked up.

"I just think your sister should be able to welcome your new beau into the family." Nic said, her eyes still on Jerrik.

Jett chanced a glance at Jerrik. She hadn't wanted to look at him after he set eyes on her sister. Jett's whole life, had been an exercise in crushing disappointment. Every boy she'd ever had a crush on. Every boy she'd ever loved. Every. Single. One. At the first sight of her sister, had pushed Jett to the side to try to date Nic. Or worse. They'd pretended to be with Jett in order to get close to Nic. It's what Shawn had done. He'd just been the only one to take the farce as far as he did.

Brown eyes filled with apprehension rose to the handsome Viking's face. What Jett saw there punched her in the gut. She blinked rapidly.

Jerrik looked down at the small woman with complete and utter disdain. Nic smiled sweetly at him and his upper lip curled. He turned to Jett and his expression softened. He took her hand, lifted it to his mouth, and kissed her knuckles. He looked back down at Nic.

"Are you serious right now, Nic?!" Shawn nudged her arms as she continued to gaze longingly at Jerrik.

"I'd break you, little girl. And why would I forsake a goddess for a peasant?" Jerrik turned to Jett, fully dismissing her twin sister. "Trust me, my love. In this time or another, there will never be anyone else."

The world fell away.

A small, shy smile danced on her lips. She understood exactly what he meant. 'In this time or mine.'

"Let us dine."

"Let's." Jett smiled at him. Jett looked back at Dez. "You coming?"

"As if you could stop me."

Jett chuckled.

"How do you do that?" Jett asked Jerrik.

"Do what?"

"Make the world disappear, so there's no one left but the two of us?"

"When you figure out how you do it, let me know."

Jett grinned happily as Jerrik guided her to a large, round table near the small table where her parents sat.

~~~

They filled themselves on delicious food. Their bodies loosened as they drank copious amounts of alcohol. And conversation flowed around the table.

Jerrik looked at Jett. She was engaged in an animated conversation with her best friend about Dez's new man. Her warm, dark skin was luminous. Her bright smile and infectious laughter drew eyes from every section of the room. And her regal beauty held their gaze for longer than was polite.

Jerrik assumed that was why her sister shot daggers at her from across the room. And Jett's soon-to-be ex-husband pouted sullenly.

He instantly had a dislike for the pair. During nights in bed, Jett had told him stories about her sister as well as her estranged husband. But even without the backstory, Jerrik still didn't like them. Being able to lead a large village required the ability to read people. And Jerrik had become proficient at it.

Something about the two made the hairs on the back of his neck stand on end.

Jerrik reached over and clasped Jett's hand. She glanced at him for a moment. They'd removed their masks while they ate and chatted, so he got an unobstructed view of her lovely face. She smiled sweetly and winked at him before going back to her conversation.

Jerrik pressed a hand to his abdomen. It fluttered erratically.

He'd never experienced what he felt for Jett. No one had ever spoken of such feelings in his time. He was ill-prepared to feel such things. It brought out his protectiveness. His curiosity to know everything about her. His lust to claim every inch of her.

His world had once revolved around leading, protecting, and defending his family and village. It now revolved around her. She had become his nucleus. His center.

And for the first time in his adult life, the man who hadn't been afraid of anything. Who stared death in the face and smiled. That same man was terrified.

I cannot lose her.

Chapter 32

After dinner, they danced. Jerrik was a quick study. He twirled her and pulled her in close. He held her hand warmly between them as they swayed.

All eyes were on them as if they were the couple of honor. But Jett didn't notice. It was just the two of them on the dance floor.

Jerrik's free hand lifted to cup the side of her face. Jett nuzzled his palm. His fingers slid behind her neck and pulled her in. They kissed softly. Jett felt his tongue flick against her lips and her lady bits immediately jumped to attention. She quickly pulled away, remembering they had an audience.

"Don't even think about it." She scolded. "We are in polite company."

"If we were in my time, I would lift you over my shoulder and carry you away to ravish you. I may consider it still." Jerrik teased.

"My parents would flip the fuck out. Especially my mom."

"That will not matter for much longer." Jerrik said flippantly and grinned.

Jett frowned and pulled back slightly. "That's not funny or cute, Jerrik. Leaving behind everything and everyone I know and love isn't to be taken lightly."

"But you will not be leaving everyone you love. You will be with me. Am I not enough?"

"That's what I'm trying to figure out, Jerrik." Jett looked away.

"'Trying to figure out'?" Jerrik asked. "So, you are still deciding?"

"It is a big ask. To leave my best friend, my job and the kids I'm teaching. And they may not be perfect, but leaving my family isn't easy either. To leave all the creature comforts I'm used to for a rustic, dangerous life with no electricity or indoor plumbing. I'm terrified." Jett defended.

"You will get used to it. And I will protect you." Jerrik said firmly.

Jett could tell that he was in full stubborn Viking mode. But he'd met his match today.

"And what if that isn't enough for me? What if I decide I want to stay?"

"You will not." Jerrik's eye flashed with anger.

Jett caught the hurt behind it.

"How do you know I won't change my mind?"

"I am not saying you will not change your mind. I am saying that it does not matter if you do. You will come with me. I command it."

Jett stopped dancing and pulled out of his arms completely. She grasped his arm and pulled him to a more private corner.

"You don't run shit here, Jerrik." Jett hissed under her breath. "You are not my laird. I have free will and if I decide that I don't want to go with you, that's the end of the discussion."

"I will not live without you."

"Then you can stay. Did you ever think about that?"

"You know I cannot."

"Yes, yes. I know. It's your duty to run your village. As if you don't have two perfectly capable brothers to lead your village."

"The responsibility was left to me. Not them. It is what my father wanted."

"Then go back. Live for your father. But leave me out of it."

Jett moved to turn away from him, but he grabbed her arm tightly. She turned back and stared at his hand as if it were offensive. He refused to let go.

"Let me go." She gritted out.

"No." Jerrik said just as intensely.

Jett knew the battle of wills was more than about his hand that clutched her arm almost painfully. It was about letting her go completely.

"This isn't 11th century Iceland. If I scream, the cops will be called."

"And I will battle every one of them."

"I am not your property. Now, let…me…go!" Jett ripped her arm from his strong grip. "And do *not* follow me."

Jett turned on her heel and stormed out of the room and building.

Grrr!!! Stubborn fucking Viking!

Jett took a deep breath when she reached the courtyard. She let the cool evening air fill her lungs. She sighed heavily and continued out past the gates to the sidewalk.

She'd chosen a modern, hip hotel around the corner from The Mill when they'd decided to stay in a hotel instead of her parents' or Dez's place. With the way her and Jerrik couldn't keep their hands off each other and fucked like the beast with two backs, she'd figured a hotel nearby was best. So, she decided to walk the short distance. She needed to blow off steam anyway.

The Mill and their hotel, The Raven, were butted up against each other. It only took her a few minutes to reach the entrance, but that was long enough for her feet to swell up further in her heels. Once she got inside on the tiled floors, Jett kicked off her shoes.

She smiled at the desk agent and padded to the elevator bay. Jett walked into the first elevator to open. She pressed the button for the third floor and leaned against the wall of the elevator. The doors started to slide close. A gloved hand shot through the doors to stop them. They reopened and two men dressed in Halloween costumes stepped in. Jett gave them a brief smile and nod. She slid further into the corner.

One man who was a few inches shorter than Jett, was dressed in black robes with a hooded ghost face mask and the man who was about Jett's height was in a mechanic's jumpsuit and hockey mask like from their respective movies. Neither spoke as they pressed the button for the fourth floor.

A bad feeling rushed through Jett's veins, but there was nothing she could do. She didn't have her phone or anything else to protect her or call for help if they tried to attack her in the elevator. She'd left all that in their room, since anyone she'd need to contact were at the party with her.

The elevator dinged her floor and she breathed an internal sigh of relief. The doors slid open and she quickly stepped off. She quickly padded down the hall to her room. She fumbled for the keycard that she'd shoved into her bustier before they left. She slid it into the slot and the green light lit up and the lock opened.

As she pushed down on the handle, a hand smashed over her mouth and an arm banded around her waist as she was lifted off her feet. Jett's heart jumped into her throat. Survival mode immediately kicked in. She kicked back and tried to use her shoes as weapons. Another set of arms grabbed her legs.

The men pulled her into her hotel room. They tossed her onto the bed. The man dressed like the ghost tried to grasp her foot and pull her towards him. Jett used her other foot to kick him in the groin. She didn't quite hit her target, but it grazed him enough to make him yelp in pain. He pulled back his hand and his fist connected with her jaw. Jett felt pain explode across the side of her face and blood fill her mouth as her lip split and inner cheek tore against her teeth.

"You fucking, bitch!" The man screamed.

Jett clutched her cheek as she whipped her head around to look at the man with the familiar voice.

"Shawn?!?"

"Shut up, fat bitch!"

It was definitely her estranged husband.

Jett lost it and clawed at his mask. It ripped away to reveal his face. He grabbed her neck and squeezed until she stopped fighting.

"It doesn't matter anyway. It's not like you'll be alive to identify me."

Jett drew back and spat silva and blood into his face. Shawn slapped her hard and the sting made her cringe back.

"Hold her arms, Josh." Shawn ordered his friend.

"Don't say my fucking name, fool!"

"Hold her fucking arms!" Shawn bellowed.

His accomplice got on the bed above her head. Jett fought as hard as she could, but once he got a hold of her wrists, she couldn't match his strength.

"Now, before I strangle the life out of your ugly ass, I'm gonna fuck you as a reminder that a white man can't replace me." Shawn sneered.

"Motherfucker, what white got to do with it?" His friend asked indignantly.

"Shut the fuck up, Josh. Ain't nobody talking about you."

Jett didn't hear anything after he basically told her he was about to rape her. She went wild. She bucked and screamed as tears began to stream down her temples.

Shawn grasped the neckline of her dress and rent it until her black bustier underneath was exposed. He continued to tug until the dress ripped completely down the middle, exposing all of her.

"Shawn, please!" Jett switched from fighting to begging. "You don't wanna do this."

Shawn leaned down until he was only a few inches from her face.

"Actually, I really do. Now, shut. The fuck. Up." He growled as he grasped her jaw.

He released her with a cruel shove and Jett cried out in pain at her already bruised face. His hand trailed down her lace covered breasts, over her stomach, and stopped at her black lace panties.

God, please! It can't end like this.

Chapter 33

Jerrik walked over to the bartender after Jett had stormed out the building. He needed another drink.

"Mead, please." Jerrik ordered.

"Huh?" The bartender looked at him strangely. "You mean beer?"

"Aye. Beer, please."

The man handed him a bottle of the amber liquid. Jerrik lifted it to his lips and gulped it down in two swallows. He slammed it down.

"Another."

The bartender handed him another. The second bottle Jerrik drank a little slower as his thoughts drifted to Jett.

He didn't mean for the conversation to escalate the way it did. But he hadn't been prepared for Jett to say she didn't really want to go with him. He knew it had more to do with other things than it had to do with him. But he couldn't help the pang of hurt that had squeezed his heart. It felt like she didn't want to be with him.

Jerrik sighed and was about to turn to asked for another beer when his eyes caught sight of a red dress. His eyes followed the movement. Jett's sister, Nic, was in a corner. Her eyes on him.

Arctic blue eyes scanned the rest of the room. He didn't see Jett's estranged husband anywhere. Jerrik's stomach plummeted and his heart shot into his throat. He placed the empty beer bottle on the bar and started towards the doorway.

"Jerrik!" A voice called out.

He turned and looked down at the petite woman who had emotionally tortured Jett her whole life.

"What?!" He barked.

"How about a dance?" She said coyly.

"Did you not hear what I said earlier. I wouldn't touch you. Ever." He sneered. "Now, where is your man?"

"I-I don't know." Her voice wobbled as her eyes shifted guiltily.

"You do." Jerrik narrowed his eyes. His hand shot out and he gripped her upper arm. "Where is he?!"

"I-I swear I-"

"I swear to Odin, if you say you don't know, I'll snap you in half right now." Jerrik squeezed her arm tighter.

"Ow! Your hotel. Your hotel!" Nic cried.

Dez appeared next to them.

"What happened?"

"Shawn has Jett in our hotel room. Watch her." Jerrik shoved Nic into Dez.

He turned and sped from the building. His long legs ate up the sidewalk. He burst through the front doors of the hotel. He ran to the elevators and pressed the button over and over until one finally opened. He paced back and forth like a caged animal as he rode up to the third floor. The short ride felt like it took an eternity. It might as well have been the 100th floor.

The doors dinged and slid open. Jerrik squeezed through them before they could fully open. He ran full speed down the hall to their door. He had to skid to a stop in his dress shoes. He pressed down on the handle to their room and it didn't budge.

"Shit!" Jerrik hissed as he remembered he needed that keycard.

His hands frantically felt his pants and jacket for one. His memory went back to Jett sliding a card into the top of her dress, but he didn't take the second one because they'd planned on returning together.

At Jett's cry of pain Jerrik's head jerked up. He placed his palms against the door and heard a muffled masculine voice. Jerrik clenched his jaw and his lip curled with rage. He backed up and then ran towards the door. He turned at the last second and slammed his shoulder into it. The door shook with the force but didn't budge.

"Jerrik?!?" He heard Jett's voice call out.

"JETT!" He screamed back.

Jerrik heard a slapping sound and Jett's shout of anguish.

He heard a roar and realized it came from him, only when he felt the pain of it through his throat. He backed up and charged the door again. This time the door cracked at the force. He ran back and charged once more. The door split under the force of his weight.

Jerrik stumbled into the room. His eyes quickly scanned the area. One man with a hockey mask jumped off the bed with his hands up.

"It was his idea." He lifted one hand in surrender with the other hand pointed at the man in black robes that was on top of Jett's prone body. "They paid me."

The other man turned and Jerrik saw that it was Shawn.

Jerrik stepped towards him. Jett's crazed estranged husband dragged her from the bed. She was in nothing but her undergarments. The coward placed her in front of his body and wrapped his hand around her throat. The skin of her jaw was darkened with a bruise. The side of her bottom lip was split. And tears streamed down her face.

The edges of Jerrik's vision turned red and zeroed in on her abuser.

"I'll kill her right in front of you." Shawn warned nervously.

"Then I will kill you slowly." Jerrik said it as if it was a discussion over coffee. "Slowly or quickly. Either way, you will die this night."

Shawn's eyes widened with terror as he tried to figure out what to do. He shoved Jett hard at Jerrik and ran for the door. Jerrik grasped Jett with one arm. The other shot out like a bullet. He snatched Shawn by the throat. Jett stumbled back freeing his other arm.

Jerrik pulled Shawn to him and held him to his chest. His other hand snaked around the back of his head and he twisted with enough force to snap Shawn's neck and ripped the tendons, practically ripping the man's head from his shoulders. The whole brutal assassination happened in the span of time it took Jett to flinch in shock.

Shawn's body crumpled at Jerrik's feet. Jerrik stepped over his lifeless body and headed for the other man. Shawn's accomplice cowered in the corner.

"Don't kill me, man!" He sobbed. "I swear to God, they paid me. They paid me. I didn't really wanna do it, but I needed the money."

Jerrik reached down and ripped the mask from the man's head. Tear-filled green eyes looked up at him in fear through shaggy, dirty blond hair that had flopped in his face. The Viking grabbed a handful of his jumpsuit and pulled him up to his feet.

"Jerrik, don't."

Jett's soft voice and hand on his arm were the only things that stopped him. The haze of red around his vision disappeared.

"He's a witness to what happened. You can't kill him." Jett pleaded.

Jerrik slowly released the man. His knees gave out on him and he crumbled back to the floor where he'd been.

Jett sprang into action. With shaky hands, she found her phone charger and tossed it to Jerrik.

"Tie him up! I'll call the cops and then you have to get outta here." Jett directed him.

Jerrik stooped down in front of the man. The man willingly put his arms behind his back and Jerrik tied him tightly.

"Shit! Too late." Jett hissed as she looked out the window.

Blue and red lights flashed outside.

"Someone must have heard the struggle and called the cops. You have to get outta here, Jerrik." Jett started to push him from the door. "You have to take the stairs. Go back to the party, find Dez and tell her what happened."

Jerrik stopped and turned to her. He clasped the good side of her face. He desperately wanted to hold her. To make sure she was okay.

"Jerrik there's no time." She lowered her voice so the man couldn't hear. "They can't find you in here. There is no record of you. They'll be suspicious and take you in. But with no record, you can be a ghost. They'll never be able to find you."

"Alright. Ek elska pik." He said in Old Norse before releasing her face.

Jerrik turned and ran out the room. He ran down the hall to the stairwell.

The cops poured out the elevators just as the door clicked shut.

Chapter 34

"So, you never saw the man in your life and you didn't get a good look at him?" The detective asked as Jett sat on the back step of an ambulance.

He was a gruff and grizzled looking Black man. The kind with the rough, hard exterior but with a soft, mushy center.

The paramedics had finished checking her over. They'd deemed her able to go home. The lady EMT applied a liquid bandage to her lip, and then gave her an ice pack to press to her bruised and swollen face. She'd changed into her favorite comfy sweater dress she'd arrived to the city in.

"Mr. Wagner said the same thing." The detective said suspiciously as he jerked his chin in the direction of Shawn's accomplice. "So, I am to believe that some lone hero heard you screaming, broke down the door, saved your life, and then fled?"

"I don't know what to tell you, detective. That's exactly what happened," Jett said.

Before the cops ran through the busted doorway, she'd told Shawn's sidekick, Josh, to say he hadn't gotten a good look at Jerrik. And that if he stuck to that story that she wouldn't press charges. She was certain that the man was so terrified by Jerrik that he'd never attempt to come after her.

"Alright, young lady." He gave her a knowing look. "Whoever he was, you were lucky to have him. We'll leave it at that. Case closed."

"Thank you, detective."

He turned away and Jett sagged in relief.

Two uniformed officers walked up to the detective with a handcuffed and sobbing, Nic in tow.

Josh had sung like a canary. He'd told Jett and the cops that Nic and Shawn had plotted to have her killed for insurance money. And that they'd paid him. He'd showed them the money transfer app on his phone for $1,000. Jett had thought, *Wow! What is this, an episode on the Crime Investigation Channel? And I'm only worth a thousand bucks. Nice.*

"Jett, please! You know I didn't mean it. It was all Shawn." Nic begged as they pulled her towards a police car.

"You paid Josh from your own account, Nic. I can't save you. No one can. And honestly, I hope you rot." Jett got up and turned away.

Dez ran up. Her eyes filled with worry.

"Jesus, Jett! Are you okay?" She wrapped Jett up in a comforting hug.

Jett swallowed her emotions and nodded.

"I'm alright."

"He's at my place waiting for you," Dez said cryptically.

"Thanks."

"Nicky!" Jett's mom cried out as her parents ran up.

Some uniformed officers blocked them from running to their daughter as she was shoved into the back of a cop car. Gloria's eyes scanned the crowd that had gathered. They landed on Jett and they turned icy with hatred.

"This is all your fault," she yelled as she walked towards Jett and Dez.

"No, mother. It's your fault. I warned you that letting her get away with everything and never facing any consequences was going to come back to haunt you. And now it has.

"And the fact that you don't even care that she tried to have me killed and almost succeeded is just…"

Jett sucked in a ragged breath. She blinked rapidly.

"I'm done."

Her father looked lost. His family had blown up right in front of him and he didn't know what to do. Jett hoped he found the strength to walk away from her mother before she destroyed him.

But as far as Jett was concerned, she wouldn't be around to find out.

"Come on." Dez said as she wrapped an arm around Jett's waist.

They turned their backs to her parents and walked away. The red and blue lights reflected on their retreating backs.

~~~

Jerrik paced Dez's small space as he waited for them. The lock on the door scraped. Jerrik stopped mid-step. The door opened a moment later and the two women walked inside. Jerrik ran the few steps it took to reach the door. His arms banded around Jett's waist and lifted her off her feet.

The moment she was securely within the circle of his arms she broke. Her entire body shook with sobs. She tried to suck in precious air but choked on her tears.

Jerrik carried her to the couch and sat with her on his lap. Dez was there with a glass of water and some tissues before she disappeared to give them privacy.

His big hand rubbed her back soothingly. He whispered words of love in an attempt to calm her.

"Just breathe, Jett. It is okay. You are safe. It is over. I promise, elskan mín."

Eventually, she fell asleep. Her face nestled against the crook of his neck.

~~~

A nightmare featuring the replay of what had happened, jarred Jett awake. She gasped into the darkness. Strong arms already wrapped around her tightened.

~ 227 ~

Jett lifted her head. Jerrik still sat on Dez's couch, cradling her on his lap. He'd fallen asleep with his head back. But she'd woken him when she'd flinched awake.

"Are you okay?" He asked.

"Yeah. Well, as good as can be."

"I do not believe I have been more afraid in my entire life, and I have often run head first into battle. So, I cannot imagine what tonight was like for you." Jerrik leaned forward and gently kissed her bruised cheek.

Jett braced her hands on his shoulders and lifted her leg to straddle him. He rubbed her back. Her arms slid up and around the back of his neck. And she rested the good side of her face against his shoulder and melted into him, trying to absorb his strength.

"It was pretty fucking awful. But thank you. Thank you for saving me." Jett said into his neck.

It was the first time a man had ever rescued her. In recent years, women were into saving themselves. To be the hero of their own story. But when she'd never been loved enough for anyone to want to save her, it felt good to be rescued.

I mean, I think I would've preferred figuratively than literally, though.

"You do not have to thank me." Jerrik kissed the top of her head. "I was saving myself as well. Because I do not know what would have become of me had he succeeded."

Jett breathed in deeply. She drew in his scent. He smelled of his shampoo, soap, and all man. She nuzzled his neck and raised her lips to his skin. She felt his pulse jump on her lips.

Jerrik's hands squeezed her a little tighter. They slid down her back and cupped her ass. Jett felt him grow hard against the apex of her legs. She pushed back to sit up and look at him.

"We do not have to. You have been through a lot."

Jett couldn't think of a better way to erase or at least forget briefly the events of the night. She leaned forward and rubbed her lips across his.

Jerrik forgot himself for a moment. He clutched the back of her head and deepened the kiss hungrily. Jett cried into his mouth in pain. Jerrik jerked back.

"Shit! I am so sorry." He kissed her cut gently in apology.

"It's okay."

Jett pulled his lips back to hers. They kissed softly. His mouth trailed down to her neck as his fingers gathered up the material of her dress. Jett raised slightly to assist him with freeing her bottom half from the fabric. Her fingers found the fly of his tuxedo pants. They nimbly unfastened him. She reached inside and caressed him through his boxer briefs.

Jerrik growled and quickly set his cock free. Jett raised up and lowered herself down to his fat-tipped cock. She sunk down onto his long length. Her head fell back, exposing her neck. Jerrik bit and licked the available skin.

Quiet little mewls passed her lips as he guided her up and down his erection. She lifted her head and looked down at him. Jett pressed her forehead to his.

"Take me with you." She breathed against his lips. "I'll go with you."

Jerrik stopped and searched her eyes in the darkness. He must have seen that she was serious, he encircled her waist and buried his face in her chest. He pumped up within her harder and faster. Jett wrapped her arms lovingly around his head.

Her pussy fluttered with the beginnings of her climax. Jett rolled her hips to create more friction. Jerrik thrust up to meet her. She shuddered as her body shattered. She buried her face in his hair to stifle her cries. Her wet walls flexed around him and Jerrik groaned into her chest as he exploded inside of her.

"Ek elska pik," Jerrik's muffled voice said against the fabric of her sweater dress.

"And I love you," Jett said.

Jerrik looked up at her. He smiled softly.

"How did you know?"

"Just a feeling." Jett smoothed a loose strand of hair back from his face.

"I do. I love you." He finally said in English.

Jett took in the first of many healing breaths.

~~~

Dez walked out of her bedroom the next morning. She found the two sprawled on her couch. Jerrik laid on his back shirtless. Jett laid on top of him. Her legs straddled his hips and a throw blanket draped over her backside and fell around them.

They both blinked at her as they came awake.

"You fucked on my couch, didn't you?!"

Jett cringed.

"Send the bill to my father. We wouldn't even be on your couch if they hadn't raised a psychopath," Jett said.

"You've got a point."

Jett sat up, but was careful not to expose anything. Although Dez tried to look. She shrugged when she couldn't even catch a peek of skin.

"So...uh...we need to talk." Jett gave Dez a serious look.

Dez sighed. "You're going back with him."

Jett's face registered shock.

"How did you know?"

"Unlucky guess. But whatever you need from me, I'll do it."

Chapter 35

"Come on, Mason!" Caleb called out to his best friend.

Jett smiled as Caleb waited for Mason as he got his brace, and then followed their friends out of the classroom after school. All in their wizard robes and wands.

After Jerrik's talk with Caleb, everything had changed. The boys had become fast friends. Mason had pulled Caleb to the wizarding side and now the whole class was obsessed.

Jett wiped away a tear that had escaped unbidden down her cheek. The next morning, they were scheduled to leave. The new moon was expected that evening. The fog seemed to appear the dawn of every new moon.

The last few weeks had been a blur. Jerrik got her as prepared as he could. She spent time with Dez and had even seen her father the previous weekend. It had been hard for him, his family splitting down the middle, but he'd finally left her mother. Everything that had happened had shown him just how toxic his wife had become. Or always was.

Jett still wasn't sure going to Jerrik's time was the right thing. Especially as she watched the children goof off before getting on their respective buses or in their parent's cars. She was a teacher. She wanted to change lives, one student at a time. She didn't know what good she'd be in 11th century Iceland.

But she also knew that being separated from Jerrik wasn't an option.

Jett sighed and started packing up her things for the day. For the last time.

She cleared her throat and frowned. Her eyes widened and she sprinted for the bathroom across the hall. She made it to a stall just in time. She threw up her lunch and anything else that had been in her stomach.

"Ugh. Jesus!" Jett flushed the toilet and leaned against the stall wall. "What did I eat?"

Or...

She froze.

Her head calculated.

Her mouth popped open.

"Fuck."

~~~

"Shit!"

The word "pregnant" stared up at Jett from the pregnancy test she'd bought after school. She had no idea how to feel.

She was elated. She hadn't thought she could get pregnant after she'd learned years ago that she had a cluster of fibroid tumors blocking the path to every egg she released each month.

She was excited to be a mom. And for Jerrik to be a dad. When he'd interacted with her students, her ovaries had fairly exploded.

But the feeling that overrode the rest was fear. She couldn't imagine having a baby in the 11th century. Her father not being there to meet his granddaughter or grandson. Delivering a baby without modern medicine. Diseases. Or worse.

"In my time, unfortunately, the little boy with the cane would be left to die in the wilderness."

There was no way that if anything were to be wrong with their child that she could leave the baby to die in the wilderness to be some wild animal's dinner. She bent over the toilet and puked again at the thought.

Jett pressed a hand to her mouth as her heart broke.

~ 232 ~

~~~

"Hello, sweet lass." Jerrik kissed Jett's neck. "Dinner smells delicious. I am certain I will miss the food here."

She chuckled awkwardly as she worked on dinner. She didn't turn to look at him or lift her face for their customary kiss when he got home from work.

"It took much convincing to get Sam to come back early. He wanted to stay out another day." Jerrik talked to fill the silence as he leaned against the opposite counter.

"Hmm…" Jett hummed absentmindedly.

"Are you okay?"

"Yeah. I'm fine."

"You are lying. I know when you are lying."

"Jerrik, let's not talk about it."

"Are you scared for the morning."

Jett's shoulders sagged.

"I can't go."

Jerrik stilled. His heart shot to his throat and then raced as if he were running.

"What do you mean you cannot go?"

"Just what I said."

"Is it because of the baby."

Jett whipped around and stared at him in shock.

"How did you know?"

"I guessed. But your reaction is the answer."

"You guessed."

"I am not a dense man, Jett. I noticed your monthly had not arrived."

Jerrik pushed off the counter and wrapped her in his arms. He kissed the top of her head and then her nose.

"You and the baby will be fine." He looked down at her. "What would you have done if you got pregnant in my time? Leave and come back here?"

"I-I didn't think I could get pregnant."

Jerrik scoffed. "I am certain my seed is strong."

"Apparently," Jett grumbled.

"So, there is no problem. We leave in the morning as planned." Jerrik kissed her head and then walked over to the couch.

"No, Jerrik. I'm not going."

He stopped and turned back.

"I didn't think getting pregnant was a possibility. But now that I am, I can't do it. I can't risk my life and the life of my baby. You said yourself that if the baby isn't perfect that your people leave the baby to die. And we don't even know if the fog will take us to the right time. It's not like we can set a time traveling clock like some fictional movie. I can't risk it. I won't risk it." Jett's eyes filled with tears.

"The baby will be healthy." Jerrik walked back to the kitchen.

"You don't know that. There are so many terrible things that could happen. And it scares me too much. Hell, we have medicine here that helps numb the pain of childbirth. I can't get that in your time. No, Jerrik." Jett choked. "You can go if you choose, but I'm staying here for our baby. It's your choice. You decide if your duty to your village is more important than your duty to your new family.

"I'm gonna be sick." Jett ran from the room to the half bath.

Jerrik stood in the middle of the kitchen. His world tilted on its axis.

Chapter 36

Jett had gone to bed without dinner. Her stomach too queasy for her to trust food in it. She also knew she wouldn't be able to look at Jerrik's face without being destroyed. She'd already cried herself to sleep.

The bed dipped and pulled her from a fitful sleep. Jett felt arms band around her. She was slid to the middle of the bed. Jerrik didn't speak. Instead, his lips found hers in the darkness.

Jett opened for him like a flower to the rain. Tears streamed down her temples as he made love to her like she was the most precious and delicate of creatures. The Viking barbarian turned tamed goliath. Jett tried to burn every touch, sensation, and emotion into her memory to pull out to examine later when she missed him and craved his touch.

She came hard on his throbbing flesh as he spilled his seed within her depths. He then pulled her into his chest as she sobbed. His lovemaking had felt like goodbye.

Once more she cried herself to sleep.

~~~

Jett jerked awake. She shot up. It was still dark. She slid her hand across the mattress but found the space empty and cold. She grabbed her phone and it said it was 5am.

"What have I done?" Jett jumped out of her bed and ran to her closet. "Why didn't I beg him to stay? Why didn't I fight?"

Because you were scared he'd say no. That he'd choose someone else over you. Old habits die hard.

Jett shoved her legs into a pair of gray sweatpants and pulled on one of his thermal shirts. It smelled like him and a sob escaped her lips. She blindly pulled on her white sneakers.

Her feet pounded down the stairs. Her keys in hand, she slammed out the door, and locked it as an afterthought. Her coat forgotten.

She sped to South Portland harbor. It was where they'd planned to leave. The car screeched to a halt in the parking lot. She threw it in park and jumped out of the car. Her heart pumped as she ran as fast as her feet could carry her. She reached the dock where the little motor boat they'd planned to rent was tied off. The spot was empty.

"It's gone. He's gone."

A wail ripped from her throat as she collapsed to the warped wood beneath her. A few fishermen that hadn't gone out for the day looked over at her. A couple ran over to her.

"Miss, you okay?"

Jett hiccupped as she tried to find her voice.

"D-Did you see the big blond man that took the little motor boat that was tied here?"

"Yeah, he left a few hours ago or so."

Jett nodded sadly as tears fell unbidden down her cheeks.

"Are you sure you're okay, ma'am?"

"I'll be fine."

The two old men helped her to her feet. Jett walked listlessly back to her car. She got in and took several minutes to breathe. Every breath hurt. But she wiped her eyes and started the engine.

Jett drove back to Cape Elizabeth. She didn't pay much attention to the drive. A horn blared at her when she blew through a stop sign.

Pay attention. You have more than yourself to take care of.

She turned the wheel away from her house. She wasn't ready to go back. Not to a house that had been filled with his commanding presence. It was too much.

Without much thought, Jett found herself at the scene of where it all began. Portland Head Light lighthouse.

She parked the car and got out. The fog hung thick in the air. But this time it was regular fog. Instead of the eerie mist that brought him to her and took him away just as quickly, this mist was more depressing than anything.

Jett stepped down the big boulders to where his ship had been. She found one flat enough for her to sit on. The rock was cold and damp against her hands and backside as she sat in the dreary November morning.

She didn't know how long she sat there. It was long enough that the mist began to lighten and lift. The sound of a motor reached her ears. Jett glanced up. She spied something white moving towards the water's edge. She squinted to get a better look.

Her heart jumped in her throat.

Chapter 37

Jerrik couldn't tell the difference between the real fog and the fog that had brought him to the 21st century. He turned off the engine and grabbed the oars to row slowly through the mist. His arms, back, and chest flexed with every stroke through the water. The chilly air slipped down the collar of his cream sweater. Jerrik shivered. He didn't know if it was from the cold morning air or something more ominous.

Fingers of white vapor broke from the natural fog and crawled towards the boat. The supernatural fog shot out and Jerrik fell back. It narrowly missed him. He quickly restarted the engine. It roared to life and he pulled away from the mist that wanted to pull him back to his time. Or unknown time he wasn't prepared for.

Once he was far enough away, he stopped the boat and untied the smaller row boat he'd towed along with him. He pulled the rope and the little boat floated to the side of the motor boat. The smaller vessel held his Viking clothing he'd arrived in. As well as his father's sword. Hidden within the folded clothing was a message for whomever may find the boat.

Jerrik gripped the side of the row boat. The fog crawled forward and he used all of his strength to push the boat into the fog. Its nebulous tendrils wrapped around the boat and pulled it into its mysterious depths.

"Goodbye brothers. Goodbye mother. I pray this finds your well."

He grabbed the tiller on the motor and steered the boat away from the fog. He sped away just as the fog overtook the spot he had been. He disappeared into the morning mist.

~~~

Jett stood up as a motor boat appeared. The mist parted and Jerrik emerged. The morning breeze blew his long blond locks back. He grinned when he saw her. Jett had never seen anything more beautiful.

Jerrik pulled up to the rock she was standing on at the shoreline. He stopped the boat and stood up. He stepped to the edge and stretched his arm across the space between them. His hand raised palm up waited for her to take it. As if he offered her eternity.

Jett reached across the space and took it.

Jerrik lifted her into the boat and directly into his arms.

"What made you stay?" She asked.

"You. The baby. This place and time. You." Jerrik shrugged. "It was written in my destiny. Everything says we are meant to be together. My 'death,' the fog, you being here when I arrived, your boss knowing people who could tell you who I am, all the way to your belly being filled with my child when you believed you could have none. It was fated. I will not fight it. I do not want to."

"Will you be happy here? Without your family?" Jett asked quietly, fearful of the answer.

"I will miss them. But life without you... That cannot be."

Epilogue

"Push! You can do it, Jett!" Dr. Clark encouraged.

She was a pretty Black female OBGYN that Jett had picked meticulously and had immediately fallen in love with. She meant business and she cared about her patients.

"Aaaaaaargh!" Jett gritted as she pushed.

"Ow!" Jerrik howled. "I did not think it were possible for you to crush my fingers, but you have proved me wrong."

"Shut up, ya big baby! I'm pushing two watermelons out a hole the size of a lemon." Jett howled.

"I was just pointing out that you are strong." Jerrik cringed.

He ripped his left hand out of hers and shook it. He quickly removed his black wedding band and slipped it into his jeans' pocket before she broke his pinky finger against it.

"Why do you think I'm not holding her hand, Rik?" Dez said over Jett's head.

"You both can get out!"

"There, there." Dez also cringed and dabbed the sweat from her bestie's forehead.

"You can rest." Dr. Clark said.

Jett collapsed back in exhaustion.

"You are doing really good, sweetie." Jerrik kissed the top of her head and then her nose.

"Thanks, babe. I'm sorry for yelling. Can't guarantee I won't yell at you again though."

"You go right ahead. Yell as much as you want."

Jett's eyes widened and she crushed his hand again.

"We got another one. Let's make it the last one." Dr. Clark said. "Come on, Jett. PUSH!"

Jett bared down with a snarl.

"I swear to Odin, Thor, Freya, and whoever else that your big Viking ass better not touch me ever again. I don't care how good the dick is. This shit is ridiculous!" Jett screeched.

"Sweet-"

"Shut. UP!"

Dez nearly fell out.

"Dez, I swear to God if you keep laughing..." She stopped talking as a scream ripped out of her.

Seconds later, the strong wail of a baby rent the air.

"Oh, listen to those strong lungs. We've got a boy!" The doctor held up the baby boy before handing him to the nurse to get cleaned off.

"Stian Thorin Rolfson." Jerrik said proudly as the nurse placed him in Jett's arms.

"Jerrik, take him. She's coming." Jett said as her face scrunched in pain.

Jerrik quickly took his son. He kissed the top of his full head of slicked down dark waves. He rocked him and placed his pink finger in his little mouth. Stian sucked greedily.

A few minutes later, another strong cry pulled his attention to the doctor.

"You've got a beautiful and perfect little girl." Dr. Clark announced.

After she was cleaned and placed in Jett's arms, Jerrik leaned over and kissed the top of her blonde head.

"Alva Dagmar Rolfson."

Jett looked up at Jerrik with tears in her eyes.

"They're beautiful." She sniffled.

"They are." Dez agreed as she looked over Jett's shoulder.

"And I'll make sure that they're close and adore each other."

"You're gonna be a great mom," Dez said.

"A perfect mother." Jerrik agreed.

"I think your brothers and mom would be proud." Jett said to him.

For the first time in his life, Jerrik had to gather himself. He nodded and unashamed he wiped his wet eyes.

"Aye, I think they would be."

~~~

1052 A.D. Iceland

Dag sat alone on a cliff overlooking their village. He felt restless. From the moment all threats had been taken care of and Thorin now ruled all of Iceland, life in the village had become stifling. Dag craved the open sea, battle, and adventure. He wanted his own land to rule. The thought of overthrowing his baby brother had never crossed his mind.

Thorin was settled with Ellie. They had little Jerrik and she was pregnant with another. They didn't need Dag anymore.

But where would I go?

Dag gazed down at the water. His frown deepened. He sat forward and squinted into the distance.

On the water below, a mist eerily crawled across the water. The hairs on the back of his neck stood on end. He shook off the shiver that slid down his back.

Just as quickly as the fog had come, it began to slither back out to sea. It left behind a strange white boat, the likes of which he'd never seen before.

Dag hopped up and ran down the hillside. He ignored those who tried to stop him as he jogged through the village. As he reached the water's edge, the boat had floated closer. He waded into the water and pulled the boat all the way to shore.

His heart stopped, stuttered, and then raced at the items that were inside of the boat. He looked around and found a boy tossing a net into the water.

"Boy! Watch this boat. Do not touch it!" Dag shouted out.

The boy nodded and Dag ran back up through the village to Thorin's longhouse. He burst through the doors. Thorin had Ellie in his lap and was kissing her soundly.

"You two are going to populate the whole village." Dag rolled his eyes.

Thorin smirked when he came up for air. His dark blond hair hung loose around his shoulders and his green gaze searched Dag's silver eyes. Ellie looked up at him. Her warm brown skin glowed with her pregnancy. Her jet-black curls a wild mane around her shoulders. She was stunning. She made Dag consider finding his own woman.

"Leave your brother alone," Gyda grinned. "I want as many grandchildren as I can get before I leave this world."

"What has happened, Dag. I can see something is bothering you." Thorin asked.

"I have to show you something. All of you. Come." Dag jerked his head towards the door.

They followed him down to the shore. The boy had taken his job very serious as he stood guard over it. Dag walked to the boat.

"Look." He nodded to the small vessel.

Thorin and Gyda stepped forward curiously. Both their eyes shot up to Dag. Ellie peered in, but looked up in confusion.

"Is it?" Thorin asked.

"I am sure of it," Dag said.

"What is it?"

"It is their brother Jerrik's sword. The sword their father gave to him." Gyda explained.

Ellie's eyes widened. A look of understanding crossed her face.

Thorin lifted the sword from the boat. He turned it this way and that.

"It is Jerrik's." Thorin confirmed.

"Is there anything else in there?" Ellie asked.

Dag frowned. "The clothes he was in when he died."

Ellie stepped forward and grabbed the clothes. She placed them on the ground and began to unfold them as they surrounded her. She pulled back the animal pelt and found a sandwich bag.

"Oh my God!" Ellie gasped.

"What is it?" Thorin asked.

"Something from my time."

She opened the baggie and pulled out a photograph and a letter. Words were written on the back of the photo.

"It says, 'Jerrik and Jett.'" Ellie read it.

She turned it around and showed them. They stumbled back.

The photo was of Jerrik smiling happily next to a beautiful woman with skin darker than Ellie's and closely cropped hair. Each one of them took turns staring at the photograph. Gyda looked at it the longest. Tears streamed down her face.

"Holy shit!" Ellie exclaimed. "I remember him. I recognize his face."

"What?" Thorin asked.

"What do you mean?" Dag asked at the same time.

"Right before I was pulled from my time, I saw a Viking longboat pass by the ship I was on. It was engulfed in flames, except for in the center. Inside it, a man lay still. But he didn't look dead to me, just asleep. This..." Ellie pointed to Jerrik's image. "...was that man. I had forgotten until just now. Seeing him brought it all back."

Dag and Thorin looked at each other.

"Can you read it?" Dag held out the letter to Ellie.

"Of course." She opened it and began. "'Thorin, Dag, and mother. I hope this letter finds you well. Somehow, I have found my way to the future. The 21st century. You cannot imagine the life here. I have found a woman who saved me as if Freya herself sent her to me. I love her deeply and she is with child. I would have come back, but she is my life and my future now. I know that Thorin will lead just as well as I ever could. The sword is yours, brother. As it should be. Mother, trust that I am happy. Dag, I know you have a restless heart. Explore the world, brother. I love you all and will carry you in my heart in this time or the next. I will meet you in Valhalla. Jerrik.'" Ellie finished and looked up at them.

Thorin nodded his head. "Jerrik is alive."

"And happy." Gyda added as she sniffled.

Dag's eyes lit up. "And in the future…"

The End

If you enjoyed Jett and Jerrik's story, please leave a review at the online retailer where you purchased the book. Just a few words are always appreciated.

Acknowledgments

Thank you so much to my trusted beta readers for continually being there for me. Nadia, Grace, Cosalyn, Squash, Kim, Simone, and Michele. Your encouragement and love for my characters and books keep me going. Each one of you bring something to the table that helps me in more ways than you know. I love you ladies.

Without Mom and Dad, I would never have been able to get this writing career off the ground. They continue to support and uplift me. They literally believe I can do anything. And that means the world to me. And an added shout out of appreciation for my mom while I wrote this while it was just the two of us in Mexico. You had no one to talk to as I powered through writing this. I know that had to be boring as heck. So, thank you for your patience.

A big thanks to my new readers who just found me. Thank you for reading this book. And if you loved it and my voice, thank you for sticking around.

And finally, to my loyal readers. Thank you from the bottom of my heart. You all have stuck with me for several years now. You've watched me and my writing grow. You cheered me on and reminded me why I do this. I love you all more than you know.

About the Author

Twyla Turner currently resides in Arizona. She was born and raised in Joliet, Illinois, a Midwest girl at heart, though constantly moving from place to place, and always thinking of where she wants to go next. Having been an avid romance novel reader since junior high and minoring in Creative Writing. She felt that it was finally time to start combining her love of travel and writing, as well as her life experiences and putting them down on "paper." Which experiences, she'll never tell…well maybe, if you ask nicely.

Other Books by Twyla Turner

SERIES

<u>The Struck Series:</u>
Star-Struck
Awe-Struck
<u>Damaged Souls Series:</u>
Scarred
Open Wounds
Healed
<u>Chasing Day Series:</u>
Chasing Day
Catching Day
<u>The Curvy Girls Club:</u>
The Red Scot
The Bravest Hero
<u>Bound Through Time - The Viking Brothers Series:</u>
Past
Present

STANDALONES

THR3E
<u>Curvy Ever After:</u>
Forbidden Curvy Girl Fairy Tales
Winter's Beast
His Muse
Rock the Curves

NOVELLAS

Love in the Wild
The Rescue
Love Bites

Their Secret Desire: The Princess & The Gladiator
The Holiday Boyfriend

Connect with Author

Website:
www.twylaturner11.wix.com/novelswithcurves